D1460523

Claire Macquet is a journalist working on developments in technology, industry, trade and social welfare in the Third World. She was born in South Africa in 1941 and has lived in London since 1965. In the late 1980s, she began writing fiction with a collection of short stories, *The Flying Hart*, published by Sheba in 1991. *Looking for Ammu* is her first novel.

Looking for Ammu

Claire Macquet

Published by VIRAGO PRESS Limited 1992
20-23 Mandela Street, Camden Town, London NW1 0HQ

Copyright © Claire Macquet 1992

The right of Claire Macquet to be identified as author of this
work has been asserted by her in accordance with the
Copyright, Designs and Patents Act 1988.

All rights reserved

*A CIP catalogue record for this book is available from the British
Library*

Printed in Great Britain by Cox & Wyman Ltd., Reading,
Berkshire

Lines quoted in the text are from the following works:

'Jane, Jane . . .', from 'Aubade', by Edith Sitwell, in *Look!
The Sun*, Gollancz, 1941; 'I'm tired of love . . .', from
'Fatigue', by Hillaire Belloc, in *Faber Book of Comic Verse*,
1974; 'Poor Bess will return . . .', from 'Mad Bess of
Bedlam', Anon, seventeenth century, music by Purcell; 'A
woman can be proud . . .', from 'Crazy Jane Talks to the
Bishop', by W. B. Yeats, in *Yeats, Selected Poetry*, Macmillan,
1964; 'There was a bloody sparrow', quoted in 'Wyn's Song',
in *Collected Letters of Dylan Thomas*, Macmillan, 1985; 'I doubt
na, whyles, . . .', from 'To a Mouse', by Robert Burns, in
Collins Albatross Book of Verse, undated, but circa 1970.

For Catherine Rae Arthur

Acknowledgements

For advice on medical issues, thanks to Dr Susan
Labrooy and Dr Harold Behr; to Sister Sandra Beevor
of the Hampstead District Nursing Service, thanks for
far more than information about nursing. Caril Behr
gave me an idea for the plot which is so important that I
can't give details without spoiling the story; Christina
Veronica McCarthy gave both encouragement and
much help on the text. As always with Virago, I had
excellent editing, from Ruthie Petrie and Becky Swift.
And my lover Catherine Arthur gave me time, and
motivation, to finish this book.

We can only learn to love by loving.
Remember that all our failures
are ultimately failures in love.

The Abbess in *The Bell*, Iris Murdoch

Thursday evening,
3 November

Five cracked steps lead to the door. Seven bell buttons dangle from the woodwork, some with half-legible scribbles of names – none of which say 'Ammu Bai'. Here we go again, more of London; so strange, so horribly familiar; a scene from a dream about falling.

'Loves me, loves me not. Loves me –' Harriet's fingers ran over the buttons and pressed the last.

'– not', she added as footsteps as unlike Ammu's as footsteps could be thundered against floorboards.

'Yeah?' The woman opening the door was big and louring, fiftyish, bleached hair cropped to the skull, wearing a crumpled yellow kimono: a used-up unhoping figure, offering Harriet no hope.

Harriet could feel London pressing close behind her – a clammy mist creeping up, cars charging, banging of dustbins, somewhere a woman shouting – the bronchitic wheeze of an ageing city where it was dark for half the day and cold even at noon. Nothing was quite real; not even Ammu. Ammu, the centre of her life for almost five years had called Harriet to London. And when she had come, Ammu was nowhere – gone.

For all that, she trotted out the well-practised opening: 'Good evening. I'm Harriet Weston from Mauritius. I've come to see Dr Bai, Dr Ammu Bai.'

'She's out.'

'Out?' Harriet's heart jumped – Who was out had been in. And here, the least promising of the places she had tried in her three frustrating days in London.

'Will she be long?'

The woman shrugged her shoulders.

'Would you mind if I wait?'

The woman looked her up and down, rocking the door in a movement which made Harriet desperate to put her foot against it. 'You got a lot of patience?'

'Yes, why?'

'She's been out since Thursday the twenty-first of October.'

Harriet's heart fell back. 'Out for two weeks – but she lives here?'

The woman shrugged again. 'Her things do, what there is of them.'

'Where's she gone?'

'Don't ask me. I'm only the landlady.'

'Did she go off to a conference, on a holiday?'

'Then she travels light – no bag.'

'Why did she go?'

'I said I don't know shit. Only know I haven't seen five weeks' rent.'

Harriet's heart was pounding. This was the third place Ammu had gone from. It was only another cold spoor, but it smelt different, closer, dangerous. At the other two places, Ammu had been staying with friends, old friends, people with families who wrote letters, people who listened to Harriet's story, thought something odd was going on, and wanted to help. Harriet glanced quickly at the woman rocking the door. This was different. If there was something wrong – something bad – this woman, this awful place, could be important.

'I've been looking for Dr Bai for three days,' Harriet said carefully, 'I'm very anxious to make contact.'

'So am I, sweetheart.'

'I came from Mauritius to meet her. It's important.'

'Important to you?'

Harriet nodded.

'No wonder I took you for a fool.' The woman smiled in Harriet's face, a fleshy, whisky-raddled smile, perhaps ironic, perhaps something else; certainly not sympathetic.

Harriet struggled on. 'It's very strange the way she seems just to have disappeared. I'm afraid something might have happened.'

'Could be you don't know the Ammu Bai I know, darling.'

'Then you know her well?'

'Like I know crap.'

All of London's traffic opened up in a roar, swamping the narrow doorstep. The night was suddenly unbearably clammy. The soft white face opposite was still smiling. 'So that's it, then,' the woman continued. 'Goodnight dearie, and happy hunting.'

'Just a minute –' Harriet grabbed the door with a shaky fist. This woman knew Ammu, knew the clever, beautiful, battling Ammu, knew her 'like crap'. 'Just a minute –' Harriet fought off the urge to push her other fist into a face '– if you please.' God, she thought, Londoners are revolting people. This woman knew something. She knew Harriet wanted what she knew (perhaps it was something important, more likely not amounting to very much) and she took pleasure in taunting her with what she would not give, at least not for free. Five years in Port Louis – a place where everybody talked incessantly and excitedly to everybody else about everything – had put Harriet out of touch with her home town's sour reserve. This woman would have to be courted, every scrap of information wheedled out of her.

Harriet made up a polite face. 'As you know her well, you may be able to help me.' A smile would be inappropriate, but Harriet tried to muster an open, engaging look:

'Will you give me five minutes?' The woman looked blank. 'Can I come in and talk to you about it? You see, I'm sure there's some mistake about the rent, and perhaps I could in some way assist...' (Careful here; Mauritian rupees did not stretch very far in London.)

The woman laughed. 'That's really something. I love it. You can sort out Ammu, sort out the rent. So if Ammu's off on a bender, far as she can get from those dreary sick children, I'm supposed to help you drag her back?'

So this woman did know Ammu, at least well enough to know that she worked with sick children. 'A "bender"?'

'You ought'a do your homework, Florence Nightingale; or is it Miss Marples; or both? Could be there are things about Ammu Bai you don't know.'

Harriet jumped at it. 'Could you tell me?'

'Why? So you can sort her out?' The rocking of the door became more violent, then stopped. 'Get lost!' she said, quite softly, then: 'I'm not having anything to do with this. It's nothing to do with me.'

A stab of fear, and Harriet's grip on the door tightened. 'Ammu's in trouble, isn't she?' she countered in as soft a voice. 'And you know she's in trouble, don't you?' The woman looked away. 'I don't want anything from you except some way to help Ammu. Let me in.'

A moment of doubt. Harriet stood motionless, allowing the woman to look her over, her eyes travelling down to Harriet's feet and then up again, making Harriet sharply aware, in turn, of her ginger hair (as usual working itself loose from its bun), her almost colourless pale eyes, her skin, dry and reddened between its freckles, her body, skewed by the weight of the duffel bag on her shoulder, long and awkwardly jointed as a puppet – the whole, surely, harmless, inoffensive.

Brusquely, the woman turned into the house. Harriet was on her heel. She followed her down a hall that smelled strongly of wet dog, perhaps dead wet dog. A light snapped on, clarifying the smell into that mix of uncleaned carpet, fishy cooking oil, damp, tobacco, boiled cabbage, weeping – the ugly smells of English poverty.

So Ammu lived here, or had lived here: why? Why had she left Paul's pretty house in Camden Town where the geraniums she had put on the doorstep were dying of frost; why had she then left Dr Ramgulam's comfortable semi in Gunnersbury, to come to this place? Did she know she would come here when she had written, on jasmine-scented paper in her loopy hand that was more comfortable with Tamil than Roman script, the letter that had called Harriet to London and been the promise of a new life? That letter had not mentioned any need for a forwarding address.

'What's wrong, Ammu?' she whispered to herself as she followed the yellow kimono down to a half-basement heated to a scorching like singed human hair by a bulging gas fire. A huge, and very dusty, paper lantern swayed in the waves of heat, its bulb revealing three shabby upholstered chairs, lumpish sideboards, a great deal of mess, and a number of cats. There was a strong smell of rot.

The woman flopped into the biggest, messiest chair and lit a cigarette. She didn't offer a chair to Harriet. Harriet hesitated, wishing herself back on the cold step. In Mauritius, even the very depressed were clean; they had to be because a room like this would be host to hundreds of dangerous creatures – spiders, scorpions, rats, snakes, and (to Harriet worst of all) cockroaches. She made an effort, determined to play it by the book. 'May I sit down?'

'Help yourself.'

Harriet quickly examined the seat of a chair, and sat. She lowered her glance over a heavy body draped in yellow, hairless calves (that descaled fish-belly texture of sunless European flesh), rubbed turquoise slippers sunk into a carpet loudly patterned with triangles. All around the feet, like the remains of a plague of worms, lay little rolls of cigarette ash. On the mantelpiece above the fire, behind the woman's head, and in a temperature which must have been half way to boiling, sat a huge fat-faced tabby, staring. Clearly, little happened to disturb the air in this room. Little was happening now.

On the doorstep, Harriet had begun to form a set of questions which might lead somewhere. Down here, nothing but the oppressive room seemed to have any shape at all. Ammu would not have been dislocated by this room; to her, anything that carried the impress of a life was interesting. But Harriet did not have the same skills, except when by Ammu's side. For all that, she would try to get the discussion back to where it had been. 'You mentioned that you knew Ammu well. May I ask how you met?'

The woman took no more notice of this question than the cats did.

Harriet raised her voice. 'Have you known Ammu long?'

The woman turned and stared her full in the face. 'What the fuck have you brought to drink?'

'Sorry!' Harriet almost jumped. 'I have some Mauritian rum.' Harriet realised that her voice sounded silly, nervy, prim – far too much the nurse – but she pressed on, drawing a bottle out of the bowels of her duffel bag. 'I brought it over for Ammu. She was fond of it, and I don't expect you can buy it in London.'

The woman snorted again. 'Ammu was fond of anything over 40 per cent proof, like me.'

Harriet dumped the bottle on the floor beside the hairless white legs. It was unpleasant to think of Ammu drinking anything with that woman, and impossible to imagine her being like her in any way.

The woman picked up the bottle tenderly. 'What does this label say? I don't have my glasses.'

' "L'Esprit de Maurice" '.'

'Is that Indian?'

Harriet felt a touch of compunction. 'No, French. But it's only cane spirit really, though it calls itself rum; not a sophisticated drink, but it's powerful.'

The woman nodded.

'And it's cheap; this bottle cost the equivalent of about eighty pence. Spirits are so expensive here, aren't they?'

The woman nodded again, feelingly.

Harriet began to feel she was making progress. It was still very heavy going, but she was beginning to be able to make vibes that could get through the dead weight of the room. 'Mauritians say it's scented with the breath of the dodo,' she chatted, to fill a lengthening pause. 'You know about dodos – flightless pigeons bigger than turkeys? European sailors killed them off 200 years ago. Ammu claims that their remains still give a pungency to all medicinal herbs in Mauritius, and increase their healing power.'

Harriet could well remember Ammu telling her that story, one night at the clinic, after they had treated with some extremely poisonous-looking herbs a dozen wedding guests stricken with alcohol poisoning, not from L'Esprit de Maurice, but from banana spirit, its country cousin, no doubt distilled behind the chicken yards of some tiny farm.

Often, late at night, when the last of the patients had left, Ammu, her skin shiny with sweat, would stretch out her legs, pulling the skirts of her sari to her knees, and drink rum straight out of the bottle, all the while talking furiously about ancient cures for diarrhoea, rheumatic heart disease, or about the 'scumbags' in the Ministry of Health – not often about dodos.

The woman in the chair opposite didn't comment. With a violent twist of the wrist, she tore open the bottle. 'It smells like cats' piss,' she said.

Harriet's confidence had risen. 'It's an acquired taste.'

She began again, still weighing her words. 'Thank you for agreeing to talk to me. Something strange has happened to Ammu.' The woman nodded. 'She wrote to me only a week after she had arrived in England; that was in September. She asked me to join her here. She wanted me, you see, to go off to work with her in Mozam – in another country.'

There was no nod in response to this. Perhaps the woman was thinking. 'You know Ammu started up more than two dozen people's clinics in Mauritius?' (No response.) 'But when I arrived to join her, she had gone from – from the place she was staying. I'm trying to find her.' (Still no response.) 'I hope we can be on our way before Christmas.'

'What a romantic story. Should I wish you both happiness?' The woman sniffed at the bottle again.

Harriet tried another tack. 'I'm from London, Palmers Green actually, but I've been in Mauritius for the past five years. I've come home – though it doesn't feel like home to me any more – just for this. Well, for a long time I've wanted to work full time with Ammu. She isn't much appreciated in Mauritius, you know; her ideas about health care are rather radical. It sounds a bit childish, I guess, but I would follow her to the ends of the earth. Has she talked much to you about her work?'

The woman laughed. 'Do I look like the kind of person a doctor would talk to about work?'

Harriet paused, looking into the pale face. It struck her that Ammu talked about little other than work. 'You said you knew her well.'

'Intimately,' the woman said, with emphasis.

Harriet cut in, 'My name, as I said, is Harriet Weston. And you are?'

'Sophie.'

'Pleased to meet you, Sophie.' Harriet half rose, extended a hand, and then drew it back again. 'How did you get to know Ammu?' The cat on the mantelpiece blinked.

'God, you're stupid for someone supposing herself to be playing detective. There's only two ways you meet somebody in this concrete hole: you take an ad in *City Limits*, or you take them off somebody else. I took Ammu off another woman.'

'You what?' A horrible image of Ammu as some kind of hostage, exchanged between rival gangs of Sophies, shot into Harriet's mind. But she was determined not to be rattled, or frightened, by the woman's offensive language, and ploughed on, 'Is this person someone you know, a friend?'

Sophie pursed her lips. 'You could say that.'

'Is it possible that this friend might have "taken" Ammu back?'

'Nope.'

'Or have any idea where she might be?'

'Now you sound like some fart in "The Bill". So let me give it to you on a bloody plate – if you knew my friends, you wouldn't ask such stupid questions.'

'I beg your pardon.' Harriet noted fingers that clung to the glass, trembling in some mute fury. She noted the eyes, too puffy, smoke-stung, tired to give focus to the flat sarcasm of the voice. But whatever Sophie thought of the questions, she answered them and, Harriet believed, up to a point honestly. So Sophie had friends, in spite of her vile manners. What was she now saying? Were her connections, and her friends' connections, with people so superficial that they forgot them the day after meeting? Would the friend Sophie had 'taken' Ammu from be angry? Her first fear predominated: was there something odd, perhaps criminal, about Sophie and her friends which would make curiosity dangerous? Anyway, what was 'The Bill'?

'I'd like to meet this friend.'

'You can cut it out now; I'm bored with it.' Sophie

slopped rum into a glass already a quarter full of brownish-yellow liquid, and drank. 'The stuff also tastes like cats' piss. You'd best pack up and go back to Mauritius and those gangrenous old men and coughing babies you and Ammu get so turned on by.' Another slug. 'You're wasting your time, girl.'

'Oh. Why?'

'If Ammu wanted to be with you, Ammu would now be with you. Have you ever known her to let anything stand in her way before?'

'But that's why I'm worried. You see …'

'You're chasing after Ammu. That's wasting time. Catch an eel with your bare hands if you want something less slippery. Make it an electric eel – easier on the nerves.'

'I don't understand.' (In a small voice.)

'You love Ammu. You're wasting your time.'

Harriet scoffed, her fear beginning to yield to irritation – the woman was no worse than an ill-natured neurotic. 'Ammu is the most impressive person I have ever met, ever in my entire life. Anything else is wasting time.'

'Ah yes, I'm with you. Got it.'

'I rather doubt it. Ammu has done wonderful work. Hundreds of people owe their lives to her. She started from nowhere, just with the idea that people's health belonged to themselves. Do you know how original this is? You see, our health systems come out of two narrow technologies – surgery and antibiotics. They've become so powerful that we think our bodies were designed to be stuffed with pills and carved up with knives and ruled by doctors. Ammu has fought that …'.

'Well, then she certainly takes the bacon. But I didn't know she liked them so young, and so vanilla.'

'Vanilla?' Ammu had been much in favour of the reintroduction of vanilla in Mauritius, and had encouraged the peasant farmers trying to grow it. 'What vanilla?'

'Not part of your vocabulary, darling. But then maybe

you're also not so young.' Sophie leaned closer, peering. 'Lesbians all look eighteen till they hit the menopause. And then, baby, with a crash comes the real world. When's it gonna hit you?'

'I'm thirty-five;' (politely) 'I am not a lesbian.'

'Sure?'

'Of course I'm sure.' (An image of long-forgotten Martin rose wanly in front of Harriet's eyes.)

'Then you can leave now, darling. My cats take care of the other kind of rat in the closet.'

'But Ammu, surely Ammu ...?'

'You know nothing about Ammu. You know nothing about nothing. Fuck off, and take your bottle of pisswater with you. Come on, move.'

Harriet sprang to her feet as Sophie rose and lumbered towards her.

'Sophie ... just a minute. I must find Ammu. I didn't mean to cause offence. Something has happened; I'm afraid something bad might have happened. When she came here, it's possible she may have come to hide. Please. I'm not put off by anything you say.'

'What a generous soul!'

Harriet was shaking. 'Please just help me find out where she might have gone. Tell me how she came here, and, if you know, why; anything about phone calls, letters, anything. Did she stay in the house during the day? Was there anything – a quarrel perhaps – with somebody, this other friend? Did anybody, anybody odd, come here for her? Was there any trouble about money, about the clinics. Please.'

Sophie fell back in her chair and Harriet, taking the cue, perched on the edge of hers, now occupied by a cat. 'Perhaps,' Harriet struggled on, 'I might be able to bring her back here. And there's the rent.'

'Fuck the rent, you prissy little girl guide,' hissed Sophie. The cat on Harriet's chair took off. 'I want her bloody arms around me. It's been fourteen days of hell. She's killing me.'

'Oh, I see.' Harriet didn't see at all. Her whole brain was blanked out in some awful shock.

'We were together every night for almost a month. Now it's like we've been apart for almost a lifetime.'

Sophie's words dropped, like pebbles in a pond, into Harriet's ears. 'Every night for almost a month,' she repeated. Surely this was a real piece of information; Harriet could make nothing of it.

Sophie, head bowed low over her drink, was absently swilling the stuff from side to side of the glass. That was a gesture of Ammu's, something Ammu did expertly to save from drowning the clouds of gnats and fruit-flies that swarmed into every glass in Mauritius. Mad as she was, this woman did know Ammu well. This woman had sat up late, drinking with her.

So many times, so many many times, when dawn would soon begin to threaten, Ammu had pleaded with Harriet to stay, for another drink, another few minutes talk. But Harriet, panic-stricken at the thought of the forty bright-eyed student nurses to be faced at 8 a.m., would flee when Ammu's talk shifted to subjects that could go on forever, promising to be back to help at the clinic after work, bringing another few rolls of stolen bandages.

So Ammu was here, drinking with Sophie, not talking about schistosomiasis but things Harriet knew nothing of, while Harriet's letter lay unopened at the house with Ammu's geraniums in Camden Town. In that letter was the announcement that Harriet had given up her job, her friends, her security, her life in Mauritius, to go penniless with Ammu to start new clinics at Guija in the south west of Mozambique.

Harriet's mind raced back over Ammu's letter to her: was there anything she could have misunderstood? For the first three pages, it was typical Ammu – rage against the sanctimoniousness of the British charities that had paid for Ammu's visit to London and would meet many of the costs of the new clinics in Mozambique. Ammu was always at war, always girding up for the next battle. But on the fourth page, her tone had changed. 'I can do it,' she had written, 'with or without their rulebooks of stupid "priorities". I don't need anybody to help me – except you, Harriet, except you. Will you come with me?' Then, scrawled up the margin: 'Take the first flight to London. I need help with organising the equipment. I've got a CWT of supplies from Save the Children and even a firm promise from those tightwads at Oxfam. Bring all the cash you've got. And get your jabs up to date – there won't be time to do it in London – you'll need malaria tablets too.'

Harriet had given in her notice the day she received Ammu's letter, and put herself on a diet of spinach and chapattis to save every rupee for the fare. She had also written to the Abbey National in London that she would be cashing in the whole amassed £1,750 of her savings account. And, of course, she had replied immediately to Ammu, to the address at the top of Ammu's letter.

When Ammu moved to Sophie's place, why had she not telephoned Paul at Camden Town to send on any mail? Why had she not travelled the few miles to collect it? Why, if she had to change her plans, had she not written again to explain? Why was she staying in this place at all, with this rude woman, this woman who now seemed to have some kind of claim over her. Ammu's arms around her: Harriet found this revolting, incredible – no, only absurd.

Harriet had seen Ammu holding the stick leg of an old peasant, probe a poisoned swelling and then lance it with a movement so swift and sure his face expressed nothing but surprise. She had seen her press her fingers into swollen, suppurating labia, and then enquire delicately into the sexual habits of the husband. But it was not possible even to begin to think of Sophie in Ammu's arms.

But what could have been in Ammu's thoughts while Harriet was trying to telephone her from Mauritius, getting worried and then frantic as the days and even weeks passed?

Harriet's expensive phone calls had led to nothing. International Directories couldn't give her the number in Camden Town since she didn't know Paul's surname; the offices of Save the Children, Oxfam, Christian Aid, Help the Aged, ActionAid and half a dozen other charities promised to give messages when they saw her, but they never saw her. Ammu had not written. Ammu had not returned to Port Louis. The officials at the Ministry of Health could barely contain their delight.

Could someone like Ammu merely abandon the clinics she had fought so hard to build; casually forget a deal for which Harriet had paid with her career? These things were unthinkable. But so was the thought of that ugly woman having any kind of hold over Ammu. Everything was wrong like a bad dream.

'Gone for two terrible weeks. Just gone.' Harriet looked up sharply. Sophie's voice was languid, almost sleepy. 'Went, just as she came – from nowhere, to nowhere. She was only lent to me. I knew it at the start, but it was her – it was her made me forget the price to be paid.

'It was near the end of September, still hot, but the year was beginning to die. I wasn't doing anything, looking for anything, just quietly drinking myself to death. Then one night, Brucie picked her up, at a club or someplace; said I had to put her up. I didn't ask, no point in knowing what could only mean trouble. Nobody but Ammu ever explains nothing to me, they just give me orders. I stuck her in the attic.

'Next day she came down here and asked me if it was okay if she washed her clothes in the bath. I said sure; I mean, what's a few pints of hot water? Then I thought it was a bit rum that this little wog wanted to wash the clothes she was wearing when she didn't have nothing to change into. So I went in to give her a dressing gown.' Harriet moved quietly across the room and refilled Sophie's glass.

'Thanks.' Sophie kept her head low, almost as if she was crying. 'She was on her knees by the bath, bashing yards and yards of blood-red silk, just with her fists; not using soap, like she thought I was too mean to let her have any. I saw her from the back, you see, wearing nothing but one of those stupid little tops Indian women wear under all that other stuff. Her skinny brown arms were stretched out in the water. It gave me a real shock to see how hairy her armpits were; I thought all that lot was sort of smooth. Then I noticed her bum had these deep dents in the side, like a kid's little arse. But, funniest of all, it was sort of pale and looked terribly naked. You know, I didn't figure till then that blacks got suntanned. I guess I laughed.

'Anyway, she heard me, and she grabbed her funny old petticoat off the floor to cover herself, and she looked up at me with those big puppy eyes that are so black they are all pupil. Eyes like that, you know, they drag you into them, just drag you in. I didn't even think to try to peep round the petticoat thing, check out the rest of her; isn't that odd? I just sort of went into the eyes like they were the whole of her. I didn't know for ages she was some kind of doctor. I didn't know what she was into, as if I would care, anyhow.'

Harriet didn't look up. She was trying to control the furious beating of her heart, control the surges, appalling in a trained nurse, of wanting to blind the eyes that had looked at Ammu as at an animal.

'Who is Brucie?' she said icily.

'My friend, my tenant; occasionally my lover. You can meet her if you stay.'

'*Her*?' Harriet started, found her eyes caught by the stare of the cat on the mantelpiece. 'You want me to stay?' Stay in this horrible place to hear more of this impossible, sordid story? 'I'm due back at Gunnersbury tonight; at Dr Ramgulam's place. She's Ammu's friend.'

Sophie spoke slowly, her head still bowed very low. 'I'm Ammu's friend. I'm Ammu's only friend. I'm the only person she's really trusted, really opened herself up to.' Sophie's knees were spread wide apart, opening the kimono on a deep shadow. Harriet's glance turned back to the cat. 'You don't believe that, do you? You don't believe Ammu could love someone like me. Well, let me tell you, sweetheart, Ammu did. She said once to me, she said: "I've brought you back to life Sophiji, and I love you for that." She said, "You've given me the greatest gift anyone can give a lover: to let her give you life." I think she said that was something Indian, something from a holy man.'

Harriet half shook her head. This woman *did* know Ammu; this was something only Ammu could have said; it was also something she would never have said to Harriet.

'So she gave me life. But then she took it away again. Because she went, on that Thursday, and she left behind the gift I gave her. And when I had it back, it wasn't life any more. It was a murdered thing; not cold and dry like my life had been before, but all red with screaming inside.' Sophie, chin still sunk into her breast, lapsed into silence.

Harriet shook her head slowly while pictures of her own taken life formed and broke up in her mind, of her dream of life with Ammu in Mozambique.

Sophie lifted her head: 'But, you see, we both knew. We both knew that Ammu had to pay. No difference if the bill was run up a long time ago.'

This was something different. Harriet snapped. 'What did Ammu have to pay?'

'I could tell you something of that, if you stay. Why not? What's left?'

What was left?

'The last tube will have gone by now. You can stay in Ammu's room.'

'Okay, I'll stay.' Harriet looked at the face slowly turning up towards her, showing not tears but a crooked smirk; Sophie was warming, wanting to talk, even seeming solicitous about Harriet's welfare while Harriet grew more and more depressed. 'I might as well find out what happened, and where she's gone to, before I try to get back to Mauritius.' She elbowed a cat off the arm of her chair. 'And since you're so well informed, tell me this, why didn't Ammu write to me, tell me not to come?'

Sophie shrugged. 'Can't say. She never said a word about you, sweetheart.'

Harriet glared back at the cat on the mantelpiece. 'All right then,' she drawled savagely, 'You want to talk, so talk. But just give me the facts – the facts about Ammu, you can keep your life story. So you met Ammu as Brucie's, um, associate.'

'Brucie's bit of stuff.'

'Bit of stuff,' Harriet echoed. This, if true, was a fact. She pressed on. 'This Brucie met her at a club, you said. What club?'

'I dunno. I said I didn't ask. Some place where dope is cheap and leather cheaper.'

'A low place?'

'An arsehole.'

'I want to speak to Brucie.'

'Bleat your heart out to her for all I care. Brucie couldn't see what I saw in Ammu. Brucie's your age, no, younger; a shallow, selfish fool. I was mad for Ammu, sweetheart. I never needed somebody so hard. You think, don't you, girl, that at my age you run slow on passion. Not so. When it comes, it kicks like a mule. Fuck your kids' moonlight and roses. Fuck Brucie's parading about like she was in the Paraguay police, needing a woman hanging on to her to prove she's tough. I'm not talking about any of that. I'm talking about love. I'm talking about dying of it, about cutting your throat for it.' Sophie was panting. 'You know that kind of love? No; not you, never. You never will. Well open your fat ears. I can't live without the feel of her mouth. It's my death sentence.' Sophie paused, looked away. 'I'll never see her again.'

'Why not? If I can believe half of what you say, she found some pleasure in your company.'

Sophie, like the cat on the mantelpiece, was still staring at nothing. 'You don't have to believe nothing of it, except that it's all over, everything.'

Sophie poured out another great slug of rum and then rested the teetering glass between her outspread thighs. So it, whatever it was, was over for Sophie. And it, whatever it was for Harriet, was fading like the Cheshire cat while the eyes of the real cat on the mantelpiece narrowed and hardened.

'So', said Harriet, 'It's over. Ammu went "out" one morning. She had some kind of bill to pay? What bill? To whom? Where? What did she tell you? I might need to have a few words with her about a bill owed to me.'

'She didn't say. There's things you just know.' Sophie raised the glass to her mouth.

'She said' – Harriet almost yelped as a deep but strangely girlish voice sounded behind her – 'that Sophie is the mother and father of all pink elephants.'

Sophie spoke, her mouth still round the glass, 'Piss off Brucie. I'm talking business.'

A youth, tall as Harriet, but stout and muscular, smelling of tobacco and leather, marched into the dim room, seized the bottle of rum by the neck. The cat on the mantelpiece disappeared. The others kept well clear of the boots. The figure sniffed the bottle, then swung round at Harriet, presenting a jutting jaw, and the downy outline of the cheeks of a young woman. 'You gave her this – why? You can't think it's good for her?'

Harriet scrabbled to her feet. 'You're Brucie. How do you do. I'm Harriet Weston, nurse tutor from Mauritius.' Harriet half extended a hand. 'I came to London to join up with Dr Bai, but I haven't been able to make contact yet. I understand you've met her.'

The young woman grunted.

'I'm sorry it's so late, but I would appreciate a few minutes of your time. Later tonight would suit me well, after Sophie and I are through.' Harriet made a half-turn towards Sophie. 'Sophie's been very helpful.'

'Sure, sure she has; Sophie's all charm. Come on Sophie, time to shut your face and do the apples and pears. And time' – to Harriet – 'you buggered off. I'll ring you some time about that talk.'

'She's staying,' said Sophie. 'She's okay. She's Ammu's friend.'

'I'm staying,' said Harriet with a firmness she wished she felt, 'in Ammu's room.'

The big woman looked thoughtful, then nodded. 'Okay. If that's the way it is, I'll take you up.' Harriet, marched off by Brucie, was spared the need to bid Sophie good night, thank her; was given no chance at all to find out what on earth was going on.

Late Thursday night,
3 November

Brucie left, after flicking on the lamp and gas fire, and, with a movement whose rawness made Harriet wince, yanking back the covers of Ammu's bed.

The door closed. Quietness – of white walls, a crooked ceiling, a narrow bed pulled tight – fell over the little garret as the thump of boots diminished down the stairs.

Harriet put her hands to her eyes, and they filled with merciful water, rinsing out the burning points of the stares of half a dozen cats. Sophie's legs, etched on her eyeballs in the outline of a pair of plucked hens in Port Louis market; Sophie's mouth, shapeless as an open bruise, dissolved in the wash of tears.

Gradually, Harriet began to get the sense of where she was: in the room of an Ammu she didn't know, couldn't imagine. Now she should try to get some grasp of what she had heard, some idea of how much she had to believe: some sense of how bad it was.

But Harriet found herself without thought or plan as she moved around the small space, touching here in the window the lace cloth on a small white escritoire, there an over-large wardrobe, a kitchen chair with a worn, embroidered cover; the bed she didn't touch.

That was all there was. Yet, although Harriet had never been inside Ammu's private spaces before, the room pulsed with the sense of Ammu – the sense of her alienness. The bed, its covers rucked by that Brucie: the covers Ammu did not crumple, because, according to the madwoman in the basement, she lay, not here, but in the woman's bed, thinking – God knows what – certainly not about Harriet mad with anxiety in Mauritius, running up a huge telephone bill trying to find Ammu somewhere in London.

In a sudden movement, Harriet swung round, seized the chair, and thrust its back under the handle of the door. She had to have a while to be alone, alone with this room, all she could now grasp of Ammu.

Ammu owed her an explanation. Ammu had asked her – Harriet – to share her life with her; but, she was now supposed to believe, Ammu had shared her body, in some unnatural intimacy, with an ugly drunkard. How could this be possible? How could the clever, beautiful Ammu find release in such a soiled place?

As this thought came to her, Harriet almost heard Ammu's voice, sharp as a rap on the knuckles – Ammu had always found her release in soiled places. To the coterie of society doctors, she was alien as a scorpion. It was to the poor and desperate, bodies fouled by disease and suffering, that she gave herself. But this thing that Harriet had heard tonight was not of that giving. This was Ammu herself sinking into the foulness; this was not what Ammu meant when she said there was no distance between herself and the people she tended. Surely this was not what she meant.

No, Harriet could not believe Sophie's story. If only there were not things in that story, rays of light in it, that could only have come from the mind of Ammu.

No, Harriet could not disbelieve Sophie's story either. If she had to find Ammu now, it was to force her to say why she had done whatever part she had done of this thing. The pulse in Harriet's stomach – that old associate that never let her forget that her body was an often awkward partner in the business of her life – throbbed aloud in the silence. Her fingers twined in her tough ginger hair.

Freni, the old mad woman, thin as a strip of dry pemmican, had squatted in the dust outside Ammu's clinic at Rivière Sèche, just like this, tearing at the few tufts left on her skull, mouth open in a dry howl. She would sit there for days, hoping for nothing, but waiting for Ammu.

Freni was dead now, but Harriet could clearly see her, on that first meeting, five years earlier, not long after Ammu had finally succeeded in bullying Harriet, the nurse, the cold professional, into making her first visit to one of her clinics, the newest one, only a month old. Just to look, Ammu promised, not to compromise Harriet's professional ethics in any least way.

They must have seemed a peculiar couple on Harriet's scooter, lurching along the track to the village. Harriet was stiff and resentful. People on the dusty path lowered their bundles of firewood or mangoes to wave to Ammu and then stare after the white woman, so tall and red, her hair, escaped from its bun, flying into Ammu's face while the skirts of Ammu's sari threatened to wind themselves round the wheels. Ammu, unconscious as ever of Harriet's states of mind, threw greetings to every person, chicken or goat in hailing distance. And she laughed in anticipation of the surprise of her patients that she, who usually walked, or hitched a ride on a donkey cart, should arrive on this machine.

The temple turrets, crammed with painted flowers and parrots, came into view; then the verandah, where a crowd of peasant women sat in the shade, and a scouting party of children was half way up a pawpaw tree, cheering them on.

With some hundred yards still to go, Ammu called 'Woah', as if to a horse. Harriet braked sharply. 'Thank you, Sister Weston.' Ammu was off and running up to what seemed to be a heap of rags by the roadside.

Harriet switched off the engine, leaned the scooter against a bush and tagged after her.

Ammu was squatting down beside an old ragged bald woman. A leper perhaps? Coming close, Harriet detected no signs of leprosy, but clear indications of dehydration, and the woman's bearing suggested some severe disorientation, perhaps schizophrenia – without any doubt, a hospital case. Beyond, in the tree, the children watched, silent now.

'Namaste, Freni.' Ammu folded her hands together in the respectful greeting.

The woman's fingers twitched in the fabric of her sari.

Ammu continued, speaking in Tamil slow and simple enough for Harriet to understand. 'It is very hot in the sun, Freni. Why are you not at the temple?'

The fingers twitched again, in response to this, and to Ammu's following remarks, made at long intervals, a mixture of pleasantries and enquiries about her health. Harriet felt more at ease. Ammu was now behaving like a doctor.

Then Ammu stood up and signalled to one of the children. A girl of about thirteen, wearing a school uniform, came running.

After finding out the girl's name (Leilane), Ammu asked her somewhat fiercely: 'Why is Freni not at the temple?' Leilane shuffled her feet. 'Were you here last week, Leilane, when we all agreed that she should stay at the temple?' Leilane nodded. 'And when you children promised to bring her tea every two hours with sugar and sometimes a little salt?' Another nod. 'Freni has had no tea today.'

Leilane shuffled. 'She spat it out.'

'Why? Did you give it to her in a cracked cup? You know she can see the spirits in a cracked cup.'

Leilane was stung. 'There were no spirits in it. She spat

it out because she's evil; and the tea was good. She couldn't swallow something good.'

Ammu put a hand on Freni's shoulder. 'Are you evil, Freni?'

Freni opened her mouth, and, after a minute of dry mouthing, out came, in a cracked croak: 'Ye-a-es.'

'Do you want to be evil, Freni?'

Freni nodded.

'Why?'

Freni's mouth moved furiously before spitting out the words, 'I killed my baby.'

'She didn't,' interjected Leilane crossly, 'She doesn't have any baby. She had one grown up son, a fisherman. His boat sank in the hurricane.'

'Her son, used he to feed her, and care for her?' Leilane nodded. 'Do you think Freni is evil, Leilane?' Leilane nodded again, but uncertainly. 'Do you think, maybe, Leilane, if you children fed her and cared for her again, and prayed to Vishnu to let you all be her son, then Freni's evil would go away because her son's spirit would be doing its work in the world again?' Leilane looked more uncertain than ever, an uncertainty echoed by Harriet.

At the end of a session at the clinic that went on until very late – long past the hour the children should have been in bed – the two holy men poured unused quantities of their foul smelling liquids into old kerosene cans, rolled up their handkerchiefs of red and purple pastes, and came to Ammu with outstretched hands to collect their payment. Harriet watched their departure with relief.

But meanwhile Freni was back under the verandah of the temple, her whole body eased with quantities of tea. A swarm of children was pushing and shoving to make for her as comfortable a bed as they could of one blanket on the rough stone.

'God, I could do with a drink,' Ammu muttered as they made their way back to the scooter. Harriet had to face her bright-eyed students in far too few hours, but she was by now so intrigued and confused by Ammu's ideas about health care, that she had to stop off at Ammu's home, a couple of rooms smelling of jute sacks, and half a verandah, at the back of a tenement. The mosquitoes must have relieved Harriet of near a pint of blood as she and Ammu sat under the stars till dawn.

Harriet wanted details about Freni's condition, but Ammu volunteered little more than that she was glad the mental hospital hadn't got the chance to poison Freni's brain with drugs and glad too that Freni had broken a silence of many months, even if only with five words.

Instead Ammu talked for hours – until Harriet's head swam – about what she would always talk about: her ideas. Mental illness, she declared, was an infection of the soul caused by despair. It could only be cured by love, because despair was grief at the death of love, and the giving of new love invoked the gentle gods. The newly healed person could only be made strong again by work, because good work was an exchange of love with the earth. Indeed, all healing, she said, was of this nature. She quoted something by Ivan Illich, which Harriet looked up in the library when she got to the hospital that morning:

> The medical monopoly of health care has expanded without checks and has encroached on our liberty with regards to our bodies ... Society has transferred to the physicians the exclusive right to determine what constitutes sickness, who is or might become sick and what shall be done to such people.

Harriet faced her students in a very muddled state of mind that morning. The only thing that was clear was that she wanted to talk more with Dr Ammu Bai.

Harriet came to, sitting on Ammu's narrow bed in

Sophie's house in London, her hands still covering her eyes, her eyes still oozing tears, but the pulse quiet in her stomach.

Freni had, as Ammu predicted, got much better. She had even, a year or two later, had a brief moment of glory when the temple priests raised her to the status of minor holy woman with especial powers to protect seafarers. She died shortly after of chickenpox caught from one of the children who by that time brought her fruit and rice and flowers as well as tea. Ammu and Harriet watched the throngs of village women and children wailing and beating their heads as they followed Freni's bier to the burning ghats on the river; Ammu was happy, believing that Freni's spirit was proud to be guest of honour at this last festival.

Slowly, Harriet opened the duffel bag and took out of her wallet her one photograph of Ammu. Against a background of palms and giant water lilies of the Botanical Gardens at Pamplemousses, it showed a small figure in a rumpled sari, the childlike face with its huge eyes and delicate bones belying Ammu's forty years; standing four-square, with the tense smile of someone who had waited rather too long for the photographer to press the shutter.

Harriet looked desperately at the picture. 'How could you, Ammu? You have always shocked me, but with this? Why? Was my loyalty, my service, not good enough for you?'

Ammu had battled hard to win Harriet. She had fought and won against a decade of training in hospital medicine. She had destroyed all Harriet's old certainties, because Harriet had discovered herself, made her place in the world, as a nurse in the Western allopathic tradition. Now, the thought of administering order and pills to a succession of cases briefly confined to hospital beds seemed cold and empty. She couldn't go back to what she had been. If Ammu had abandoned her, what would be left of Harriet's life?

She flopped onto the chair, head in her hands. Without Ammu, she had no job, no home, no cause. She was not herself, she was driftwood. And she had already drifted so far into nothing that she had not even telephoned her mother in her three days in London. Mother! It seemed a thousand years since Harriet had dreamed, with innocent amusement, of teasing Mother with something that would have made Martin seem a comfortable contrast: dropping in on her with Ammu, saying, 'Hello, Mother, this is the Ammu I've written so much about; we're going to Mozambique. We're going to start people's clinics there.' Because of Ammu, even her poor mother was betrayed.

And Dr Ramgulam, the decent Dr Ramgulam, Ammu's good friend for so many years, who had given her Sophie's address, and sensed that it was a bad place? Dr Ramgulam had wanted so much to help.

All these betrayed people; Harriet wished them away, to disappear, like Ammu; to be nothing, like herself. 'Ammu, I have to believe that you have treated me worse than Sophie,' she said aloud, 'Why? And are you so ashamed that you have run away from me? Have you run off with another Sophie, another Brucie?'

Why?

Harriet's head filled with dozens of fractions she had not added up before: they made powerful round numbers. Ammu, who embraced everybody else, had never embraced her. Ammu kept her busy seven nights a week, but never paused to ask if she was tired. Ammu talked, almost always about her work, seldom about herself, never about Harriet. Ammu knew nothing of Harriet's past; would no doubt be surprised to find that Harriet had one.

In Ammu's letter there was no touch of sentiment about the Mauritian clinics. They could now, she said, run themselves perfectly well. Someone who could so coolly cut herself off from the children who ran out from tin shanties calling her name, could surely as coolly cut herself off from Harriet Weston, a mere drudge. Only the last paragraph, an afterthought, had turned to Harriet as herself, not just someone in the audience: 'I want to start them again', she had written. 'I want to start clean ... I don't need anybody to help me, except you Harriet, except you.' And then, in a postscript scribbled up the edge of the page, the sketchiest of instructions. Would any sensible, grown up person have taken such a letter seriously? Harriet had swallowed every word.

She swung round and grasped the edge of the lacy escritoire. The top was bare but for a dead begonia, with its blackened stems bowed to the cloth and its flowers, papery dry but still strangely red, scattered. Harriet picked up a flower. Surely this would cause Ammu pain, because, although Ammu did not love Harriet, she truly loved plants. Perhaps, when this was still in bud, Ammu had touched it, spoken to it in her Indian way, encouraging it to grow big and strong. Her fingers felt about for something else Ammu would have touched. There were so few objects in the room. How very strange that Ammu, who was so messy in her person, should leave no mark on the place she had occupied but a plant in a pot.

She opened the drawers of the escritoire. Fresh green lining paper; nothing else, not even the odd hairpin or paperclip of any normal abandoned desk. Being someone who lived so much in her own head, had she put nothing down that needed to be taken up again? 'Every night for almost a month,' Sophie had said. Had Ammu been so busy with Sophie that she had scarcely used the room? Harriet, her arms heavy, pushed the drawers roughly to, and nudged the door of the wardrobe.

It fell open. Nothing in it but a black cloak. She touched it, a cheap, coarse fabric. But her touch released from it a faint scent of jasmine – Ammu's scent. Somewhere, Harriet's Ammu was still here, in this room. Tears rushed into Harriet's eyes as she took down the cloak and buried her face in it: Ammu's for sure. 'Oh, Ammu,' she said into it, 'I would have done anything for you. When you called me to England, I came; but you had abandoned everything, and me.'

But what was this? Ammu had left the house, moved off to fresh fields, packed up and gone, in England, with winter coming on, leaving behind her cloak? Ammu had gone, leaving a plant to die? Was that possible? And she had gone without a bag; Sophie had said as much. Furiously Harriet ripped open the drawers at the base of the wardrobe: a pair of socks, a camisole, a sari of red silk, neatly folded. She recognised it – Ammu's 'smart' sari, the one she was wearing when she left Mauritius and was doubtless wearing when she arrived at Sophie's. But she wasn't wearing it when she left. Why, if she was going somewhere important?. She had come with nothing to change into. Why? She had then acquired a few things, and left them behind. Why?

Something was not right. Something was definitely not right. Whatever was wrong for Harriet, something was definitely not right for Ammu. Harriet sat on the bed, her stomach fluttering. Even up here, at the top of the house, she was still aware of the nauseous smell of Sophie's whisky, Sophie's cigarettes, Sophie's cats, Sophie's appalling house, the last place Ammu had been. Somewhere, in a corner of her mind, the scene kept on playing itself, as it had for the past hour, of those soft tentacles of arms wrapping themselves around Ammu. But all this – the smell, the arms, the house – Harriet put firmly away in the effort to think of what could have happened to Ammu.

Think, think. Try to get it clear. What did she know? Surely she knew that Ammu was in trouble? How could she have thought that Ammu would walk out on Paul, walk out on Dr Ramgulam, just to give Sophie a few words from some Indian holy man? Surely Ammu was running away from something, or worse, had been taken. Sophie was what? A drunk, presumptuous, pitiable, manageable. Guija was real. If it was conceivable that Ammu would abandon Harriet, would she abandon Mozambique?

Harriet seized the cloak in her arms. Think.

A new set of fractions rushed towards whole numbers – Ammu tidying up all the administrative details of the clinics before she left Port Louis; Ammu buying a year's food in advance for the little orphanage; Ammu in tears at the airport saying she did not expect to see Mauritius again. Why had Harriet let that little voice inside whisper to her about all the fussing of Indian emotionalism, so unlike her British stoicism; why, above all, had she for one second doubted that Ammu's call to her was a sacred contract?

But then, what of the little voice now that was saying that her proud Ammu, the voice of the sick and poor in Mauritius, believed in some very funny things about medicine, and seemed to have lain in a sweaty bed with the appalling Sophie? So, if she did; so what if she did, so what? Why did that make her want to break Sophie's ugly head open? Harriet shook the cloak. Don't let me think about those things, she said to it.

Just think about Ammu. Forget, for the moment, about Harriet, Harriet's hurt, Harriet's guilt. What could have happened? Brain: function. Think, think like a nurse, 'define the problem; search for the causes; give emergency help with the problem, long-term help with the causes.'

Ammu had disappeared. She had walked out of the house, and not returned. Why? Because she had run away, or been taken. If Ammu had run away, what could she be running away from? If Ammu had been taken, who could have taken her, and why? Harriet could hardly begin to answer these questions. While she knew a great deal about Ammu's work, and much about her ideas, she knew very little about her life.

Could anyone want to rob her? Ammu was poor as a

nun, with no possessions of her own, at least as far as Harriet knew. But some rather questionable healers did make questionable profits out of the sicknesses of the poor at Ammu's clinics. And Ammu, if she took against one of these healers, cared nothing for the anger she aroused, nor that a healer she rejected would be ruined for life. Harriet acknowledged that Ammu's enemies included some desperate and dangerous men.

Could any jealous lover want to injure her? Sophie? Brucie? Some other strange passion? With a sinking feeling, Harriet acknowledged that Ammu seemed to have been trawling in murky waters.

Could the Mauritian Government want to silence her? Ammu saw her aims as revolutionary: empowering the people, dethroning the doctors and bureaucrats, demytho-logising Western medicine. But Ammu had set up no party to fight for these aims, so while to her the Govern-ment was an enemy, to the holders of power she was at most a troublemaker, more often just an eccentric, a woman with a bee in her bonnet, a source of amusement. Harriet acknowledged that Ammu was an important leader only to Harriet and a group of peasants – women, children, invalids and old people – whose views carried no weight in society.

Could anyone want to prevent her from setting up clinics in Guija? In her letter, Ammu had explained that this was an area so wrecked by the Renamo dissidents that even those brutal bandits had been forced to abandon it. Ammu's aim was to help a little bit of the region back to life. Renamo would not be pleased to find a green hole in its scorched earth policy. And Renamo was backed by a powerful fascist faction in the South African Defence Force. Could men so hardened to murder and pillage be expected, if they knew of it, to exercise tolerance of a powerless Indian woman who would, mole–like, under-mine a little bit of their order?

Harriet was shivering. She wrapped herself in Ammu's cloak. Dark, awful things were coming into her mind, monsters made out of ignorance and fear, leading to no useful answers. Why – Because she didn't know what to do; because Sophie had shaken her trust in Ammu; because she could still not think as she had been trained as a nurse to think – objectively.

She decided, instead, to try to follow Ammu's movements since her arrival in London in early September. As scheduled, Ammu had attended the Save the Children conference. People had been disturbed and impressed by her speeches (people always were) and had given money for the Mauritian clinics, which Ammu had transferred, by banker's draft, to Port Louis. She had arranged for a team from Save the Children to visit Mauritius, inspect the clinics. She had made no plans to meet them there. Her lieutenants were delighted to be given the job.

Ammu had then, out of the blue as far as they were concerned, Save the Children told her, rushed up to the rostrum and said, 'We can't just stand and watch.' Shaking the Unicef report like a fist, she had said, 'A child dies every three and a half minutes in Mozambique and Angola through the destabilisation backed by South Africa. I am going to go there to fight wounding with healing. The Mozambican authorities and Father Chipani from the Notre Dame Mission at Matola want me to do it. You must give me money, and protection.'

There was a great uproar in the room, but no promises. Then the charities set their lawyers and sleuths to check Ammu out, talk to their field staff in Mauritius and Mozambique. Within a week, offers of money and protection were pouring in, and Ammu, full of excitement, wrote to Harriet, offering her a job.

All this while, Ammu was staying, as arranged, at Paul's house in Camden Town. And at Paul's house, Harriet's reply still lay, unopened. Because, on September twenty-third, Ammu had moved on, giving Paul no forwarding address, not keeping her promise to be in touch.

She had gone to Dr Ramgulam, the old friend whose telephone number Paul had found scribbled on the pad beside the telephone, and passed on to Harriet.

But, scarcely twenty-four hours after moving to Gunnersbury, Ammu had called, very late, from a payphone, to say she would not be returning. This time she had left an address, the address Dr Ramgulam had given to Harriet under a vow of secrecy, because Ammu had asked her to reveal it to nobody – Sophie's.

At Sophie's place, Ammu had stayed a month. Sophie surely had more important things to tell than of sweet-talk with Ammu. Harriet, now boiling hot, flung off the cloak. There was more questioning and searching to be done in Sophie's house.

She glanced quickly around the room, then reached over, and put her hand under the bedclothes. They were cold. What was she expecting? To feel some warmth of the body that had perhaps rested there once or twice in the afternoon? She stripped the bedding, dragged the mattress to the floor. Inside the base of the bed was a concealed drawer. She lifted it out: a douche, half a dozen used syringes and several pairs of surgical gloves, the rubber old and perished. Beside them lay a yellowed jotter pad. In a crabbed, ill-formed hand were lists of men's names, annotated with pictographic codes and sums of money. She could look no further. A wash of cold fear for Ammu, exposed to such a house, to people like Sophie and Brucie, flooded over her.

What could she do? When she knew something horrible had its claws in Ammu, how could her mind be so opaque as not to see what was to be done? She decided to search the house, giving another half hour for Sophie and Brucie to fall asleep.

Throwing herself furiously back onto the chair, she wriggled and twisted, then tried to mollify her stomach by conjuring up images of the Bunnikins wallpaper in her childhood bedroom, a trick that sometimes worked on that queasy partner in her life. But this time she blotted out the recollection that she could do this without shame because Ammu regarded such games as no more than sensible psychic management. Thirty minutes later, she was calm and determined.

Quietly, she made her way down the stairs to the half-landing below and entered the first room. It was empty. There was nothing of any interest in it; just rather dirty lodging house furniture. She didn't look under the mattress. The room beside it gave the same result. Why did a woman who let rooms for a living have three of them empty?

On the floor below, a ceramic sign read 'Bruce'. Harriet passed without a sound. Opening the next door, she heard heavy, difficult, breathing – Sophie. She passed quickly. Beside it was the bathroom she had visited earlier; it was cold and dank, with a rather smelly lavatory, a washbasin (which she remembered as grimy and avocado coloured) and a white bath, glimmering in the street light. She felt among the crumpled linen in the airing cupboard, under the basin, inside the cistern, behind the two rather stiff towels hanging from the rail. Then in the kitchen, where two cats watched her, she fumbled among jars of powdered coffee, and the empty whisky bottles beside the waste bin. The doors of the two ground-floor rooms were locked, a normal enough precaution against burglars, but seeming sinister enough for Harriet to struggle to make out something through the keyhole.

In Sophie's den in the half-basement, she put on the light. There was Sophie's chair, with its crumpled cushions surrounded by little worms of cigarette ash. The big tom cat which had stared at her from the mantelpiece now lay in Sophie's lost warmth, still staring. She ignored it. There was Ammu's rum, the bottle now half empty. Harriet pulled out the few books, felt around the television set, under the pictures.

Oh Ammu, some sign. Something. She put out the light, casting a look at the cat, and crept back up to Sophie's room. The same troubled, hoarse breathing. How drunk was the sleeping figure? In the streetlight that filtered through the dirty window glass, Harriet could just make her out, a lump on the bed. She froze: there were two heads – 'Ammu!' But the ghostly shape didn't move, and, as her eyes reached further into the darkness, she recognised the cropped outlines of Brucie's skull.

Still as she could keep herself against the thudding in her stomach, Harriet watched, till she could make out the outline of Brucie's face, detect, underneath the rasp of Sophie's breathing, long sighs from Brucie's lungs. The rhythms of their breathings crossed and counter-crossed, the slow music of night duty on a hospital ward. Harriet stood there, relaxing into the familiar vigilance of one who watches over sleepers. She moved closer. Their arms were entwined. She leaned almost close enough to check a pulse. Yes, they were asleep, Sophie heavily, Brucie with eyelids twitching in a dream. She would search the room.

Ears honed in expectation of a sharp yell from Brucie, Harriet's fingers reached into a drawer, filled with the softness of fabrics. Another, stiffer fabrics. Listening to the double breathing, she felt along shelves and inside drawers, plastic shopping bags, even an overflowing laundry basket and a pile of newspapers and magazines on the floor. She found nothing. What did she expect? Bits of Ammu's body? About to give up, she noticed, hanging on the back of the door, under Sophie's yellow kimono, a candlewick dressing gown. Could this be the gown Sophie had lent to Ammu that first day? She took it down. There was a bulge in the pocket; her fingers lifted out a package of papers, envelopes, tied with a silk cord. She brought it to her face: a soft breath of jasmine.

Quickly as she dared, Harriet hung up the gown and exited.

Friday, 4 November

Tock. Tock. Tock. Tock. Bubbling up from the throats of frogs on the giant water lily leaves. Frogs, big and glossy, their soft bodies absolutely still except for the huge bubbles rising up their throats. Then one of them had plopped into the water, rocking the lilies, rocking Harriet into a gentle wakefulness. She stretched out a hand to lift the mosquito net – that was not there. God no! This was London. Her knees jerked against a ton weight of bedclothes. Ammu!

Tock. Tock. 'Breakfast!' The low growl was familiar. A big woman swinging round at her, a bottle of rum held by the neck, swirled into her consciousness. It was that Brucie. The door rattled against the chair jammed under its handle.

'With you in a sec.' Harriet leapt out of bed, stuffed Ammu's letters into the bottom of her duffel bag, and thrust the bag deep into the bedclothes. Then she straightened herself and her yesterday's tracksuit, crumpled with sleep. She looked again at the open bed, then roughly shoved the bag under the pillow and straightened the blankets. 'Who is it?' (This she knew perfectly well.)

'Me. Open up.'

'Coming.' Harriet ran her fingers through her hair, scrabbled for her shoes then, still dissatisfied, squashed the bag hard under the meagre pillow and heaped the blankets over it.

But time to gather her thoughts was not to be given. Brucie forced the door open a crack, and her booted foot was pushing away the leg of the chair. Then her form, huge and dark, filled the doorway. She too was in yesterday's rumpled clothes, minus the leather jacket; but she was holding a little tray laden with steaming mug, fingers of toast and a boiled egg. 'Sophie got this stuff together and sent me up,' Brucie muttered. 'She wants me to talk to you.'

'What time is it?' Harriet looked about vaguely.

'Somewhere around noon, maybe two o'clock.'

'Two! Good God!' That was late afternoon in Mauritius. She had slept the day away. How much time lost; how long had she slept? She had dropped off to the whine of a milk float.

Brucie levered the tray into her hands, and bustled round the room, lighting the fire with her zippo lighter, pulling back the pale curtains. She still smelled of tobacco and hash, and London-sweated clothes. Then swinging the chair round and perching astride it, her chin on the back, she intoned:

'Jane, Jane,
Tall as a crane,
The morning light breaks in again.
Comb your cockscomb ragged hair,
Jane, Jane, come down the stair.'

Harriet decided to take this for solicitude. 'Thanks, I'd like to wash later, if the bathroom's free.' Her eye moved quickly to the pillow to make sure the duffel bag was out of sight.

'Right. Eat your breakfast'.

'Brucie rolled a cigarette without taking her eyes off Harriet. She watched closely as Harriet unwrapped the spoon from its roll of kitchen paper, laid it beside the egg, then picked up the mug. 'Drink,' demanded Brucie.

Harriet took a sip of the strong, dark, milky and very sweet tea – thé Anglais they called it in Mauritius; she had drunk it often, keeping pace with Ammu, drinking rum. For all that, her stomach gave a lurch at the scent of buttered toast, reminding her that she had missed a couple of meals or more. No chance to assess the woman opposite; Brucie's attention was too busily devouring her. So far, neither of them had smiled.

'She wants me to talk to you, help you, you know.' Brucie paused, but Harriet was not yet ready to show any reaction. 'Sophie's a right punk of course, but she's gone a bundle on Ammu.'

'So I gather.' Last night's talk with Sophie broke open in Harriet's mind like a festering wound. 'I'm not very hungry, thank you.'

'Eat!' Brucie narrowed her eyes as she lit her cigarette, inhaling deeply. 'Why you so keen to find her?'

Anything to gain time. Harriet swallowed hard to quell the fluttering in her stomach. 'I'm supposed to be going with her,' she said, 'to start new clinics.' Brucie nodded encouragement. 'In Mozambique.'

'Oh yeah. Well, maybe she's gone on ahead. Maybe you should get on a plane.'

Did this mean anything? 'Why do you think that?'

Brucie didn't answer. She took another long draw on her cigarette. 'What do you do?'

'I told you last night. I'm a nurse.'

'Is that what you are for Ammu? Is that it: a nurse?'

Harriet's heart was low. 'That's it. That's what I am; that's all I am.'

Brucie chortled. 'That's rich. A bloody nurse comes half way round the world to get this woman out of trouble when her lovers sit on their arses.'

'What do you mean?'

'More'n I can say.'

For once, Brucie's eyes moved away, and Harriet could search her face. She had strong features under a pale and rather spotty skin. The cropped haircut gave her cheeks a piggy fullness, but also brought out the powerful line of her brow, straightness of her nose and the gentle curve of her downy, though fleshy, chin. Harriet recognised something of intelligence in the dun-coloured eyes. It was difficult to connect this slow-speaking, ponderous, but somehow direct young woman with the list of men's names and cash values. 'I'd be most grateful to know what you meant by that.'

'I'd need to know you better. It's a long story.' Then, sharply: 'Have you been to the police?'

Harriet's heart jumped. 'No. Why?'

'Are you going to?'

'I don't know. I wouldn't know what to say. I suppose I could report a missing person.' Harriet hesitated. 'But what would they make of that? A foreigner, black, travelling around asking for money … wouldn't they scoff her off as an intending immigrant or something?'

'Well, don't do it. Not if you want help from Sophie. And that's what you came here for, innit?'

'All right.' (Harriet made a mental note to write the numbers of the local police stations in her diary.)

'But you have talked, or you wouldn't be here. Who to?'

Harriet looked away. It would be so nice if this woman were somebody she could trust, at least up to a point. What else did she have, apart from the precious bundle in her duffel bag? Brucie was so short with her, controlling the discussion, giving nothing but a promise as yet undefined. But then, she thought for a second, Brucie was with her, was there, something solid and somehow detached, in a way Sophie wasn't. 'Paul, in Camden Town – don't know his surname – Ammu stayed with him and his friend, another man, when she first arrived.

People at Save the Children; they don't know anything. Their conference is over. They've given Ammu the money. And' (Harriet paused before bringing this out) 'Ammu's old university friend, Dr Jasbir Ramgulam, at Gunnersbury.'

'Is he looking for Ammu?'

'She. She's worried.'

'Well, get her to back off, okay? Also that Paul. Get rid of them. Tell them you had a letter from Ammu from Kampala, or wherever Mozambique is.'

'A big, poor country on the south-east coast of Africa; we're going to a place there called Guija. There's a civil war there and the health services have broken down – where we're going everything's broken down.'

'Sure. I heard about that, some politics stuff. And that always means two geezers want to run the place, so they each make sure they fuck it up for the other guy. Right up Ammu's street – place sounds a genuine hole. For my mother's tits I couldn't tell you why Sophie wants me to give you this. I wouldn't do it. But then, I'm not the sort to fall in love.'

Harriet felt something almost like warmth for this woman. 'You are going to help? Do you know what's happened to Ammu?'

'Enough, I reckon, to get you going. Any more is up to Sophie, but mainly up to you. I'll get you started, then I'm off, okay? Then you're on your own, okay?'

'Okay then.' Harriet almost smiled. This was better. This was action. 'And thanks. But what do you mean by "enough"?'

'You'll see tonight. I'm taking you to the Purgatorial Fires, where you can meet the creep of all time, Ammu's Uncle Robertie. Then I bugger off. If, ever after, you ever try to lay something on me or on Sophie, you can forget Gweejeewhatsitsname, got it?'

'Uncle Robertie? Ammu has an uncle, here in London?

And you know him?'

'You'll know him yourself soon enough. And you haven't touched that bloody egg. It's okay. It's free range. Me and Sophie don't eat anything that's been made to suffer. I'll pick you up here, around eleven or so tonight. You all right on the back of a bike?' Brucie rose to her feet, and yawned. 'You'll need about fifty quid. I'll leave you some gear. Make yourself scarce till then. But don't say anything about this to that Paul or that Dr Jazz woman. And don't try to talk to Sophie. I'm handling this, and I won't have any messing. Got that. Till then, I'll be downstairs, waiting to hear you out the door.'

'I haven't got fifty pounds.'

'Get it.' Brucie stabbed her cigarette out in the begonia pot and went, leaving Harriet confused, even ashamed of her early morning prowl, the accusing package of letters, and her firm intention to tell everything to Dr Ramgulam. Things kept changing around. Now Sophie and Brucie, her first contacts with whatever bad had happened, were beginning to seem, in a funny sort of way, almost like decent people. And Harriet, having stolen the letters, was now being offered help by the people she had robbed. If only she had read them straight away, then returned them. But last night it had seemed important to deal with them out of range of Sophie's house.

Well, things were moving. She had half a day to get the letters read and, with luck, put back into the dressing gown. And, there were things to be done, practical things, and that made a measure of order. She jotted down a list in her diary which began with fifty pounds to be withdrawn from the building society and ended with telephoning her mother and Dr Ramgulam.

Making up the bed, turning the sheets with good hospital corners, she thought how odd it was that, though she was now certain that she was nobody of much importance in Ammu's life, she felt excited, for the first time in four horrible days, to be searching for her.

Sophie was nowhere to be seen when Harriet carried the tray down to the kitchen, so Brucie's injunction was easily obeyed. Harriet had rather hoped to get a glimpse of Sophie, as if to check that she was still the person Harriet had met last night, but she was pleased, so far, to keep in with Brucie. Her head was full of the possibilities Brucie offered. She wanted to get a clearer picture, too, of this strange woman. For a start: was she young, younger than Harriet? With that haircut, clothes and manner, those late-night eyes, she could be anything between twenty and forty. Was she being honest in her offer to help? She dressed and talked like a thug. She lived in a furnished room. She rode a motorbike. She came home late. She smelled of drugs. She demanded money. She was not the sort to fall in love. What, if anything, did she do for a living? What, if anything, did she care about? Although so many things counted against her, some part of Harriet believed she was being honest.

In some odd way, Brucie reminded Harriet of Ammu. They could hardly look more different – Brucie was big, slow, cumbersome, Ammu so slight. That nervy energy pulsing through Ammu, the jaunty thrust of her chin and firm plant of her feet cut across the message of her delicate bones, just as her big voice defied the little ribcage that produced it. Brucie was, somehow, given by nature, in voice and bone and weight, a power Ammu made for herself. Yet the essence of Ammu's power was her passion, poured out so lavishly for the poor and hungry. Brucie had a power that could go into nothing.

Harriet tipped the egg and toast into the bin. It was so caked with grease that her fingers stuck to the rim. Gingerly, she poured out the tea and rinsed her fingers and the mug under the tap. No, Brucie's power didn't quite go into nothing: Brucie was angry that Harriet gave Sophie rum; she seemed truly to care for Sophie; and so,

Harriet had to believe, did Ammu. Brucie cared, as Ammu did, about the sufferings of animals, though Brucie had no Hindu background to bring her up to it. And, despite her smell, her manners, her language, Brucie was not disgusting. Brucie was even, in her awful way, quite pleasant looking and intelligent. Cleaned up a bit, she could have made a passable student nurse; faced with the things nurses have to face, Brucie wouldn't squeal. This, to Harriet, was the essence of courage. Harriet was sorry to have deceived her about the letters, because Brucie's offer of help made everything seem a bit healthier somehow.

The package safe in the bottom of her duffel bag, Harriet let herself out into the damp, cold street. She called at the building society. Then, although it was already darkening, she walked all the way to Kensington Gardens and settled herself on a bench in a remote copse. Huddled tight in her lilac-coloured anorak, she pulled out the letters.

It was a package of seven envelopes, tied with a slightly greasy silk ribbon, the sort a child might have left behind at a clinic and Ammu absent-mindedly picked up to hold back her own heavy mane. The scent of jasmine was blunted by the cold, but still faintly perceptible.

The back of the last envelope had an address stamped on it in purple: Pointe-aux-Sables, Ile de Maurice. Official, but imprecise: perhaps a temple or a peasant co-op. The letter on the top was addressed in a florid hand. It read

> Mme le Docteur Ammu Bai, Physicienne (Liverpool)
> Malthouse Mews, 9
> Camden Town, Londres
> Les Iles de Grande Bretagne (England)

Harriet scrutinised the envelope. Its brightly-coloured stamp, with a picture of a pineapple, read 'Swaziland'. All

Harriet knew of Swaziland was what she had found when looking up Mozambique in the out-of-date atlas at the nursing school; it was a small, squarish African country south-west of Mozambique, where presumably, despite the Anglophone name, they spoke French? Perhaps this letter? ... Harriet's fingers moved to the ribbon, then hesitated at the neat bow. She had never before read someone else's mail.

She had certainly never before searched somebody's bedroom while that somebody was asleep in it, and with a partner who might attack if awakened. But medical professionals learn to take liberties with bodies (one of the things Ammu objected to about her profession). Letters were different, private. And these were Ammu's. She lifted the package. 'I'm sorry Ammu,' she whispered.

Harriet was already engaged on something foreign to her nature – searching for Ammu, chasing after her, entering her private places; taking on, uninvited, a dramatic and important role. Yet she had done it, and was about to do more. Almost angrily, she tore open the ribbon. But she pushed the letter from Swaziland aside and started at the bottom of the pile. The first letters were written in Creole French; she translated as she read:

> Sister in God,
>   I acknowledge receipt of your cheque for £159 (Rupees 7,155). I enclose a statement from the *Banque Nacionale de Maurice* showing the sum credited to the clinic at Pointe-aux-Sables, with full rights of withdrawal delegated to Mr Nand Moogum.
>   Your good heart, enlightened by the Goddess Lakshmi, will have observed Mr Moogum's record in financial matters. Your eyes will have noted that this cheque was issued to cover your expenses in London. Unless the Gentle Goddess has provided you with another source of income, will you allow me to mention

this to Save the Children?

I shall assist Mr Moogum to spend the money on two gas bottles and a refrigerator for vaccines, to ensure that your requests are met in full.

May the Gracious Goddess and the Holy Virgin St Mary guide you in a city prone to crime, dissipation and Godlessness.

Your brother in God,
Vishwa Seeballuck

Dear Ammu Doctor,

Brother Vishwa gave me paper to say thank you for the crutches. I would like better to have walkman and the heavy metal rock. I can go almost to river now, but crutches get stuck in mud. Brother Vishwa says it will be alright in dry season. But it is monsoon and Christmas is next. So please will you send the sugar lumps to take away my polio like you did for the other children. They haven't got it even now. I also want thalis with goats' milk.

With most respectful salutations,
Shastra B T Y Rampertab

This was the Ammu she knew. Ammu would never give up on the wretched Moogum. Like little Shastra, whom Harriet fancied she remembered as a girl of about twelve, he was disabled (in his case, river blindness), but he compensated for his disability with guile. Knowing he was a thief, Ammu continued to trust him. And, after a while, Moogum, in his way, rewarded her. Harriet believed he would buy the refrigerator, and the gas bottles, but bargain hard on the price and pocket the difference. Ammu would be content with that, see no need for Brother Vishwa's supervision.

The second letter, and the third, which was like it, made Harriet burst with some kind of fury. Everywhere Ammu went in the villages, she was followed by a swarm of children yelling '*Madame le bon medicin*'. Children on crutches were not last in the race to catch her attention. And Ammu would turn, look them over expertly, point to some child at the rear, and say 'Tell your mama to see me about that cough.' The mother in question would be tugging the child to the clinic within an hour. For someone who believed in people's independence, Ammu exerted a powerful discipline in the villages. For someone who had made hundreds of people love her and depend on her, Ammu had left the Mauritian clinics with very little to show of personal regret.

The fourth letter gave Harriet a very odd feeling. It was a typewritten letter, her own typing of five years ago, annotated in Ammu's loopy hand. How strange that Ammu had brought this unimportant, and now pointless, letter to London with her. It read:

Dear Dr Bai,

I regret that I was not able to meet you at the Ambassador Hotel, but understand that the porter let you into my room and served you there. I am in receipt of the brochures you left for me.

I appreciate your wish to bring this matter to a quick conclusion. However, I am in the employ of the Ministry of Health and am not at liberty to alter the curriculum for nurse training in Mauritius. I am new to this country and have a full schedule. None the less, I am, as I explained on your three previous visits, interested to see your clinics, of which I have heard reports. Thereafter I will be in a position to make a judgment about involving my students.

May I suggest that you telephone before visiting again, as I find it helpful to be able to plan my appointments.

Yours sincerely,
Harriet Weston

Harriet grimaced with embarrassment as she read this letter. Ammu still remembered their beginnings, perhaps she still held them against her. Along the margins, Ammu had written, '25 second-year students, 40 first year, one English tutor, devoid of imagination but vulnerable through overmuch of politeness. Note – make sure she sees clinics when we're doing child inoculations.'

Another annotation, dated three months later, read, 'H has visited six clinics. Is confused, impressed, but has not yet brought any students. H a real nurse, was up and helping in five minutes, but does too much for people, and doesn't talk. H said she might bring students during the holidays, but hear they find her a bit of a prig so maybe none will come.'

Another, undated, but clearly much later, read, 'Still no students; H is a stuffed shirt. But she's hard-working, well-trained and loyal, and doesn't ask questions. Vishwa agrees to keep her on if my Mozambique idea comes off.'

The unfairness of this made Harriet wince. She had given hours and hours of unpaid labour to Ammu's clinics. She had allowed Ammu to overturn her whole view of health and medicine. She had made Ammu the centre of her life, and had thought that she was a figure of some importance in Ammu's. She wasn't. That was very clear – even in matters of work, she played second fiddle to Brother Vishwa. And now the dutiful Vishwa was running the Mauritian clinics, and soon he would be putting his own stamp on them, easing out Moogum and all the other undeserving disabled, then casting aside the advice of the old women, the holy men. In the hands of the good Vishwa, Ammu's clinics would soon be indistinguishable from those of any charity.

In a freezing rage, Harriet stamped her feet furiously – of all Ammu's followers only she, Harriet, really understood what Ammu was trying to do. How could Ammu herself not know this? Yet, at some point, Ammu had begun to see things differently: Harriet was the helper she had chosen to go with her to Mozambique. Why? Why did Ammu say 'only with you'? Because a stuffed shirt doesn't ask questions?

The next two letters, postmarked London, changed Harriet's mood from frustration to a real excitement. Also in Creole French, but mixed with English, they were from a 'Tonton Robertie', a semi-literate with an old man's hand. His first letter welcomed Ammu to London, with many promises to 'show her the sights'. The second spoke of 'deepest disappointment that you treat le bon Maréchal so bad; now won't even see him.' It went on to complain of this causing 'embarrassment to me and you and bringing shame on the family name'. What Maréchal? What shame? Tonton Robertie's second letter was addressed to Ammu at Sophie's place; so he knew she was at the address that was supposed to be secret. Why? Perhaps she would soon have answers, for surely this must be the uncle she was to meet that night.

The last letter, the letter from Swaziland, postmarked 15 September and so probably received just before Ammu left Camden Town, gave Harriet a spooky feeling. Written in correct though old-fashioned French, it read:

Dear Miss Bai,
Your uncle Monsieur France Du Deffand has powerful friends who have supported him through many trials. He also has enemies: he is himself the chief of them; you might ask yourself if you are not the second. I shall have completed my business and will be in London when this communication arrives, ready to receive you. Everything at issue is negotiable. Your uncle will arrange our meeting. I wish you to have this message in my own hand.

Several lines of deeply respectful salutations preceded a signature which Harriet deciphered, with difficulty, as 'Yves de Wet de Haas'.

How many uncles, in London and available to 'arrange meetings' or show her the sights, could Ammu have? Was Mr France Du Deffand the Uncle Robertie of the two previous letters? What family business? What enemies? What Maréchal? Could this Mr de Wet de Haas who was so intimately involved with her uncle's friends and enemies be he? Harriet struggled to clear, in her mind, her image of Brucie and to find in it a true offer of help. Because if Brucie was to be trusted, what happened tonight was going to be very important.

Nightfall was filling the park with fog. The bundle of letters was limp and wet; her hands, numb with cold, were not able to knot the cord. Stomach pulsing from hunger, anticipation, a jumble of thoughts, Harriet made her way back to the lighted streets, and found, with relief, a café with steamed up windows, its dim interior reverberating to the roar of an old gaggia machine. It was 5 p.m., still six hours to go before she was to meet Brucie. She chose a table deep in shadow, and warmed her lips and hands against the thick scorching earthenware of a cup of milky tea. She should phone her mother. She should phone Dr Ramgulam. There were phone boxes in the street, not all of them vandalised. But only tonight, 11 p.m., mattered to her now. The tea was wonderful. Apart from a sip with Brucie, she had had nothing to eat or drink but a slug of foul-tasting water from the tap in Sophie's bathroom since noon the previous day. Cup still pressed to her lips, she leaned back against a light-starved rubber plant and closed her eyes, inducing calm with the thought of the Bunnikins wallpaper in her childhood bedroom.

Harriet was indeed, in her own way, as tough a professional as Ammu. In Mauritius, the students called her 'Sister Frigidaire'. If someone had told them that Sister Frigidaire had a nervous stomach and would bring herself under control by conjuring up images of wallpaper rabbits in tailcoats flying kites, they would have squawked like a flock of mynah birds. So what? Ammu, who understood the psyche better than anyone, was not above using such tricks, so Harriet had no need to feel ashamed of hers.

There was a small room above the front door in a house in Palmers Green which had been Harriet's since the Whittington Hospital had released her as a squalling baby. It would always be hers, and always freshly papered with Bunnikins, because Mother promised that that pattern would be in stock at the Army and Navy Stores until the end of time.

The only child of a quiet couple who had lived all their married life in that same house, Harriet had been a runt of a girl until she hit thirteen. Then all at once her bones extended themselves, bursting through the sleeves of school shirts, until she was taller than the Headmistress and gawky as a dumb-waiter. She knew her parents' love through the regularity of meals and reheeling of her shoes. This also showed their disappointment: all the signs showed that she would be no more successful in the world than they were.

For their sakes, the adolescent Harriet longed to do well. But she was too tall, her blue eyes too pale and staring, her hair too wild a ginger flame, her brain too like a rabbit, starting in fear at mathematics, grammar, French, and the scolding of too many teachers. Only in swimming and a few games not too reliant on fine hand-and-eye coordination, did she achieve any success.

Harriet's mother accepted with resignation her daughter's gracelessness. In the same spirit, she greeted her decision to become a nurse, a calling at least formally known as a profession. And so Harriet exchanged

Bunnikins for a cell with an iron bedstead at the nurses' home in Lincoln.

She didn't do well at first. She hated sleeping in a bed in which other women had lain with their lovers, or just with their own sweaty bodies. She was horrified by the rings around the bath, and, worse, the pubic hairs wriggling away from the plughole. (These she removed with tweezers.) She would pile pillows over her head at night to blot out the carousing of her fellow students. She made herself as small as someone 5′ 8″ could be and, though she was physically somewhat clumsy, very neat, leaving no markings; even her dressing table was clear, her comb and bottle of antiseptic mouthwash stuffed into a toilet bag inside a drawer.

For all that, her student days brought her her first sense of herself. She was a good nurse. Although she was still sickened by the smell of the bin into which she tipped her used sanitary towels, on the ward she had no horror of blood, incontinence or death. Though she didn't chat, and the patients perhaps found her cold and uncertain, they liked the strength of her hands. For all her nervous tummy, she was the first student in her year to be able to lay out a body – without tears, giggles, nausea – without fear. She was pleased; she had found herself – tough, independent, solitary.

Martin came into her life by ambulance, with a foot crushed under a tractor. A local boy, he patched up ploughs and harrows and dreamed of working in the museum, repairing instead Roman pots and Viking bracelets. He was not handsome and, when he was not fooling around, he was shyer than Harriet. They visited the stereo-blasted pubs favoured by the youth of Lincolnshire, and celebrated birthdays in the wine bar that served Liebfraumilch and prawn sandwiches with chips.

Harriet felt good about Martin – because he never looked at any other girls, not least because he never kissed her, except in public. In the long summer evenings when he was scouring the banks of the Car Dike for Roman glass rings, Harriet studied her nursing textbooks. She wanted Martin to take a course in archaeology, but he was ashamed, he said, of his bad writing. Harriet took a nursing degree, part time, and became a nurse tutor. They celebrated their thirtieth birthdays at the wine bar.

But ever so gradually, Martin was slipping out of Harriet's mind. She saw on the television scenes of famine in Ethiopia and, while picnicking with Martin along the sunbaked canals, would dream about struggling through the desert to reach emaciated children with beautiful faces. By this time, years of practice at nurse authority had given Harriet a sense of real power. She had also discovered that she had a good stock of physical courage, a quality to which she would like to give greater expression. She found herself irritated when Martin's motorbike found its automatic way, through fog and rain, to the wine bar. She couldn't understand why Martin was so upset when she answered the British Council advertisement for a nurse tutor in Mauritius.

She wrote a few times; he sent postcards of Lincoln Cathedral and made a short and nervous telephone call on her birthday. But when Ammu came into her life, there was no space for such things, and Martin was forgotten. Even letters to mother became brisk monthly notes on the affairs of the clinics.

'You want some more tea, miss?' Harriet rushed back to consciousness.

'Ah – with milk, please.' (Milk, also potatoes; the only things that tasted better in England.)

Five and a half hours to go. Nurses are good at waiting – at a bedside. But Harriet had learned the tempo of the lecture room, and of Ammu's clinics where the action was frenetic because everybody was involved in it.

Impatiently, she pounded the cold streets. Her confidence in Brucie rose as she warmed herself under the hot air hand-dryer in the lavatories at Notting Hill Station, diminished as she marched shivering across Holland Park, rose again when she came across a young woman, dressed like Brucie, playing the flute in Kensington High Street – remaining generally positive. She was getting closer to Ammu. She definitely felt that. Brucie would lead her to Uncle Robertie; he would lead her to the Mr de Wet de Haas, perhaps le Maréchal, and there would be Ammu, the princess in the tower. Harriet was going to free Ammu; they would go to Mozambique, where they would do great work, and perhaps one day Ammu would learn to care for her.

Still a lot of hours to go. Harriet was passing Earls Court tube station. Why not? On impulse she jumped onto the first District Line train heading west, towards Gunnersbury. Dr Ramgulam ought about now to be winding up her evening surgery.

Early Friday evening, *4 November*

Jasbir Ramgulam was the easiest person in the world to talk to, because she took nobody completely seriously. Big, motherly, untidy, with a voice like a sergeant major's, she saw the human race (herself excluded of course) as a listless flock of dear things without direction or moral sense. Her father's conviction that she would have made a famous psychiatrist was probably well founded.

Harriet, not herself a good conversationalist, found pleasure in the company of people who talked a lot about the things that interested her; and she was used to taking orders from doctors. She would have found her brief stay at Gunnersbury enjoyable if she hadn't been so worried about Ammu, so worried about herself. Dr Ramgulam had asked many questions about the Mauritian clinics – of which she fiercely disapproved – and scoffed at Harriet's replies. She had elicited a surprising amount of inform-ation about Harriet's past, even about poor Martin, whom she disposed of with, 'Better off without him my dear; young women never develop properly when attached to a man – no more than a nation does under colonialism, no matter how benevolent. When I'm prime minister, no woman will be allowed to marry before the age of forty.' But she had herself married at twenty-three, and only her father, and Ammu, had protested. Ammu, she said, was always protesting about her.

She and Ammu had met at medical school in Liverpool; they were the only Mauritian women students in the college at the time. That, and a furious drive to make their mark, was all they had in common, because Dr Ramgulam's was a very different Mauritius. It was the big family house with a dozen servants and peacocks in the garden where Jasbir spent the long holidays away from school in France and Switzerland. Ammu's Mauritius, on the other hand, gave her, in Dr Ramgulam's view, nothing but a vast ignorance of, and contempt for, English ways; plus a few well-worn saris – 'Made out of nylon, my dear; remember that nasty stuff? After being washed with cheap soap it smells like corpses.'

Their stormy but enduring friendship began a day after Ammu's arrival. That night, in the common room, Ammu, looking fixedly at the clock on the wall (she had no watch) had said, 'In the last forty minutes, Miss Ramgulam, you have begun five sentences with the words "My Uncle the Prime Minister".'

Jasbir Ramgulam, stung, had responded, 'You would do the same, Miss Bai, if you had any uncle worth naming.'

To which Ammu had replied, softly, 'I have an uncle who takes photographs which may not legally be sent through the mail.'

The other students had buzzed about at this, according to Dr Ramgulam. Such an uncle was far more interesting than the mere prime minister of some obscure Third World country. Anything Ammu said was always the more interesting; Ammu was the student the lecturers most liked to dispute with. She barely scraped through the exams, but everybody considered her brilliant.

'And she hasn't changed a tittle, my dear. I have changed – I've softened, I expect less; I see now that good intentions can do great harm. Just look at Islamic fundamentalism – yet what religion could be more sensible, more bourgeois, than Islam? But we grow older; we all learn to suspect our most passionate aspirations – except Ayatollah Ammu. Ammu is set hard, an Iron Lady.'

Ammu couldn't wait to get back to Mauritius, and did her elective year there, at the hospital in Port Louis. By the end of the year she had such a reputation as a trouble-maker that she had no hope of a job in the National Health Service (although the Government was keen to employ as many nationals as possible), and was forced into private practice.

Once again, she confounded expectations, starting up under a tree in Rivière Sèche, the driest and poorest quarter of Mauritius, and taking her fees in half-bags of rice or a few vegetables. That was the beginning of the Dr Ammu Bai series of People's Health Clinics which grew to have more and more to do with Ammu's version of Hindu philosophy and less and less with Western medicine. Until her night at Gunnersbury, Harriet had known none of this, not even that Ammu had studied in England, and at the very college that ran the correspondence course through which Harriet had earned her nursing degree.

Dr Ramgulam, who came out of school with a battery of distinctions and awards, stayed on in England, disappoint-ing her father by marrying an obscure GP and by degrees taking over his practice as heart disease steadily reduced his capacity to work. Widowed early, she kept in touch with Ammu through long but infrequent letters and her occasional holidays at the family mansion. She quarrelled furiously with Ammu about the clinics, but met her de-mands for large financial contributions to them. 'The only thing to do with peasants, my dear, is to shut up the howls of their bellies with rice so that they can hear the voice of their heads. Then they will take care of their health – through sensible, old-fashioned scientific medicine.' Ammu's near mystic attitude to the body, her love of tradi-tion and Hindu culture were, to Dr Ramgulam, tommyrot.

'So we've had, my dear,' said Dr Ramgulam, only minutes after she had greeted Harriet with a bear-like embrace, tapped her all over to make sure she hadn't been accosted on the previous night, shoved her into an enveloping armchair and thrust a tumbler of scotch into her hand, 'utterly glorious dingbats for more than twenty years. This silence of hers is hardly characteristic. Usually, when she's in England, she's fighting to get on the radio to tell the Brits their charities are run by nincompoops.'

Harriet took a gulp of Dr Ramgulam's whisky; it hit her stomach like a football. She took a breath and said quietly, 'I think Ammu might have been kidnapped.'

'Kidnapped!' Dr Ramgulam roared. 'Now that's more like the Ammu we know and love. But why on earth would anyone want to kidnap a penniless quack?'

'I found some letters, and talked with two people who saw a lot of Ammu in October. I don't know who's taken her, or why, but there is something very odd about an uncle and about a Monsieur Yves de Wet de Haas. Do you know anything about this Mr de Wet de Haas?'

Dr Ramgulam slowly shook her head.

'And she's not a quack. She's a true healer.'

'Of course, my dear. And a true leader too if you are typical of her disciples. But I distract us from the point. Why would anyone want to do something so bizarre to a healer, no matter how true?' Dr Ramgulam leaned forward, elbows on her knees, displaying a pair of surprisingly hairy and muscular forearms.

'I hope you may be able to help answer that. I have some views, no more. I think it would be useful if I could get some information about this de Wet de Haas.' Harriet dug into her duffel bag, pulled out the package of letters, and handed Dr Ramgulam the envelope from Swaziland.

Dr Ramgulam read it quickly, then again, slowly, looking thoughtful. 'Ye-es,' she said. 'I don't much like the look of this.'

'See these too.' Harriet handed over the notes from Tonton Robertie. Dr Ramgulam looked them over briefly, then turned back to the Swaziland letter.

'I wish I could say something useful.' She scrutinised the signature. 'He has a Boer name – it means something like 'law of the rabbit' – but those charming gentlemen go in for double barrels in a rather different arena, and they certainly don't speak French.' She glanced over the text. 'And this is cultured French, though rather stiff.'

Harriet nodded. 'Please go on.'

'Well, he knows, or thinks he knows, something about Ammu's relationship with her uncle, and he seems to have had some communication with Ammu, but it's not clear if they were personally acquainted. Even if he had met her, he surely didn't know her well. What else can one say? They are on different sides in some dispute involving the uncle. That's obvious.' Dr Ramgulam looked up. 'My dear, I do wish I had some insight to offer.'

'Please continue.' Harriet's tone was insistent.

Dr Ramgulam sighed. 'His hand,' she peered, 'could have been formed at a convent school. French nuns in Mauritius teach that italic flow. It is possible that he could be a Mauritian of South African descent; no, more likely an émigré from Mauritius adapting his name to a new culture. If so, I suspect he's a white man – no self-respecting black would choose a Boer name. Or – let's think – he could be of mixed race but South African affiliation. That would explain the connection with Swaziland, a small country bullied by a mob of South African spies. But perhaps I allow my speculations to be led by some instinctive dislike. Why the dislike? Well, the letter to Ammu is a threat, isn't it? The reference to Tonton Robertie is insulting, isn't it?'

Harriet nodded agreement, and encouragement, while Dr Ramgulam paused and slid the letter back into its envelope. 'But then, a lot of Mauritian whites emigrated to Madagascar or Natal, and a few to Zululand and Swaziland early this century. They took a touch of Franco-Indian snobbery, of the "de Wet de Haas" order with them.'

Dr Ramgulam returned the package to Harriet. 'He sounds dangerous. Let's see. Ammu got his letter at Camden Town, perhaps only a day or so before she came to stay with me.'

'She didn't mention him to you?'

'Not a word. We spent our time quarrelling about that harebrained scheme for Mozambique – as if Ammu hasn't already done enough damage in Mauritius! I knew, of course, that something was up – she was nervous as a lamb and distinctly uneasy about giving me Sophie's address. Now let's think. Tonton Robertie says she was refusing to see "le Maréchal"?'

Harriet nodded. 'So you also think this man could be he?'

Dr Ramgulam shook her head. 'It could be anyone.'

'But you suspect?'

'My dear, we have nobody else to suspect. Yes, I suspect.'

Do you know the uncle, Mr Robertie France Du Deffand?'

'Ye-es.'

'Do you think he was the uncle who took photographs which could not legally be sent through the mail?'

'My dear, Mauritian families are enormous. The entire island consists of uncles, godmothers and whatnot.'

'But he is the only uncle you know to be closely connected with Ammu?'

Dr Ramgulam nodded.

'What do you think of him?'

'I think he was programmed to suck blood, gurgling like a baby at the breast.' Dr Ramgulam was now more comfortable. 'I think he's soft, selfish, greedy, emotional – rather sweet, in fact. What's he got to do with it? He doesn't have the stomach for real vice. Anyway, he adores Ammu.'

'Does Ammu care for him too? Do you think she would protect him if there was some family scandal?' Harriet felt her blood rising. 'Do you think she would stand in for him, allow herself to be held hostage to give him the chance to clear himself?'

'My dear girl, who do you think Ammu is? Jesus Christ, taking on the sins of the world?'

Harriet was stung. It was not the first time Dr Ramgulam had mocked her admiration of Ammu.

'If Ammu's up for canonisation, my dear, it's quite sufficient virtue that she, someone who hurls brickbats at the toss of a hat, never once said a bitter word to him or about him.'

'Could that be out of loyalty, Indian family loyalty? Could loyalty also lead her to protect Robertie?'

'Indian family loyalty, indeed! What makes you think Ammu's an Indian?'

Harriet's mouth fell open. 'What – '

'Now, I'm an Indian,' (Dr Ramgulam thrust out one muscular arm and poked it with the fingertips of the other) 'but you aren't, even if you spout the Panchatantra, truss yourself up in a dhoti and put a ring through your nose.' Dr Ramgulam gave Harriet a hard, one-way stare. 'I think I'd better fill you in on Ammu, dear friend of mine though she may be.'

Harried nodded coldly.

Ammu, Dr Ramgulam explained, was one of the dozen or so children of a half-Indian woman and a poor-white man. 'Bai', meaning 'woman', was not her surname at birth; it was the village nickname for her maternal grandmother, who had given birth sixteen times. Her father's name, like Uncle Robertie's, was the aristocratic

Du Deffand. ('The lower you go down the social scale in these remote colonies, my dear, the grander the names and titles. The Indians are just the same as the Franco-Mauritians, every other roadsweeper claims to be a Brahmin.') Marie-Louise was her given name.

Du Deffand was the assistant of a small jobbing printer in Rivière Sèche. ('Mauritius, my dear, eats print. Only a million people, but they sustain six newspapers – in French, Creole, English, Tamil, Chinese. I think each Mauritian reads all six. So, if you want to get rich in Mauritius, give up nursing for publishing.') His younger brother Robertie ('He acquired a camera from some visiting photographer in return for unmentionable services') did whatever he did in a darkroom at the back of the shop. Du Deffand had a drink problem. His wife was often ill. ('Such common "communicable diseases", my dear, as black eyes, broken nose and jaw, bruises round the throat.') Du Deffand had an arrangement with his employer: he would never be sacked, but was not paid when he didn't turn up for work. So the family often went hungry. From the age of about eight, Marie-Louise worked at the print shop, earning small sums doing what she could for her father's work, and helping Robertie.

When Marie-Louise was about ten, her mother died, of a broken heart, they said in the village. Ammu, in retrospect, diagnosed the cause of death as subdural haemorrhage consequent to a head injury.

Du Deffand, relieved of his black wife, immediately emigrated to South Africa, accompanied by Robertie. He loved it; there he was a gentleman, doing a job reserved for people with white skins – giving orders to black printers, unperturbed that all but the newest apprentice knew more about the craft than he did. About a year later, Robertie sent for the children. ('Shock and horror, my dear; before they'd passed through Durban docks the children were classified as coloured. In a week the whole caboodle was sent off to some ghetto for their particular stew of races.')

Du Deffand was disgraced. He lost his job and respectability, and blamed the children for his fall. Robertie was the nearest thing they had to a protector. All the while Robertie was still taking photographs, still being assisted by little Marie-Louise and, astonishingly, making a good deal of money.

'Ammu,' said Dr Ramgulam, refilling Harriet's glass, 'was the darkest of the children and her father's bête noire. But she was Robertie's darling. He sent her to a Catholic mission school, one of those awkward institutions that defied the Bantu Education Act and allowed her to learn something, even cultivate her mind. And, when she proved to be intelligent, he had her coached in all the smart subjects.'

'Then Robertie had some right to ask Ammu not to damage the family name?'

'Perhaps he had. He was good to her. Or so one must believe from Ammu's account. But what I saw of him in Mauritius was of a rather different order.'

'But when did they get back to Mauritius?'

'They didn't; at least only Ammu and Robertie did. At some point, cirrhosis claimed the wretched Du Deffand. The other children melted into the coloured community. And Ammu, who made it to medical school in Durban (the university authorities managed somehow to keep the pre-med year open to people of all races), then won some obscure scholarship which brought her to Liverpool. She and Robertie wrote to each other regularly; she was secretive about the correspondence; I thought at first it was a lover. When she decided to return to Mauritius, Robertie upped and followed her there. Maybe he thought he'd be able to set her up as a rich society doctor and retire on the profits.'

Dr Ramgulam paused to think. 'But maybe not. He needed something like Ammu in his life; and he must have known what she had in mind. You see my dear, while still at college in Durban, Ammu decided to make herself into an Indian. She spent years learning how to do it. She called herself "Ammu Bai" and stuffed her head with elephant gods, monkey gods, the whole bang carnival. I used sometimes to wonder if she wanted my friendship just because I *was* an Indian, a real one. But that was probably unjust; at that time I was trying to turn myself into a European. We were, my dear, a couple of phonies.'

Ammu had told Harriet nothing of all this. Was it on her own account, that she hadn't rated such confidence from Ammu, or from grief that Ammu should have suffered so much, that she felt close to tears? 'I can't see anything phoney about Ammu in what you say; I can only see the most amazing courage.'

'Yes, it is a very romantic story.' Dr Ramgulam stretched out a pair of legs terminating in spongy tennis socks. 'But, my dear, you should know that Ammu is not what you think. Now, Gandhi had to play the role of moral leader, because the people needed leadership. But he was afraid of the people who admired him; they tempted him to believe that he was the person he made them think he was; they lured him towards spiritual pride. Ammu is not Gandhi. Ammu is afraid of the peasants who worship her for the opposite reason, in case they find out that she is not the person she has made them think she is.' She twiddled her toes. 'Perhaps you could help Ammu more if you admired her less.'

'I don't know what you mean.'

'Ah, well,' Dr Ramgulam leaned back and looked up at the ceiling. 'Ammu is always shouting. What do you think she is trying to shout down?'

'Corruption. Bureaucracy. Slavish admiration of the West. Worship of material things. The view of the human body as a machine.'

'Yes, to all those things. You have well-organised mind

my dear, and a virginal one.'

Harriet grimaced. She was not unfamiliar with remarks of this kind.

'A virginal mind loves perfection; and it wants the thing that it loves to be perfect.'

Harriet was indignant. 'What do you mean? Do you think there is anything dishonourable in my feeling for Ammu?'

'Not at all; I speak of abstracts. If you love something imperfect, if you can find beauty in it, you can also find its need for you. Something perfect has no needs; *vide* Plato. How do you think Ammu needs you?'

Harriet looked straight at Dr Ramgulam. 'Now what are you trying to say about Ammu?'

Dr Ramgulam pulled a long strand of greying hair out of her untidy knot and studied the tuft at its end. 'You've a right to be angry, of course. But just think: there is something about obsession – with any idea, even a good one – that conflicts with sanity. Now, I'm not saying we shouldn't examine our obsessions. We should examine everything. There should be – if I may borrow a phrase – no no-go areas in the mind.'

Harriet shuffled in her seat, but no idea that would distract Dr Ramgulam from these thoroughly unpleasant personal remarks presented itself.

'But,' the strand of hair was waving in front of Dr Ramgulam's mouth, 'we should examine them without *entertaining* them, enacting them, as it were. Now that isn't easy. Especially the obsessions we fear, and rightly fear – our sadistic feelings, for one. Just think that dear batty old Freud, who was so fascinated by sex, and could be brave much of the time, decided that the sexual abuse he heard so much about from children was fantasy. I was reminded of this by Iris Murdoch – marvellous writer; do you know her work?'

Harriet shuffled again. 'No. But what are you saying? If

Ammu is obsessed, it's an obsession about healing; none of this has anything to do with her.'

'Ye-es.' Dr Ramgulam pushed the strand of hair roughly back into place, and smiled. 'I used to eat my hair when I was little, tuck it into my mouth and gnaw; drove my mother to distraction. Now, Ammu's anger is obsessive. She has an energy fed by obsession. Don't you think, my dear, that the mind needs to be humble sometimes, able to laugh at what is most precious to it. Ammu should occasionally be freed from her anger.'

'What are you saying now? That Ammu's mad?'

'No, no. That she's trapped, perhaps by people who need angels. If somebody loved her, not as a guru, just for the touch of her hand, for her presence in a room; loved even her weakness, the taste of her tears –'

If someone has loved her like that, thought Harriet, it's Sophie, not me. Suddenly Sophie's talk about Ammu, which had been so sickening on the previous night, down in the ugly den, sprang into a different kind of focus; it had in it tenderness, protectiveness. Harriet had never given anything like that to Ammu. How could she; till this night she knew nothing about Ammu's pain. If there were just another chance to show Ammu that she too could understand about South Africa, about Indianness, about pain. 'I could love her,' said Harriet softly, 'if I were given the chance. I think I know now where I failed.'

Dr Ramgulam withdrew. 'Forgive me, my dear. One shouldn't take too seriously the mutterings of an old and neglected friend; one must allow for personal vanity. I love Ammu too, but I've always been jealous of her. The world may well remember her. It will not remember me. But we digress – Robertie.'

Robertie, she explained, had pitched up at Port Louis only weeks after Ammu began her housemanship at the general hospital. On her visits to Mauritius, Dr Ramgulam noticed him hanging around the clinics, hovering in the background when she invited Ammu for cocktails at the smart hotels. This once beautiful young Ganymede, with Ammu's fine bones and wide, innocent eyes, was becoming a flabby and ill-dressed middle-aged man, yielding by degrees to his brother's weakness. Robertie always seemed to know Ammu's movements. Once, he came to join them at table at some elegant dinner.

'He pulled up a chair just behind Ammu – who, as usual, was insulting all the doctors present by demolishing the claims of the medical profession – and reached over her shoulder to take from her plate with his grubby fingers a sliver of mango. I saw this as an uncouth gesture of familiarity from someone who had not been invited to the party. But Ammu, my dear, looked as if she'd seen a ghost. So, do you know what she did? She dug into the little bag tied round her waist and handed her purse to Robertie. He pocketed it and made off. Not a word. I saw her give him money on several occasions.'

'Don't Indians – Mauritians – don't the successful ones give money to their families?'

'Of course they do. But the rich give to the poor. Not the other way round. Robertie was still coining it.'

'Taking photographs?'

'Ye-es.'

'In Mauritius?'

'Ye-es. Shooting. I saw some of his work. I was a medical witness in a manslaughter case.'

'What!' Harriet was horrified.

'No, no. Not that. There was no evidence that Robertie had anything to do with murder. One of his clients got over-excited by his pictures.' Harriet was puzzled. 'They were,' Dr Ramgulam continued, 'of little children. "Chicken porn" they call it. This was ages ago.'

'Oh my God. How dreadful. How dreadful for Ammu.'

'Yes. Robertie is her albatross. We all have one, you

know.' She took Harriet's hand tenderly. 'Except you. You are one of the innocents. Yours is a young civilization. It has clear laws of good and evil. A carpenter's son, a good and simple man, took all the complicated pain and grievance of the Jews and boiled them down to two rules, both about love. You are fortunate. You are a follower. You are what Ammu sought.' Dr Ramgulam dropped Harriet's hand and began to swill her drink in the way Ammu did, as if to give gnats beaching against the walls of the glass.

'You are what I seek too,' she continued. 'I thought my daughter would give it. But I made the mistake I see so many mothers make. I tried to create of her something for myself. She does not understand me. She does not understand India in me. She puts rings not through her nose but through her ears and thinks it is different. I find her stupid. That depresses me.'

Harriet felt a twinge of sympathy for Dr Ramgulam's daughter: it must be difficult to live with someone who peered so keenly into other people's heads that she thought she could tell them what they were thinking before they'd had time to work it out for themselves. 'I don't know what to say,' she said. 'I'm sorry.'

For once, Dr Ramgulam misread a signal. 'I've burdened you, when you have important work to do. Then I am the one to be sorry. Perhaps I shouldn't have told you as much as I have. Ammu would have told you herself had she wished you to know. And make allowance, too, for my frustration. You are asking for answers, and lead me to give them. They could be wrong. At bottom, I probably understand Ammu less well than you do. But I think I agree with you that Ammu is in serious trouble, and you need all the information you can get if you are to help her, and not fall into danger yourself. And it's not long now. I do wish I could help you.'

Harriet looked at her watch, then leapt to her feet

although, as it was only just a little after nine, there was still masses of time. 'Thank you very much. I'm sure it's very useful, everything you've told me, especially about Robertie.'

'I'd like you to stay; I'd love you to stay forever. I'd like to go with you; I truly would. But I know you have work to do that I must leave you to do alone.' Dr Ramgulam put an arm on Harriet's shoulder. 'Be careful of Robertie, he's very loose, very weak. Trust him a little, perhaps, but not his judgment. If he tells you where Ammu is, please come back to me before you do anything further.'

Harriet smiled. 'I promise.'

'Good.' Dr Ramgulam clapped her firmly on the back. 'Now, how about sausages and mash before you march on to fight the Good Fight?'

'No thank you.' Harriet, pulling on her coat, paused and frowned. 'Just one more question: why did Robertie choose children for his subjects? You don't ... You don't think he did things to them too ...? And you don't think when Ammu was little he might have –?'

'– Abused her sexually? Yes, it seems possible to me.'

'But you said he adored her!'

'My daughter, when she was little, adored jellies, especially red and green ones. They were so pretty and soft and wobbly. She liked to smash them with her fists and then gobble them up. They made her feel powerful.'

'But he put her through school; he was good to her?'

'Didn't I tell you he was sweet?'

Harriet, in no mood for riddles, felt the knot begin to tie once again in her stomach. 'Could an experience of that sort affect someone so that she ...' Harriet was struggling for words, 'she was attracted, I mean to, um, someone not at all on her level. I mean another woman ... I mean a wrecked, rude awful woman ... I mean ...'.

Dr Ramgulam looked at her fiercely. 'What on earth are you fumbling to say?'

'Nothing really, it's just that this Sophie claims, well she says that she and Ammu ...'

'So? Are you jealous?'

'No!' Harriet barked. Then, after a pause. 'Well, yes, but, I guess, shocked too.'

'Funny, isn't it, that our prejudices allow us to hate anyone we choose, but get very exercised about whom we love.'

'I didn't mean what you think,' Harriet stumbled again. 'I mean, I don't know what to think. I am sure Sophie really does love Ammu.'

'Then leave it alone, my dear,' Dr Ramgulam said gently. 'It isn't easy, but try not to be jealous. Your kind of love is good too, and very durable. Ammu is very lucky to have you.'

'Yes, thank you.' Harriet felt terribly small, close to tears. Buttoning her coat, she added, 'Do you think, Dr Ramgulam, that Ammu is in danger?'

'Ammu knows her own mind; she makes her own way. It's always been a dangerous way.'

'Do you think I might injure Ammu somehow, expose what she needs to keep hidden, by linking up with Brucie and these people?'

'I don't know. But I think you should be careful. If I was still a practising Hindu or Christian or anything, I'd say "Do what your heart tells you. I'll pray for you." '

Friday night,
4 November

At 11 p.m. Harriet was striding, with rather stiff legs, through the little worms of cigarette ash in Sophie's den. She was about to go to some weird place, to meet a man who touted disgusting sexual perversion, in the hope of finding Ammu, someone who was not at all what Harriet had been led to believe – so not herself that she was not even an Indian! How odd that Harriet felt so good. She caught the eye of the cat on the mantelpiece, and winked at it. Brucie would be along any second.

She hadn't started out feeling this way. On the journey back from Gunnersbury, her mood had changed. At first mortified that she had shown herself as a prejudiced wimp and been called to order by Dr Ramgulam, her feelings gradually quietened. It seemed very possible that Sophie _had_ given Ammu comfort. She had to believe that Sophie _did_ love Ammu. It was even difficult to deny that she, Harriet, was in some unexamined and unpleasant way jealous. All these things became by degrees thinkable, because Dr Ramgulam made them seem, though unhappy, normal. Harriet still couldn't see Sophie as anything other than physically revolting, but she told herself firmly that since she found anything to do with sex unpleasant and insanitary, she should simply close her mind to the matter. After all, she had long learned to do this when faced with the pathetic solitary sexuality of the geriatric ward.

What mattered was that she was now on her way to meet Tonton Robertie, and, if she played her cards right, this meeting could lead her to Ammu. Dr Ramgulam believed she was the only person who could do this. By the time she reached Baker Street, Dr Ramgulam's complicated messages had consolidated themselves into a simple, powerful sense that she, Harriet, had been chosen to free Ammu. Though Ammu didn't know it, Harriet was, for the moment, the most important person in her life. When she found Ammu everything would be different, better. Harriet would have won her spurs, she would be worthy of the new Ammu Dr Ramgulam had revealed to her, someone not only clever and strong but also vulnerable, hurt, brave – even more beautiful.

Bounding into the house, Harriet was greeted by a new Sophie, someone almost normal, almost encouraging, yelling from the kitchen: 'Get into that clobber on the stairs and wait for Brucie in my den.'

And, as Harriet, washed and robed in Brucie's finery, clumped awkwardly down the stairs, another yell, 'Help y'self to some Dutch courage; there's still juice in Ammu's bottle.' Harriet stomped into the room. She would, out of politeness, have called it a drawing room, but a den was what it was, retreat of a tired and shabby old lioness, but someone who, like Harriet, loved Ammu.

'Hi cats. D'you recognise me in these togs?' Harriet standing foursquare, like Brucie, presented her long, booted form to their view and rather regretted the lack of a mirror. What would the students think of Sister Frigidaire now? Harriet felt odd, but good, wearing clothes as different from her own as fabrics with similar numbers of stitches and buttons could be. She almost regretted that they weren't as close to fancy dress (no clanking metal bits) as the things Brucie wore. The trousers, made out of heavy black canvas, carried a label which said in small letters under the brand name 'Made in

Mauritius'. Surely this was a good omen, even though, to any Mauritian seamstress, they were of a size to tent a family of four. For Harriet they were long enough in the leg, but went twice round her middle, so were hitched up with Brucie's stout leather belt. Brucie's black, thick, and not very clean polo neck she had tucked in to give more effect to the black leather jerkin zigzagged with a confusion of zipped-up pockets.

'Hi mantelpiece moggy.' The big tom looked at her in a cat's version of total confusion. 'Mind if I help myself to a drink?' Casually, she strolled over to Sophie's coffee table and poured a slug of Ammu's rum. 'Like some yourself, Mog?' She reached out a hand to offer it a pat and a sniff. The cat's expression changed to terror, and it disappeared. 'We'll have Ammu stroking you soon,' she called after it. 'That'll teach you better manners.'

Sophie came in, hands deep in the pockets of the yellow kimono. 'Talking to yourself?'

'The cats, actually.' Harriet, now feeling shy, pulled the jerkin to, across her chest. The glass of rum hung awkwardly from her fingers.

Brucie appeared at the door, grinning, 'Don't you look like a nice girl!'

'Don't she; could almost be one of yours, Bruce.' Sophie reached for the rum, then turned to Harriet: 'Fancy yourself in other people's clothes?'

'Sure she does,' said Brucie. 'Don't anybody?'

'Not you', said Sophie. 'You'd die of shame in anything but leather – and the stuff stinks.'

'You say? What if I get into them shiny cycling pants for you?'

Harriet smiled at this unexpected sociability. 'You'd be a bit cold.'

'That's not why,' said Brucie. 'It's 'cos they don't let you wear what feels good if you've got a woman's bum. They make you hide y'self. They laugh.'

'Tell them to go to hell,' muttered Sophie.

'That's like I do. I dress tough and shake the shit out'a them. That feels good too.'

Harriet eased her grip on the glass. Brucie was playing up to Sophie, perhaps to quell some unease they all felt about the evening's adventure. But Harriet's mood was still confident. 'I recognise that,' she said, 'I feel safer in Brucie's clothes tonight.'

'Course you do.' Brucie looked Harriet up and down. 'Now you've packed in being the nurse, see; tonight you're tough like me; you're nobody's servant. That makes you feel good.'

Harriet smiled. Being a nurse was precisely what she did want to be. But in Mozambique she would not be a nurse with a starched cap clipped to her hair. She could be, like Ammu, the barefoot healer. Feeling elated and free in Brucie's clothes, she saw herself riding her scooter over a dusty track, Ammu holding tight behind, ducking snipers' bullets as she made ready to leap off at some nameless village to talk to the headman about starting a clinic under a tree. Ammu in her own kind of danger, free in her own kind of wildness. Ammu with Harriet. Ammu, perhaps, starting to care for her, something that had never before seemed possible.

'I like being a nurse,' she said.

'Takes all sorts.' Brucie zipped up her jacket, stuffed her cigarettes into a pocket, and held out her hand to Harriet. 'The fifty quid?'

Harriet's smile faded, but she dug into her duffel bag and handed over the sealed envelope. Brucie tore it open and counted the notes, intoning:

'I'm tired of love; I'm still more tired of rhyme,
But money gives me pleasure all the time.'

She rolled the ten five-pound notes into a sausage shape,

and stuffed them into her back pocket. 'Leave that behind,' she said, gesturing towards Harriet's bag, 'or somebody'll take if off you.'

'No, I –' (Harriet could have sworn Ammu's letters made a distinct bulge in the bottom) '– my passport's in there.'

'It'll be safe with Sophie.'

'I'd really rather ...' But Brucie seized the bag, thrust it into Sophie's sideboard, locked the door, and handed the key to Harriet. 'That make you feel any better?'

'All right then' (uncertainly).

'Let's go.'

'Take my coat from the hall,' Sophie called after them. 'That mauve thing of yours with the fluffy collar would look daft on Brucie's bike.' Harriet bitterly regretted the letters, but things were moving so fast, she could only hope there would be time to explain.

Harriet hung on tight as they roared off on Brucie's big, noisy and rather smelly machine with a body almost wide as a horse. Within minutes they were on the raised motorway. Harriet recognised it instantly, although most of the houses beside it had yielded to glassy towers of computer companies. Automatically she ran her eyes, as she had done as a girl, along the line of second storey windows, searching for the vanished bedsitter of the man who had killed himself when they built the motorway, because he couldn't stand the noise. Harriet's stomach looped as they roared down the underpass and up again to Euston, St Pancras, Kings Cross.

Everything looked huge to Harriet's eyes, attuned to the scale of a little island whose swamps and lagoons were outscaled by long-legged birds – huge, decayed, cadaverous.

Then a glimpse of Tower Bridge, far grander than she remembered it, the Tower of London nestling quietly beside it. The Beefeaters and ravens would waken refreshed in the morning to thrill new throngs of tourists with sights of instruments of torture and tales of decapitated heads on spikes grinning at traffic on the river.

Brucie charged ahead with the unconcern of a passing Boeing. Harriet tried to catch the mood, to feel only the pleasure of movement, speed, the throaty engine; to banish images of ravens picking at shreds of Ammu's sari, of lights from Tower Bridge streaking the river with red and gold, printing on those dark waters the colours of Indian silk. She dug her frozen hands into Brucie's jacket pockets.

London went on forever. They rode for miles, into parts of the city Harriet could not recognise. The streets, lined with heavily shuttered small shops, were narrow and dirty. An Asian man darted through a doorway, but otherwise there were no people about. The place gave Harriet the strange, dislocated feeling of downtown Port Louis awaiting a December hurricane.

Brucie's bike bumped over broken tarmac, its headlamps picking out cats around the leaking plastic rubbish bags. Then Brucie drew up under a streetlight, one of the few still lit.

Harriet realised that, apart from cursing the cabs, Brucie hadn't spoken a word in the past hour. 'Where are we, Brucie?'

'Where do you think? The Purgatorial Fires. Watch out for the dogshit.'

'I mean, where in London? It's very quiet.'

'By the river, Docklands. The asshole end, where the yuppies don't go.'

'Yuppies?' This was a new word to Harriet.

'Yeah, they smash up Mercs here, to keep the buggers out.'

Harriet was wary. 'Do you do that?'

'Used to. I've gone soft now, old age. Watch that puddle. But I have a good laugh when I see the kids do it.'

Harriet frowned. 'But what if the children in Bayswater or Kensington damaged your bike?'

'I'd run 'em down.' Brucie marched ahead. 'You're a kid yourself if you think it's the same thing. People like me just drift through Kensington. Chrissake, we hardly touch the sides. Here, they come with their big yellow diggers and plough everything, even the roads, into the ground. They make lawns and wine bars behind electric fences. They chuck out the people, too, shove them into tower blocks. See them up to the north? The locals call the place "Soweto".'

'You don't live in a tower block.'

'I was born in one, right here, in Soweto – that one, with square windows, just behind the gasometer; see it?' She pointed. 'Take a breath; you can smell the piss in the liftshaft for miles. They'll blow it up soon; spoils the sky-line; reminds them of what they did to me. So I tell them: if I'm rubbish, that's my choice, and you can fuck off.'

Harriet recognised this feeling from a thousand Mauritian peasants watching the building of a smart new hospital which would charge high fees. 'That's not a very practical response, Brucie,' she said softly. 'You ought to talk to Ammu about this'.

'Sure. Some day. Come on, round this corner.' They approached a dank alley.

Harriet hesitated. 'If this is Docklands, why don't I see water and ships?'

'Ships? They're up there to the south, behind those containers.'

Above the two-storey shops, most apparently abandoned, Harriet could make out the square outlines of huge metal crates rising into an orange sky; perhaps the fine, scratchy lines between were masts of rotting schooners. Chill fingers gripped her stomach. The rescue of Ammu now seemed a lot less certain. How could you find anyone in such dereliction? How could you find anything, even a corpse? 'Brucie, this seems a very grim place.'

'It's okay. I like it. You can be free here; nobody watching you, no yuppies.'

Harriet felt as if eyes were following from every shadow in the alley, all the way to the door, set below street level. Brucie, with her usual swagger, dialled some combination on a lock, and pulled open the door onto more stairs leading into darkness. 'Watch your step as you go down,' she called, clomping ahead.

The street door closed of its own accord behind them, plunging the stairs into blackness. After feeling her way for a minute or two, Harriet became aware of something, a faint throbbing – not her stomach, something else. Another door, another combination lock, a passage, bare but lit, smelling of urine, yet another door. This Brucie opened to a roar of disconnected rock music, the flashing of coloured lights, hurtfully loud and garish after the darkness – like the rush of a cane fire, or being thrown into the crushers of a sugar mill.

'Wait here. Don't move, or I'll lose you.' Brucie motioned her back against a wall. 'Gotta get you cleared, get us a drink. C'mon, don't look so miserable – just stare ahead and look stoned, then nobody'll notice you.'

Harriet's eyes followed Brucie's retreating figure as the strings inside her stomach tied themselves into the familiar, painful knot.

It was the most awful place you could image. Horrible, discordant noise, not of a drum or a voice or a guitar, but of all the instruments howling together in some nameless distress. It was dark, filthy, stinking of hash, rot and a smell she couldn't recognise but which brought a sharp revulsion from her nurse's instinct. There could be, in this place, no night or day, no winter or summer, no life. How could this place have anything to do with anyone still alive? How could such a place have anything to do with

Ammu?

Brucie had vanished. The room was seething with human forms, clumsy, heavy, unsmiling, hollow-cheeked, eyeless under the horrible lights, mouthless under the universal small moustaches, wrapped from throat to boot in dead black and clanking with chains like condemned slaves. The figures clumped together, not exactly dancing, more shifting their feet as if to find some rhythm in the music, occasionally mouthing something, looking down into their glasses as if seeking somewhere to drown themselves.

Oh God! the Purgatorial Fires: it was not, it was hell. This was what Tonton Robertie had dragged Ammu into; this was what Ammu had to face, being related to, yoked to, even indebted to, such a man.

Harriet knew herself to be a conventional woman, even a dull one. But she knew she had qualities of worth. She could work almost anybody else under the table. In that work, she could display sense, sometimes intelligence. She was physically brave, even if, as Ammu had once said, her courage came out of lack of imagination. But this place filled her with a horror she could never feel in a sacked village in Mozambique. This was appalling – oh, God, poor Ammu!

The lights changed, and the sound became more coherent, a thumping, distant crowds cheering. Shapes were moving in the air, on people's faces and, in clearer focus, on the back wall. A big square shape like a flag, now green, now yellow, now red; a heavier shape below, moving spastically, now purple, now black, now still. The sequence began again; red, purple, black. Harriet recognised the image – a cine projector was casting over the club a rendering of the last agony of a bull in the ring, rolling on its back and pierced with a hundred darts. Harriet turned away. She was going to be sick. She looked about her desperately for somewhere to go. She looked up into the face of a man who was looking at her.

He was a smallish, fattish man, in his fifties or early sixties, whose bad teeth and drooping jowls couldn't quite disguise the delicate bones of his face or his small, pretty mouth. He moved closer. He was definitely making an approach. Harriet roused herself and threw a hostile stare his way.

He was perhaps a third of the way into the room, and apparently alone. His eyes, heavy lidded with tiredness or drink, had a glazed, watery look. Harriet, staring, recognised with shock a likeness to Ammu's big round eyes. He slowly made his way towards her. She braced herself; she was almost a head taller, but a beanpole body has many points of vulnerability. He had a slight limp from the hip; polio, perhaps, or a bone badly set after a break. There was no sign of Brucie. She clenched her fists, aware of how small and soft they were, but believing that they would be a match for anything his could do.

The man, shielding his tumbler of drink against the press of dancers, moved closer, till his nose was perhaps twelve inches from Harriet's throat. He stuck out a hand and grasped her clenched fist in a movement that was something between a handshake and an arrest.

'Well – well – what have we here? Wel-welcome.' His voice, light and girlish, and sweetened by a Mauritian-French accent, took a strange twist from his clumsy bearing. 'Wel-come to the club.'

Harriet tried to shake her wrist free. 'I beg your pardon.'

'Welcome to my house. Here, have a drink!' Still gripping her fist with his right hand, he hoisted the tumbler towards her mouth with the other, splashing her with what smelled like gin.

Harriet stepped sharply back. 'Let go. Leave me alone.'

'So, we really are in England, warm, friendly England, aren't we? Where you can't even greet an old friend all the way from Mauritius.' He dropped her wrist, took a step back and stared up into her face. His mouth rounded as if to spit, then broke into a soapy smile. 'I miss the old place. The birds and the sun and the goats and the bicycles thick as ants, but, by Our Lady, mostly the food.' His eyes were instantly watering with emotion. 'Glad to see someone, even if it is that stuffed shirt of a nurse that pads round the villages after my Marie-Louise.'

It took a second for Harriet to recognise the name. Then her heart was pounding. 'I've never met you before,' she said, more sharply than she meant to.

The small man shook his head with big sweeps – he was certainly very drunk. 'I know who you are. But you don't know who I am?'

The pulse in Harriet's diaphragm was fast as a cricket's wings. This was Tonton Robertie for sure, but, with Brucie nowhere in sight, Harriet was not ready to deal with him. She said awkwardly, 'I don't clearly recall meeting you.'

'I know I've seen you just about every time, when I go round to the clinics for my girl.'

Harriet frowned. 'Your niece?'

'The same. We're very close, me and her, like two peas.' The man pressed his two index fingers together and thrust them under Harriet's nose. 'Close like that.'

The horrible room, the raucous noise, the lights, even the unfortunate bull, all vanished from Harriet's consciousness. Her eyes bored into the man's stained and smelly fingers. With a rush of excitement, she was ready for action. She whispered: 'Is Ammu with you?'

'Her, she's with me every second of my life! She's in my blood; she's in my heart. Nobody ever loved her more than me, nobody ever done more for her. I did everything. I've been like more than a papa to her all her life, like a brother, like a lover, like more than a mama, like a million mamas! She's a good girl. She would've told everybody about what her Tonton Robertie gave – Monsieur Robert France Du Deffand, Fashion Photographer, Entrepreneur with International Connections ... that's me.' His heels clicked together as he gave a stiff little bow, stumbled, then scrabbled against the cement floor to regain his footing.

Harriet leaned over him intently. She couldn't wait for Brucie. Every second now was precious, too precious, too dangerous, too easy to lose. 'I'm pleased to meet you, Monsieur France Du Deffand. Is Ammu in London with you now?'

'Call me Robertie, I don't stand on ceremony like some. And if it suits you too, I'll just call you Harriet.'

Harriet started at the sound of her name. She caught a glimpse of Brucie pushing her way through the crowds. Good. She spoke firmly. 'I asked: is Ammu in London with you now?'

'Sure, we're doing business, family business. Business with international connections, Harriet girl. But, take it from me, big business doesn't always mean good business.'

'Not good for Ammu?'

'Not good for anybody, not the family cat, I tell you. Ammu's a stupid woman for all that education I filled her up with.'

Harriet racked her brains for the best way, casually, to get back to the point. Ammu was still somewhere in London. Ammu was with Robertie engaged on family business which was not going well. All this fitted in with the picture she and Dr Ramgulam had put together earlier that evening. But what business? Where was it being conducted? She ought to go back to the beginning, get Robertie to be more precise about each detail. But Brucie was closing in on them, and now Harriet wished her away, at least for a few minutes more. Quickly, she had time for one or two more questions; how could she get this man to focus? She said, 'What has Ammu done that was stupid?'

'She loves me, you know Harriet girl. She loves me with every single last drop of her blood. But she's proud. Hard proud. That's a very bad thing in a woman, it's – it's imbecile! But she'll change. She wouldn't want to murder her Tonton Robertie who's done so much for her, would she now, Harriet?'

'Obviously not.' Harriet tried another tack. 'She's with you, you said? At your house? Somewhere nearby?'

'Not so near. Gone off to think.'

Harriet could have smashed his head against the wall. Was this, then, the fourth place Ammu had gone from?

'Where to?'

'By Jesus' blood, leave it alone will you; she's gone inside her own imbecile head, like a tortoise, like the tortoise she is.'

As Brucie joined them, Harriet's eyes beseeched her to pay close attention.

'Robertie –' Brucie beside her, Harriet could be more forthcoming. She took the plump little hand into her own '– I need to see Ammu. I need to talk to her. It's very important.' She shot a glance Brucie's way. Brucie's eyes rounded; she began to whistle softly.

Robertie swayed gently, as if they were leading him in a dance. 'Well now, why don't you do that? You always were her faithful hound. Why not; maybe you could talk some sense into her.'

'All right; I can try,' Harriet said, as warmly as she could. 'What do you want me to say?'

'Tell her she's eating my heart. Tell her I'm eating rocks. Tell her to eat the education I gave her, and the international connections.'

'Yes?'

'Tell her she forgets her sacred duty; tell her what she owes to her Tonton Robertie, her family.'

'All right, Robertie, but where do I see her?'

'Here.'

'She's here?' Harriet's voice jumped an octave.

'Soon.'

Brucie seized Robertie's empty glass, sniffed it, said 'Gin?', then made off back to the bar. Harriet could have kissed her.

Harriet dropped Robertie's hand. 'When? When, exactly?'

'Maybe towards morning, maybe later. Maybe soon, Harriet girl, maybe so, so soon.'

Harriet stared hard at the watery eyes. She so wanted to be able to believe. 'Shall we sit down?' She steered Robertie's bulk towards a stool someone was just vacating. 'I'd love to hear more about the help you gave Ammu, and the education. If you could tell me about the family problem, I'd be better able to help.'

As Robertie sank onto the seat, and Harriet took advantage of his preoccupation with wiping the spills off the table before him to scour the room for perhaps some sign of a sari, she realised that for the past hours or minutes, she had scarcely been aware of the Purgatorial Fires. The crowd was much as before, a tidge denser, perhaps a tidge drunker, still shuffling, muttering, looking into their glasses – but much as before. Even the two middle-aged men, one fat, the other skeletally thin, hovering near their table, she could have sworn had been close by during her first talk with Robertie. Brucie's tall form, a firm and wonderfully sane shape, was once again making its way towards them.

'High school with the Sisters of the Order of Mary Immaculate – the best, next to the Jesuits. That's what a poor, uneducated man with nothing but a third-hand Hasselblad and tripod made out of splits of coconut palm gave her. Matriculation, too, from the JMB in Cambridge. Latin, physics, botany – all the distinguished subjects. I gave her my life.'

Robertie covered his eyes. 'My whole life. And a year at

the medical school, then Liverpool. You know Liverpool, the greatest of the universities? I did that for her, all by myself, everything. Her papa was a beast, bless his soul.' Robertie çrossed himself. 'Her mama, a cow in an apron, did nothing but chew and cry. Anyway, she was dead by then. Nobody understood; only me.

'I fought for my little Marie-Louise when Papa Du Deffand wanted to marry her off to a white man – chap had his own business too.' Harriet leaned close; Robertie was mumbling. 'I got her a big tin trunk and packed her bags and bought her a passage on the Union Castle Line for Southampton, even the train ticket to Liverpool. Everything with class, except maybe when I hid her old rosary in the shoes I was packing. Just thought she needed a bit of luck. I wrote her letters and sent her pocket money. She would only wear saris, and I put in rice and bananas when I sent them so she wouldn't have to eat potatoes. I kept faith with her, knew she'd be back.'

Brucie handed the glass, filled to the brim, to Robertie, winked at Harriet.

'Hello Brucie,' said Robertie, opening his eyes. 'I like your new girlfriend. She's been asking about my Marie-Louise.'

'Marie-Louise – that's Ammu,' Harriet whispered excitedly to Brucie. 'And Robertie says she'll be along here soon.'

Brucie responded with a lugubrious shake of the head. 'Robertie is the mother and father of all pink elephants.' Harriet remembered Brucie's using that phrase before.

'And their sons and daughters,' said Robertie. 'An elephant with international connections, and, let me tell you girl, a French colonial elephant that can hold its drink. Not many of us around since Bonaparte.'

'Ammu would be ashamed of you, behaving like this in public.' Brucie's severe voice scarcely accorded with the massive gin she had just handed over.

'She *is* ashamed of me. I gave her the education to do it.'

Harriet let her attention wander from this conversation, once more to search the room. Packed as the place was, there was so little colour it would be easy to spot a sari. There was none, not even a skirt, not even some piece of fabric that was not black. The two men were still nearby, still looming, looking at nothing much, looking bored. One – like everybody else – wore his leather trousers so tight they pushed a roll of flesh up under his shirt. The thin one, almost bald, wore a long, funereal robe. Even in this sea of ghost faces, his paleness was vivid, the skin stretched almost to transparency over the bones of his nose. Harriet's mind automatically ran through its checklist of debilitating conditions. But no; this was London. Suddenly her scientific interest was aroused; she examined his face and neck for any signs of Karposi's sarcoma, any other symptoms of Aids – till he caught her eye, and responded to her stare with a low, mocking bow.

Harriet turned away. Only Ammu could probe into a sickness with instruments handled so delicately that she bruised nothing, caused no pain. Only Ammu looked into the sick and suffering as if she was looking into herself. 'Sorry,' she muttered.

Robertie looked up. 'No offence taken, Harriet girlie,' he said. He was talking about his international connections. 'They bleed you dry.' He banged his glass on the table, spilling gin over the cuffs of his shirt, 'Everything you've got, it isn't enough for them.' Harriet leaned harder against Brucie's shoulder. Brucie seemed to know Robertie quite well. She must have been to this place before. Presumably Robertie came because he felt at home here. But why did Brucie? If Robertie was speaking the truth, Ammu would come here too. Why?

She looked at her watch: 4 a.m. How much longer?

Anyway, they were on the track, and she was pleased to have found Tonton Robertie by herself, without needing

Brucie's introduction; pleased too that Brucie acknowledged this so almost gracefully, fitting in with the programme Harriet had set up. She took another sip from the glass Brucie had handed her (something with coke) and leaned casually against Brucie's shoulder. The same shapeless music still tormented her ears but, now that she had become accustomed to it, it hurt them less; it was even, in a weird way, pleasurably disturbing. (The bullfight, thank God, was over). The door opened and closed, letting in more pale men in black leather. Nobody left. None of the people that came in was Ammu.

'You come here often, Robertie?' Harriet cut across Robertie's comments on a Chinese boy seated alone, not far from them.

As if taking a cue, Brucie seized Robertie's glass and made off again towards the bar.

'I go every place you can name; the concierge at the Ritz calls me "sir". I know all the metrolop - metropo - metropolises. I know London, Bangkok, Mbabane, Paris, Bogatar ...'

'Mbabane?' That sounded familiar.

'Swaziland, where the boys wear chaps of antelope hide.' Robertie rolled his eyes. 'The fur, it's smooth as silk one way, like porcupine quills if you rub the other way. Their feet are hard, grainy, like rocks in the sea. They all want to be great warriors. They're very pretty.'

Harriet nodded, wishing Brucie back. 'In Swaziland, did you know a Monsieur de -.' Harriet couldn't bring herself to say it.

'I know all the Barons de this and Comptes de that. I have international connections.'

Harriet swallowed hard. 'And a Monsieur de Wet de Haas,' she prompted quickly.

Robertie started. 'Never heard of him,' he snapped, 'and shut your face.'

'Okay,' Harriet said very slowly, registering the lie.

'Were you recently in Swaziland?'

'You want to go to Swaziland? The girls are good. Their tits hang over their bellies, bigger than watermelons. Brucie, she'd go for it, but most females don't understand sex these days. It's those brown shoes they wear; deaden the nerves.'

'Was Ammu in Swaziland with you?'

'Ammu!' He almost spat. 'My Marie-Louise is clean. She doesn't do that stuff. She's got education.'

'But she's been to Swaziland?'

'Never. Over my dead body.'

Harriet sighed. She could almost believe Robertie was stringing her along. 'Why isn't Ammu here yet, Robertie? It's getting late.'

'She'll be here soon. Tonight, tomorrow night, maybe the night after. Soon as she's ready to see sense, to give what she owes to her Tonton Robertie who loves her better than the world.'

Harriet's heart sank. Suddenly she hated all this: this stupid drunk; the appalling noise; the foul air; the packs of ugly men; the dragging, boring mystery. 'I want to see Ammu,' she announced flatly. 'I want to see her tonight. Where is she?'

Robertie's watery eyes roamed over the room. 'On her way. Yes, sure, she's ready and on her way.' (Harriet glanced quickly round.) 'Brucie's on her way,' Robertie continued, 'with my drink.'

Harriet muttered a curse under her breath. He *was* leading her on. She looked up sharply as Brucie handed her another glass of coke and something.

'Don't think you can get stuff out of this charley by squeezing his guts,' she whispered into Harriet's ear.

'He's just messing me around,' Harriet hissed back.

'I'm not so sure.' Brucie's hand was on her shoulder. 'He might be trying to work you out. Take it easy. I think we're doing okay. Remember what we came to get.'

Robertie, unexpectedly, took this in. 'Came to get what?'

Brucie answered: 'Ammu.'

'That's nice. I thought your girl was nice from the start. But why?'

Harriet and Brucie spoke at once: 'She loves Ammu,' said Brucie, and from Harriet came: 'I'm going to Moz – to another country with her.'

Robertie's eyes bored into his glass. 'Marie-Louise is not going to Mozambique.' His voice retreated into a mumble. 'It's a foul place where they pack the boys off to Jo'burg to slave in the gold mines and then send them back with coughs and syphilis and all their teeth broken by the boss boys. And, soon as they hit Maputo railway station with their new radios wrapped in blankets, Renamo sets on them, and takes everything they got. And the poor bastards walk miles back to their villages. And all they find is the houses and mealie fields burnt and the women and children raped or dead. Then there's only two things they can do to stay alive: get back to the mines, or join Renamo themselves and take stuff off the next lot coming home. There's no hope. Marie-Louise can't help them. God can't help them.'

Harriet sprang to attention. 'You know about Mozambique, Robertie – I mean you know about Ammu and –'

'Too well I do. And she isn't going. Anyway, the boys got far bigger balls in Swaziland.'

That was the last bit of anything approaching sense they got out of Robertie. 'We're doing great; don't worry. We'll make it,' Brucie whispered into Harriet's ear – 'I'll get this uncle another whopper, and then we'll dance, loosen the focus.'

'More gin – you'll poison him!'

'I guess.' With a crooked grin, Brucie once more seized the glass out of Robertie's hand and disappeared into the press. As if lonely for the glass, Robertie's fingers uncurled themselves, crawled across the table and landed in Harriet's lap. Harriet looked down with distaste.

'I'm a troubled and unhappy man, girlie,' he said, 'a lonely man. You do me wrong. In your soul you do me wrong. Like Marie-Louise.'

Harriet, tired as she was, returned to battle with a dozen leading questions, but learnt nothing that she had not heard a dozen times before.

Although she felt a bit silly, a bit like a schoolgirl, when she stood up to dance with Brucie, it was rather a relief to slide into her undemanding arms; it was certainly a relief to move, as much as they could, in a slow shuffle, away from Robertie's wistful voice, Robertie's bowed head. The music, whatever it was, was at least danceable, and Brucie was nice to dance with. After a few minutes, it didn't feel at all odd to dance with her; it felt just the same as dancing with a real partner. No, not true, it felt nicer: as Brucie steered her round a clump of men, Harriet recalled Martin's nervy strings of bone and muscle prodding at her collarbone. Her tired head sank against Brucie's shoulder. 'I'm not any good at dancing, I'm afraid,' she said. And then, as this sounded ungrateful when she felt more than grateful, she added swiftly, 'But it's nice dancing with you, really.'

'Yeah,' replied Brucie. 'Beats talking any day.'

It occurred to Harriet that talking with Brucie, although she spoke so maddeningly slowly and in that vulgar London slang, was in its way rather nice too.

'Brucie – I think you handled things ever so well this evening. You knew exactly when to back things up, and you made everything seem casual; you're not tense and priggish like me.'

'It was easy. Robertie wanted to talk. All shits want to be understood.'

Harriet felt herself grin indulgently. 'You know the

reason for everything, don't you?' Brucie's leather-clad shoulder was comforting as a pillow stuffed with lavender. 'So, clever-clogs – what happens next?'

'Easy. We stick by him like he was in our handcuffs. Y'see, he's all over the place, but he knows where Ammu is – that's clear as mud – and he half wants to tell. And he's lonely. Nobody talked to him tonight except us, yet he's quite a nice guy. I think we can open him up.' Brucie fell silent for a moment, then added, 'If we don't get it out of him here, we'll take him home. He says he's staying now in Highgate, a lane off the West Hill. But we'll never get the bugger out until we can carry him out. He's too scared of whatever's out there, and them –' Brucie jerked a thumb in the direction of the two men who seemed, as far as one could judge movement under the moving lights, not to have moved a muscle since Harriet last studied them.

Good God: something to do with de Haas? 'Who are they Brucie?' she whispered harshly.

'Dunno. I seen the fat one before, got some messenger work outa him. Paid on the nail, but bloody less than the job was worth. Thick as a plank and mean as shit.'

'The other one?'

'God knows. Looks like they pulled him outa a morgue.'

'Do you think someone might have put them up to watching Robertie?'

'Could be. Half the characters at the Fires are in trouble with their governors at any one time.'

Harriet started at the word 'governors'. De Haas could so easily be the governor, or the maréchal, of these two men. She glanced again at them and shuddered. This was the moment to confess to Brucie about stealing the letters.

But Brucie was holding her in a way that was so comfortable and easy that she couldn't bear just yet to say what would be bound to make Brucie cross with her, cut short this one pleasant experience of the evening. Half the other dancers were doing it, so she again sank her head into Brucie's shoulder. Brucie drew her closer. Harriet closed her eyes.

'Brucie,' she said after a while, 'you took Ammu to Sophie's place. Did she ask you to? Did you take her from here?'

'Yeah; wish I bloody hadn't. Robertie asked me. And she wanted to go. I didn't know anything was going on.'

Harriet's feet stiffened. 'What is going on?'

Brucie shook her head. 'I don't know. Something that isn't good. Anyway, I've already talked too much.'

'Because of Sophie?'

'Because curiosity killed the cat.' Brucie pushed her away. 'I ain't doin' enough for you? You bored with dancing already?'

Harriet drew her closer again. 'Sorry.' Once again she sank her exhausted head into Brucie's jacket and closed her burning eyes. 'I don't need to know anything. I just want to find Ammu.' She felt a tear welling up; the something with coke perhaps. 'Brucie –' there was something about this place with no time, no law, no society, no cause or consequence to anything, that made it possible to think anything you liked, '– Brucie, I must find Ammu; I want her to be safe; I want to be with her.'

'Sure.' Brucie's arms tightened around her.

'I mean really close to her, close as Sophie was.'

'That's nice.'

Tonight had been going on for an awfully long time. Harriet's half-closed eyes wandered over the figure of a man dancing alone, head bent low over his feet which he carefully placed, left foot and then right, on the patches, irregular as bloodstains, on the floor – a pilgrim at the Festival of Cavadee, stepping on nails.

It was Cavadee, honouring the holy Muruga. The last rays of sun had turned the lake to orange and the people on the shores to a dark mass lit only by their eyes. Harriet could feel the press of worshippers, holding their breaths as they restrained their children, waiting to know if this soul had prayed and fasted and denied his human desires long enough to step off the bed of nails leaving no trail of blood behind him. He stepped off, raised one foot and then the other to the dying sunlight – deeply pitted flesh – no blood. A sigh rose from a hundred throats.

Ammu had dragged Harriet to the festival, saying that she would be horrified; and she was. Soon she began to feel irritated. 'It's quite –' she had begun to say 'obscene' '– quite theatrical, Ammu.'

'Yes.' Ammu was smiling. 'Things look gawkish and overdone when they don't come out of the habits of your own culture. Try to see what's going on on the inside.'

Harriet looked. She saw men and women with dirty needles in their flesh and dead stoned expressions on their faces. The onlookers, fixed as in an old black and white photograph, were covered in sweat.

But Ammu and Harriet weren't there only to look. Not every pilgrim succeeded, and within an hour, they were extracting a spear from the tongue of a young man who had quite lost his ambition to conquer the flesh and was struggling only to scream.

It was after that that Harriet began to see inside. A young woman, a beatific expression on her face, was standing motionless with a hundred small needles protruding from the soft flesh of her cheeks. Her eyes focussed on nothing, she held in her hands a bowl of frothy milk, ready to carry it up to the temple, a simple offering brought to the steps by a soul that had left its body behind.

Standing beside Ammu, her hands stiff with blood, Harriet shivered with fear that this tender young face would be pitted and scarred for life. Then it came to her that this young woman didn't fear it. She wanted to be, not a beautiful face, but a pure soul. Shocked as she remained to the end, Harriet saw the appalling courage of this attempt to crush out of oneself the commonplace, the material, to see with other eyes, to become something else, something free of greed, and pride, and envy. She looked at Ammu, and said: 'Would you do that?'

'No,' was Ammu's reply. 'But you might, one day. First, you would have to learn to trust these people; their prayers, you see, would be your strength.'

'But not your strength?'

'They cannot help me. I am full of lies. They are deceived by me; they think me a holy woman.'

Ammu had so often shocked Harriet. 'Perhaps that's because you *are* a holy woman,' Harriet muttered into Brucie's shoulder.

Brucie's heartbeat had a strong, regular, reliable sound, music at the centre of a now very dreary cacophony. She pressed her ear closer.

Saturday morning,
5 November

By 7 a.m., and still no sign of Ammu, even Brucie had had
enough.

'Okay, kid,' she said, 'let's get the bugger out of here.'

Robertie, still sucking his thumb, and muttering
something like 'I could use another drink', was gripped
squarely round the shoulders (by Brucie), by the hand (by
Harriet) and levered through the now thinning mass of
black, up the stairs and out into the street. The door closed
of its own accord behind them.

Harriet took a huge gulp of carbon monoxide-laden
morning fog – the sweetest breath she had drawn since she
first buried her nose in a rathcorani flower in Mauritius.
Brucie was meanwhile burying Robertie's head in her
crash helmet.

'Not the bike, Brucie,' Harriet said firmly, 'we'll find a
cab.' The keys in Brucie's pocket jangled irritably.
'Honest, Brucie, it's not safe, three on a bike, and you
could be over the limit. And as for Robertie –' she pointed.
Robertie, swaying gently, was urinating against the back
wheel.

'There ain't no cabs here.' Brucie's voice was grouchy.
'Nothing comes this way except hearses. And it's no safe
place to leave the bike. Anyway, we all need air.' Without
looking at Harriet, she bundled the semi-conscious form
onto the saddle and started up. Robertie lurched as the

bike sprang to life, its revs echoing down the hollow street, then slumped against Brucie's back as it moved uncertainly forward. Brucie picked her way round a frozen pothole, and stopped at Harriet's feet. 'C'mon kid. It'll be okay, I promise. Just you watch out for fuzz.'

Harriet didn't move, aware that if they had to spend half the morning filling in forms at a police station, all the night's work might be wasted. Brucie offered the spare crash helmet. 'I'll drive ever so careful; won't move outa second gear, promise.'

Harriet smiled wryly. Brucie was tired like a child, and wanted, like a child, to play up to the drama, a knight on a charger. But she found herself so touched to think that maybe this tough, sensible, prematurely grown-up young woman wanted to impress her, that she strapped the helmet round her head and climbed meekly up behind Robertie. When Harriet let her fingers reach around Robertie to dig themselves into Brucie's jacket, once more finding pleasure in its reassuring solidity, Brucie revved the engine enthusiastically. The bike wobbled into motion.

Streets grey and silent as a city drowned under the ocean offered a few glimpses of sharkish cats, no police. Then they were in the London Harriet welcomed and feared, starting a new day, winding up its machines for work. As the bike gathered confidence, roaring past pick-up trucks and early morning buses, the flutter in Harriet's stomach gave way to a steady pulse of anticipation: they were in action, getting closer to Ammu.

'Panda car!' she called out gleefully. Her stomach jumped into her throat as Brucie, without reducing speed, swung into a side street. It jumped again when Brucie yelled 'Hold tight!' and did a fast U-turn round a big black Mercedes. If this was second gear ...

Robertie – presented only with his helpless back, she felt a touch of sympathy with Brucie's fondness for him. She did believe him, at least enough of what he said, to feel sure that Ammu was alive and not far away and that Robertie would not wish to see her hurt.

The picture was still unclear, but sharpening by the hour: Robertie was in trouble, and Ammu had somehow been dragged in and taken hostage. Robertie claimed to be a fashion photographer with international connections; Harriet knew he was a pornographer in a particularly sleazy branch of that sleazy business; he had enemies known to de Haas from whom de Haas claimed to want to protect him; men had apparently been watching him at the club. Why? Could he have taken pictures compromising to the rich and famous? Could he be privy to information about big crime rings connected with pornography, prostitution, drugs, arms smuggling? Could he be a spy, anybody's spy – for the Mafia, Britain, Russia, Renamo? This wreck of a man hardly seemed up to any of these roles, but Harriet, attending at important bedsides, had learnt early that the powerful and dangerous are not always impressive, or even clever.

Robertie's weakness they would exploit. They had hold of him now, and were not going to let him go until he had led them to Ammu. As the bike's roar merged into the din of the Commercial Road, Harriet's hopes surged. Never again would she let Ammu be trapped in the unwholesome mess of the lives of people like Robertie, or Sophie – from tomorrow she and Ammu would once again be medical professionals – objective voices, apart, clean.

This good feeling also had to do with Brucie. When Harriet rang Sophie's doorbell, she had entered the world that had claimed Ammu, and everything in it was corrupt, deformed, full of hurt and shame – everything except Brucie. Unlikely as it was, Brucie was wholesome somehow, like a baby is wholesome, however messy its nappies. And Brucie made her feel so very grown-up, bold, on the track, ready to tackle anything.

'I'll get you started, then I'm off, okay? Then you're on your own, okay?' Brucie had said in Ammu's room. But Brucie hadn't gone. There was nothing in it for her, but she was still there. And she was showing the way. Harriet clenched the leather jacket tighter, sensing, through frozen fingers, what she could only think of as sanity.

This time the route was full of reminders of the London that had once been home. THATCHER – SCHOOL MILK SNATCHER was still scrawled on the iron of the rail bridge spanning the road. They whizzed past Chrisp Street market where stallkeepers were innocently hanging up shirts that had fallen off the backs of lorries; then Spitalfields, a vast mass of flowers torn from their roots but still filling the air with sweetness; then, after spinning round Old Street roundabout, the market for camper vans, where the remnants of the year's pilgrims from Australia were grimly polishing up their wares, spray-drying distributor heads and rubbing away as much as they could of the signs of rust and oil leaks.

The bike's headlamp flashed on the phosphorescence of big green road signs signalling the M1, M11, M23, M40, all the points of the compass. The only one that mattered came a little later: 'The North, Highgate'.

The roads were clogged by the time they crawled up Highgate West Hill – cars in a tunnel of their own vapours inching their way towards the City, bodies strapped inside reaching for their radios to find out what had become of the world. Harriet, hearing echoes of another tumble on the Nikkei Index, almost laughed at their stupidity; passing by on the empty side of the road were two women holding between them the Crown witness in the only story that mattered.

Robertie, responding to a nudge from Brucie, roused himself and pointed out a narrow, unmade lane. It led to high walls, a mess of unkept garden, a white house. Brucie bumped up onto the flagstones, switched off. The headlamp faded, bringing into view the big, decayed square villa, rising to three storeys, its stucco cracked where buddleas had rooted themselves into its sides. Harriet's stomach gave a lurch.

'We're staying over with you, okay?' Brucie, perching the big bike on its insect leg, didn't even glance at Robertie as she spoke.

'You're an honoured guest, Brucie. Your girlfriend, she's welcome too.' Leaning heavily against Brucie, he took them up to a door at the side of the house and pushed it open with his foot. 'No lock, you see, Brucie my lovely, no need here; here you're under protection of my international connections.' Harriet grasped Brucie's other hand, and Brucie gave hers a reassuring squeeze.

Robertie flicked a switch, and half a dozen small spotlights sprang to life. They were in a big, warm ground-floor room, humming from the vibration of a boiler somewhere close. Rugs, whose intricate patterns in dark red and blue glimmered under the lights, were scattered over a floor of polished black stone; even silkier rugs shrouded the long windows. Between the rugs hung large abstract paintings, in pale yellows and greys. There was a low table in black lacquer, holding, in a pool of white light, a hookah on a brass tray; around it a cluster of pouffes in embroidered leather, and beyond, behind a delicately embroidered screen, a huge open futon. Robertie, swaying gently as he stood in his downtrodden shoes and trousers pushed low under his belly in the middle of this elegant room smelling sweetly of wax, said, 'Welcome to my house. Have whatever you want – a seat, a bed, cigars, a drink? I've got wine, gin, milk – I'll go right now to make you coffee,' and then collapsed onto the futon.

Harriet stood, fists on her hips, looking about her. 'What do we do now? Wait for him to finish his beauty sleep?

'Hush yourself.' Brucie put a finger gently to Harriet's lips. Then she knelt over Robertie, pulling off his leather jacket, shoes and trousers, and tucking him up. 'Shit, Robertie; your feet are frozen. Sure you're not feeling sick? Want me to get you a little nightcap?' Robertie was already asleep.

Harriet was trembling, despite the almost oppressive warmth. The intimacy of the scene was unpleasant. 'I don't know why you don't take up nursing yourself,' she said sourly.

Brucie grinned. 'Am I doing okay then? Used to be in the St John's at school – anything was better than needlework.'

'Loosen his tie and collar if you must. Then let's get on with it.'

'Okay.' Brucie unravelled the thin black tie; Robertie's shirt was already unbuttoned. Then she gestured at the lump under the covers. 'Get in there.'

Harriet backed away. 'I want to look around. There might be some clues. And this room makes me feel sick.'

'Easy on now. We're doing great. Get in: he's harmless, and it'll relax him better.'

'But what are we waiting for?'

'For him' – she pointed – 'to take us to her, or for her to come to him. Any other ideas?'

'Well, no, not really. But can't we just sit here and watch?'

'Do it. Act normal. Shit! What if his minders walk in and find themselves out of a job?' Brucie stood up to face her, folding her arms. It was a gesture that reminded Harriet of Ammu bullying a woman (whose menstrual cramps she had tried but failed to cure with herbs and meditation) to go to the hospital Ammu herself had so reviled. 'We gotta take it slowly now; we're real close – it's all gonna happen real soon.'

Slowly, Harriet began to wiggle her feet out of Brucie's

boots. 'No, keep them on,' Brucie whispered. 'We might have to move in a hurry.' Harriet shoved the street-soiled boots between covers of fine pale grey silk. Brucie snapped off the lights and crawled in, leather creaking, beside her.

Harriet, turned away from Robertie's sleeping form, could feel Brucie's breath in her hair. She moved her head a millimetre closer to pick up the thump of Brucie's heart – Brucie was one hundred and fifty per cent awake though her eyes were closed.

So this was what it was like to lie, a grown up person, in a bed with another grown up person, so near you could feel a heartbeat, but so separate you could fall into your private sleep. In hospitals, many people slept badly because they lay alone. How odd to be so easy with another body. Harriet doubted that she could ever achieve such closeness with anybody, and she felt sad, alone, a spiky, thorny thing.

Perhaps, if she had been softer, more like everybody else, Ammu would have come to love her in Mauritius. Was it possible that she might lie like this with Ammu one day? Why, when someone as low as Sophie had lain close with Ammu, did it seem so wrong, shocking, for Harriet to think of doing it? Why couldn't she lie as she now lay beside Brucie who didn't ask anything? If she put an arm around Brucie, Brucie would say, 'That's nice,' or 'Christ you've got sharp elbows.'

But even now, when she knew she loved Ammu, she knew too that she could no more touch her body than put her hand in the fire. Why? If Sophie could consider peeping past the towel to Ammu's nakedness, could Harriet not at least think of embracing her?

Harriet didn't know; she only knew that Ammu was a blaze that would burn into the darkest corners of her mind. Brucie's heart went thump, thump, thump; automatically, the nurse in Harriet counted its beat while she wondered how soon it would all happen. She was dreadfully tired.

Beyond the soft, dark room, muffled by the wall and the garden, London was going about its business with a throaty roar. It seemed a thousand miles away. The whole thing felt unreal, sinister, like being inside an enchanted castle, awaiting the moment to break the spell that sealed Robertie's lips. Brucie's hair smelled faintly of coconut oil; perhaps this was a Mogul palace and the boiler was the beating heart of a great elephant, Brucie's the heart of a youth tending it. She shut her eyes to quieten her stomach, reaching around in her mind now for Bunnikins. It would be horribly easy to fall, not exactly asleep, but into some pit of unconsciousness. Robertie was snoring – a lot of phlegm in his bronchial passages; he smoked and drank far too much. His heartbeat was fluttery and too fast. The purring of an expensive car sounded somewhere close; then the crunch of wheels, an engine switched off, a comfortable sound. Harriet let her body sink into the silky covers.

'Christ!' Brucie's hand thumped the pillow. 'I left the fucking bike out there.'

'What, where?'

'My bike, out there; outside the house. Shit! Shit! Shit!'

'Oh, shall we go and move it?' Harriet found Brucie's alarm mysterious.

'That car that just drove up,' Brucie whispered hoarsely, right into Harriet's ear. 'Remember how it sounded? Sure as eggs it's the Merc of those two fuckers who were watching us at the club. Oh shit! They were behind us, you see, nearly all the way to Aldgate. That's where I finally lost them. Then I just forgot about them. But the buggers must stay here too. Why the – why didn't I think of that? It explains how an old queen like Robertie could be in such a place.'

Harriet was now wide awake: de Haas's men! 'You mean those two men from the club; they live here or have followed us?'

'It's gotta be them, and if they're here they know we're here, because of that bloody bike.'

'Brucie,' Harriet said hastily, 'there's something important I didn't tell you. I know, I mean I think I know, something about Robertie's trouble. Ever heard of somebody called Yves de Wet de Haas?'

'Uh-huh; the Howard Hughes of the underworld. Shouldn't think Robertie aims that high.'

'He does. I know he does; he's very involved with him. I saw a letter.'

Brucie laid a finger to her lips. 'Tell me in a minute.' She was straining her ears.

Robertie's snores grew louder. 'Shit,' muttered Brucie, 'now I can't hear a fucking thing from the house. Swear I heard the front door pulled to. Did you hear that creak on the stairs? Now I can't hear a thing except snot running round his guts.'

'Brucie, listen, this is something very important.' Harriet sat up stiffly. 'I have a confession. I didn't have the nerve to tell you earlier. I have to tell you that I stole some letters; I stole them out of the dressing gown in Sophie's bedroom.'

'Shame. Sophie'll be well upset. But just listen.' Harriet heard nothing. 'Think that was a noise from the room above us?'

'Aren't you worried about de Haas?'

'Give me a break will you. I'm trying to hear what's going on in this fucking house.' A few seconds of silence, and then the flushing of a lavatory cistern sounded loudly above them. 'Okay, they're upstairs. Sure I'm worried; scared shitless. If Robertie's in trouble with someone like de Haas, he's chicken feed. Maybe we are too. Maybe if we had half a bloody brain between us we'd be anywhere but here.' Robertie rolled onto his back, and the snores rose to thunder.

'De Haas seems to be trying to help him.'

'De Haas help anyone? That's rich.'

'Would you recognise de Haas?'

'Only if he wore his horns and tail.' Brucie rolled off the futon and rose quietly to her feet. 'Just lie still. No, hold a pillow over his fucking head. I gotta check out what's going on.'

'Brucie, I'll go with you.' Harriet began to scrabble to her feet.

'No, stay. Back in a minute. Take care.' Brucie paused. 'Just one thing you oughta know. Robertie, he's in the porn business, around little kids.'

'I know. Dr Ramgulam ...'

'De Haas, he does big stuff: wars in Africa and central America, jobs like that. He's into arms and things. But he gets his money outa the gutter. Robertie could be a leaky kinda gutter, y'know, with his soft head and his big thing about Ammu.'

'Yes, and – ?' Brucie always spoke so slowly!

'If Ammu tried to clean up Robertie's act, y'know, they could both be in real deep.'

Harriet too had been thinking along these lines. 'And?' Brucie was still hovering.

'But I can't quite see it.'

'See what? Spit it out Brucie.'

'I mean, if Ammu got hold of Robertie, the de Haas lot would just piss themselves laughing. Why all this drama?'

Harriet didn't answer. In her own mind, she had already formulated the answer – Ammu must have tried to go to the police. The police had no positive role to play in Brucie's world; there was no point in even mentioning them.

'I just want you to know how I'm thinking, kid, just in case.'

'In case what?'

'I have to run for it.'

'Oh no!' The courage Harriet was so proud of deserted

her. 'Please don't leave me. I'm scared.'

'Join the club.'

'Brucie, I'd never have got anywhere without you.'

'You haven't got anywhere. Just lie there and keep Robertie quiet.'

Harriet didn't know boots could pad so softly. 'Shit!' she heard, as Brucie stumbled against something. Then a thin ray of foggy day broke in as Brucie drew back one of the window hangings. Harriet watched her deftly check out the rest of the room. Robertie's breathing was quieter now. He had his thumb in his mouth and was softly sucking on it. Harriet inched her body away from his, breaking the unpleasant contact between his outspread knee and her bottom. Brucie peered into the bathroom, felt behind the wall hangings, and then, on the far side of the room, pushed back a long rug, revealing a door. This opened a few inches until a chain, on the other side, pulled tight. It must lead into the rest of the house. Harriet could detect the outline of Brucie's head turning towards her, a thumb turning up to note a discovery of importance. But then Brucie was across the room once again, softly closing up the crack of light, and gone in a flash of day fast as lightning, out of the outside door.

Harriet felt a profound chill. Her eyes struggled to make out shapes in the room, her ears to detect any movement from the house or from Brucie outside. There was none. The boiler was still pulsing. Robertie was quiet. From the distant sounds of London, the day was well advanced; war was being declared, perhaps, or a Cabinet reshuffle, or perhaps Brucie was wheeling her bike over the flagstones and Harriet would soon hear its engine spring to life out on Highgate West Hill. Harriet's stomach had turned itself into a small sharp stone lodged between her ribs.

Millimetre by millimetre, she edged herself away from Robertie, preparing for fight, for flight, for what? Her senses sharp as knives, she waited for some sound, from anywhere.

Gradually, Harriet became aware of a small movement. It was Robertie's hand behind her, moving slowly towards her back. Her body froze. Robertie was awake: how much had he heard? Gritting her teeth, she let the hand wander, just in case Robertie was doing this in his sleep.

The hand drifted along the seam on the side of Brucie's leather jerkin. Harriet trembled with the effort not to kick backwards. 'I'm no good, girlie,' came Robertie's sleepy voice, 'this hand, it's a bad hand. It ought to be in chains. It's ruined my life, you know. And it's ruined Marie-Louise.' The hand was still, as if pondering its next move. 'My poor body, it's only got one organ that isn't scared to move – this hand. That sad old body, it's even frightened of little kids, little soft kids. And so this bad hand ...'

Harriet was suddenly ready for anything. 'How have you ruined Ammu's life?' Her voice was harsh and hostile.

'I love my little girl, I truly do. She has idea – idealism – she has character. It's this hand, my hand, that did it. Cut it off; I want you to get a knife and cut it off for me.'

Despite herself, Harriet couldn't help elbowing the hand away. 'Did it; did what?' The words came out like a bark.

'I should never have dragged her into it. She was – she is – my good angel. She's so pure; she can't understand this wicked world.'

'Dragged her into what?' Harriet sat up sharply. Robertie was mumbling something more about his hand. She cut across, 'What have you got her into? Where is she?'

'I've done nothing. My hand.' Robertie was rubbing his hands like some grotesque Lady Macbeth. 'It wrote to le Maréchal. He was always hungry. He was always wanting more. Until I had nothing but that to give him. But she wouldn't, you see, she went queer, stiff; she's so proud.'

'You gave him what?' Harriet grabbed the threshing hand, and pinned it to the bed. 'You gave him Ammu?

Where is she, where?'

Robertie looked up at her imploringly. 'In his house – you can't do anything – she's in the master's house – she's with him – she's here.'

'Here! In this house! Show me.' Harriet, on her knees in a tangle of silk covers, tried to drag him to his feet.

'I can't. I don't know where. It's none of my business.' They struggled. 'Help,' Robertie yelled, 'Monsieur de Wet de Haas, Monsieur le Maréchal, aidez–moi!'

'Christ!' Harriet heard herself echo Brucie's cry, felt herself turn and, with all the anger restrained against a world which had been brutal to Ammu, her two hands joined in a karate chop and, with the whole weight of her body behind them, slammed down hard against Robertie's head. They caught him at the side of his neck. 'Christ! You vile, you, you …' Her hands, stinging from the force of her blow, were up again, once more ready to strike.

But there came a soft gurgle, and Robertie's form lay limp. Harriet shook him. His head lolled. 'Oh my God!' Harriet leapt out of the bed, bounded to the window, tore the silk rug from its delicate iron loops. Leaping over the heap on the floor, she ran back to the bed.

Breathing hard to steady herself, she took Robertie's head carefully in her hands and turned the neck, just a millimetre, one way, then the other. Thank God it wasn't broken. She laid the head on the pillow and felt inside the mouth for the tongue, holding her breath against the sour smell of gin-softened gums. Breathing was laboured; but at least he was alive. Carefully, she checked the bones in the neck, the windpipe (no obstruction). The stomach was pulsing; he was going to be sick. She rolled Robertie over onto his stomach, raising his face a little on the pillow. With luck, just winded. To encourage more regular breathing, she began, gently, to mould his back in the first moves of artificial respiration; it would have cost her more than she could pay to give him mouth-to-mouth.

'Hey, what's this? You don't have to fuck with the bastard.' Brucie was standing in the doorway.

'Oh Brucie, thank God you came. I nearly killed him.'

'Really?' A low laugh. 'You're quite a girl. Too bad you didn't make it.'

Suddenly Harriet was swamped with uncontrollable, absurd, dangerous giggles. Brucie was by her side, and Harriet flung her arms around her. 'Oh Brucie, thank God you're back. Brucie, Ammu is here, in this house. She's the prisoner of de Wet de Haas. We can find her. Oh, God, Brucie, Brucie, let's go.' Her fingers were tugging at Brucie's jacket.

'Harriet, kid, listen.' Brucie's hand was gentle on Harriet's head, but her voice was careful, too careful. 'My bike's gone and the gate's shut. If Ammu's a prisoner, so are we. Those two fuckers have locked us in.'

'They've what?' The giggles cut off as if by a knife, Harriet sprang back. The covers of the futon were shaking softly, as if Robertie were silently laughing.

Brucie nodded. 'Come.' She took Harriet by the hand to the door. Harriet forgot Robertie in an instant.

Outside, it was bitingly cold, and the fog still hadn't cleared although it was probably coming up to mid morning. High wrought-iron gates barred the exit. Beyond the tangled branches, the thick ivy and the high brick wall, traffic roared up Highgate West Hill, from an unreachable world of activity and order. A blob of black oil on the terrace marked the spot where Brucie's bike had been. Nearby stood a glistening black Mercedes, its little red burglar alarm light winking at them.

'Shit!' Brucie's boots crunched on dead twigs as she ploughed into the bushes. 'We're in real shit.'

'Forget it Brucie, the bike can't be in there.' Harriet turned to the house. Five or six broken stone steps led to the main door. Two men could, with difficulty, have got the bike up there. Robertie's door was the only entrance on the south side. On the north flank, there were no doors, but a wrought-iron trap door covered steps to a heavily-barred basement window. Footmarks in the frost showed that Brucie had been up to it, walked all round, and perhaps tried to lift the iron ring on the trap.

'You didn't see any sign of Ammu, when you were looking?'

Brucie shook her head. 'Can't see much. You know what goes on at Robertie's end. Can't see a thing at the front.' Brucie paused, pointed to the trap. 'Down there, in the basement, there's a room with a bed in it; pretty bare, nobody about. At the back of the house, there's some french windows, wood rotten enough to kick through at the bottom, but bolted tight, and curtained. Then there's a stable door to a sort of scullery, frosted glass at the window. In the yard there's a coal shed, also locked, and an outhouse with a loo. It's crammed with flat wooden boxes.' Brucie paused again: 'Wine maybe, or guns. Looks like this really is de Haas's house.'

Harriet stared at Brucie's pale face. 'But no Ammu?'

Brucie shook her head.

Harriet pressed on: 'And the gate?'

'We could try climb it, but it's got an alarm.'

'I didn't notice any gate when we came.'

'Yeah. It was there. Open. I wondered about that; you'd think they'd lock it, if Ammu's here, you know. Guess that put me a bit off guard.'

'You thought she was here all the time; you didn't tell me!'

'How would I know? You really bug me with these stupid questions. Shit, I feel bad about the bike, so stupid.'

'The bike's insured of course,' Harriet said coldly.

'It ain't, but that's not the point.' Brucie, in that bleak light, looked white as a ghost, the spots on her cheeks bright as wounds. She was now standing helplessly in the middle of the terrace, perhaps in full view of two men inside. 'It's what the fuck they want with us. And why it matters so much to them that we're on to Ammu.'

'We'll rescue her and climb the wall.'

'If it suits them to let us. They're joking with us now. They must be so fucking sure of themselves.'

Harriet glanced at the upstairs windows – their panes reflected bare spidery branches; she could imagine two grinning faces, one heavily jowled, the other skeletal, behind. In a flush of rage against them, she grabbed Brucie's hand, and pulled her closer to the house, out of view.

'But maybe,' Brucie was vague, 'we just ought'a apologise to Robertie for beating him up and get him to help us. The poor bugger's caught so tight he might just do anything to shift his chains around. Hell, kid, I really did fuck this up. And we were so close; I'm sure we were so damn close.'

Harriet knew she ought to check up on Robertie, who might by now be suffocating in his own vomit, but she hated the thought of having anything more to do with him. She drew Brucie towards her and patted the heavily-padded shoulder.

'Robertie's useless to himself. And he's brought nothing but trouble to Ammu. Come on, nobody's challenged us yet. Let's search the house. After all, Robertie invited us here; we're not trespassing; we're not committing any crime. Their taking your bike's the only crime and, well, maybe me thumping Robertie.'

Brucie smiled. 'Sometimes I think the toffs like you got all the tits. Okay smartface, what do we do? Get in through that basement window?'

They ran back to the trap, and hauled at its ring. The metal seating was quite clean, free of leaves and mud; this gate had recently been raised. They pulled hard. Something yielded, and it gave a few millimetres, till a heavy chain holding it from the underside grew taut; the same system as the chain on Robertie's door. 'It just kills me; you know I got pliers and wire cutters in the bike's saddlebags.'

Harriet, peering through the barred window, could make out a big room, empty but for a tea chest and a mattress, its covers pulled tight, on the stone floor, a mug beside holding a sprig of something green, perhaps ivy.

'Brucie – look.' Harriet pointed at the mug.

'What?'

'A vase, a plant. Ammu, don't you think?'

With one mind, they grabbed the iron ring, and pulled for all they were worth. The iron burned into Harriet's hands; Brucie's face was red. The chain tightened, groaned, held tight. 'This is no use.' Brucie kicked at it with her boots. 'Come. We'll burst the door in Robertie's room.' Brucie was away before the last word was out of her mouth.

'Robertie!' Brucie bounded onto the bed. 'Robertie; where have those fuckers put Ammu?'

Robertie rolled his head slowly from side to side. 'Your girlfriend really gave me some wallop.' His voice sounded strangled. 'I think she's broken my neck. I've got a headache that throbs right down to my toes. Marie-Louise is in the basement. Her choice. Le Maréchal wanted her to stay upstairs. Get me some Panadol from the bathroom, there's a pretty boy – no, ask your girl, she's a nurse.'

But Brucie was already at the door leading into the house. She opened it far as it would go on its chain, then, stepping back a few paces, hurled herself, feet first, against it. With an almighty crash it burst open and Brucie's body shot in like a missile.

'Wazzat?' Robertie jumped.

'Shut your face,' Brucie hissed, back on her feet, but rubbing her bottom.

'No, you can't do ... No, that's serious trouble.' Robertie, holding his head, began to heave himself out of bed.

Brucie, abandoning now any pretence of stealth, flung herself on Robertie, seized him by the collar, and dragged him to the lavatory, where he fell, gasping and clutching his injured throat, onto the floor. She locked him in.

They marched into the main part of the house accompanied by banging and croaking from the lavatory.

Brucie was now herself again, once again the dynamo Harriet admired. 'Since the fuckers know we're here,' she said in a loud voice as they passed through a library and into the hall, 'no point in farting about. Ready to fight?' From a display of old weapons crossed under a shield, she yanked off two enormously long and heavy lances, and tested their weight and balance. 'Would you know what to do with one of these?'

Harriet shook her head.

'Same here. Well, we're fast learners. Come on.' Humping one lance onto Harriet's shoulder, and holding the second poised for launching, she led the way into another room, a dining room, and pulled back a thick silk rug covering french windows. This door Brucie had tried from the other side. Brucie released the bolts. 'In case we need to run,' she muttered.

The big table in the centre of the room was laid for four; on the sideboard, little flames flickered under silver tureens. Harriet wondered at this display of domestic gentility. But Brucie was at the table, seizing a heavy silver candlestick, knocking out the candle. 'Here.' She handed it to Harriet and took back the lance. 'Easier to use than that long spear.' And the lance Harriet had been holding was flung casually onto the snow-white linen.

Nobody in the hall. Nobody in the kitchen, but the smell of some aniseedy herb wafted from a pan simmering on the stove. A door between the open doors of kitchen and scullery: it yielded to a few kicks from Brucie's boots, opening on a flight of steps to the cellar.

'Brucie: they're watching this, at least listening. Isn't it better we wait a while with Robertie, then use a bit of stealth?'

'You mean come back after they've had time to move Ammu?' Brucie had firmly taken over. She was stamping down the stairs. They led to a maze – here a wine cellar, stacked to the ceiling and draped in cobwebs; beyond a room full of flat wooden crates; then some sort of chapel, and then the bare room they'd seen from the outside. But no Ammu. Harriet kneeled beside the bed, sniffing the pillow: jasmine! Brucie had meanwhile torn open the tea chest, hauling out of it a greyish cardigan, a pair of leg warmers, and a cotton sari. This she waved triumphantly at Harriet. 'Okay,' said Brucie, 'we're on the track. Let's get upstairs, to the main bedrooms. Can't be far now. Weapons at the ready?' She raised the lance.

'Ready!' Harriet had the candlestick in a firm grasp.

As they stood there, almost delirious with excitement, just above their heads, within an inch of the wrought iron trap, wheels scrunched over the flagstones as the Mercedes reversed and then, unhurriedly, rolled towards the gate.

Brucie ran to the window. 'Hey!' she yelled. 'That's Ammu, sitting perky as a fucking parrot in the back of that car!'

They ran, back through the cellars, stumbling up the dark stairs and out through the french windows. The car was gone, leaving a cloud of white vapour hanging in the path of the now wide open gate.

Saturday midday, 5 November

Brucie saw him first. 'Hold it. Here's trouble.'

In the shadow of one of the dark brick pillars supporting the gates, stood a witch-like figure in a long black cloak, its back to them. Harriet's stomach lurched as she took in the languid form and bare skull of the man from the club. 'Brucie, I think it's that ...'

'Yeah, it is.' Brucie raised the lance to shoulder height.

The man must have been working some mechanism, for the tall iron gates came silently to life, circling round on little wheels and clicking into place, shut. They watched him close and lock a little control box, pocket the key, turn, and drift towards them.

Harriet took a step back, towards the corner leading to the french windows and the dining room through which they had charged so precipitately only a minute before.

'Stand your ground,' growled Brucie through her teeth.

Although they were directly in his path, the man seemed unaware of the two women. Walking very slowly, thoughtfully, his hands clasped loosely under the fabric of his cloak like a monk telling his beads, he approached.

Brucie, feet planted well apart, squared her shoulders. As he came near, she drew back the lance, and made, into the air, two or three little stabbing movements.

The man turned his head aside, gave a small cough, paused. Then, taking another pace towards them, he said,

'You might be so good as to put that down, young lady. You would in that way reduce the risk of some unaesthetic self-injury.' His speech was lightly inflected in the Franco-Mauritian way, his words slow, laboured, suggesting that he found English a cumbersome tongue.

'We want Ammu.' Brucie's voice, although of about the same pitch as his, sounded light, girlish, slightly tremulous.

'My dear child, we all want Ammu.' He smiled, and the skin pulled tighter over the bones of his jaw and skull. His chin was freshly shaved, very close and clean, as if a nurse had been preparing him for an operation. He took another half-step towards Brucie.

'Stand back.' Brucie jerked the lance.

He stepped back, then spread a pair of very long, very slender hands. 'Do put it down, mademoiselle, I beg you. Your handling of the instrument lacks elegance. That raises in me complicated and somewhat unpleasant emotions.'

Brucie didn't move. 'Fuck your emotions. Tell us where you've taken Ammu, where you're hiding her this bloody time. And you can open that bloody gate.'

'My dear Oblomov.' He smiled again. 'My indulgence allows me to overlook that you step our of your place in the order of society, but it is grieved by your lack of concern for my emotions. Emotions direct the little theatre of our lives, my dear; even your poor role is informed by one or two rather simple ones –' He nodded his head gracefully, '– desire for food, sex, etcetera. In this case, I find myself at once distressed that you may damage a noble and beautiful object (by which, of course, I mean the lance and not your sweet young self), and equally concerned that you may do something violent. I have a horror of violence.'

Harriet stared at the man – he was surely quite mad. She thought of Freni, the very miserable people at the hospital Mauritians still called the 'loony bin', and realised that she had never before been appalled in this way by insanity. She glanced quickly towards the gate – locked and the alarm on, for sure.

'My name is not Oblomov –' Brucie hissed the next words '– I'm Brucie.'

The man was still smiling. 'How charming; an exquisite choice for you, calls to mind a sheepfarming peasant in the Australian outback. Do you also wear a hat with corks hanging from the rim? My senses inform me that you bathe only before weddings and funerals.'

'N-n-no!' Harriet spluttered. 'You can't speak to her like that ... You have no right to ...'.

The man turned towards Harriet for the first time, and gave a low bow. '*Vous ai-je offensé avec ces propos anodins, mademoiselle? Dans ce cas, je vous donne mes excuses.*'

'Make the fucker speak English,' muttered Brucie.

'Brucie has already told you what we want.' Harriet was surprised at the recovery, to full power, of her voice. 'And your words *were* offensive.'

He bowed again. 'I stand corrected, yet remain injured by your tone. Bear in mind, Mademoiselle, that I was responding to aggression, not causing it. We have much in common, you and I; between us are matters worth discussion. I come in peace.' Once again, the skeletal hands, dry leaves falling from a plane tree, spread slowly before her.

Brucie jerked back into action. 'We're only interested in discussing what the fuck you've done with Ammu. And if you're not causing aggression what about that bloody gate?'

Harriet cut across. 'Who are you?'

'My dear?' The man pointed to the lance.

Harriet looked at Brucie. Brucie looked at Harriet. Without a further word, Brucie turned and leaned the lance against the wall behind her. 'Gently, dear Oblomov,' the man said, 'don't let it fall.'

Brucie half whispered: 'I'll let it fall in your bloody guts.'

'Brucie, no.' Harriet's whisper was heavy with warning.

'Thank you. That was civil, and now –'

'Who are you?' Harriet repeated, with the same clear emphasis.

He bowed even lower. 'I hope it will not be immodest in me to suggest that you may perhaps have heard of me. I am Yves –' he smiled and bowed again '– de Wet de Haas.'

Harriet had already guessed.

'And you, my dear, are?'

'You fucking know who she is.'

De Haas ignored Brucie's remark, offered another little smile to Harriet. 'Of course I know, Madam, who you are, and am honoured by the knowledge, but ultimately the small civilities, *par exemple* formal introductions, are among life's more reliable pleasures.'

'Harriet Weston,' Harriet snapped.

'Someone of whom I have heard much, for whom I have the greatest respect, and whose acquaintance I would regard as a distinction far beyond my merit. It would please me greatly if you and your little friend were to join me for breakfast, my other guests rather abruptly having taken their leave of me.'

Harriet glanced quickly at Brucie; her blank face gave no clues.

'Now desolated by the loss of their company,' de Haas continued, 'I would be charmed if you would share my humble –'

'I won't eat meat,' snapped Brucie.

'Very good, my dear,' he bowed again, 'quite beefy and porky enough already. I have some excellent lettuce leaves.'

Harriet's stomach fluttered furiously against a frustrated urge to do something violent, while she marvelled at the calmness with which Brucie absorbed the man's appalling rudeness – directed exclusively at her – giving nothing back. If Brucie could so cope with him, the least she could do was follow.

She did. She threw a lingering glance at the lance, still propped against the wall, then meekly trooped after Brucie into the horrible dining room, where the snow-white linen now held place settings for three, and the other lance, so recently jettisoned on the cloth, had disappeared. De Haas, close on Harriet's heels, shut and locked the french windows then drew the curtains behind them. The daylight, and any glimpse of escape, faded.

And so Brucie and Harriet found themselves break-fasting by candlelight in the busy hours of Saturday morning with le Maréchal, who insisted, the other Oblomov being engaged on chauffeur duties, on serving them himself.

They were offered slender slices of melon and papaya with limes, creamy scrambled egg with a hint of basil and sage, kedgeree made with very succulent haddock, slices of cold turkey marinaded in a slightly sour fennelly liquid (which Brucie fiercely refused), bacon, kidney and liver pieces soused in grilled tomato (Brucie pushed this from her), baskets of hot croissants, then rye toast and little round rolls of very fine white flour accompanied by freshly made strawberry preserve. Very pungent, rich coffee followed. Harriet, stricken with a bone-dry mouth and throat, struggled to swallow just something, anything. Brucie, after checking out the provenance of the eggs, ate well.

De Haas was never in the kitchen for long, but even when he was out of earshot, Brucie and Harriet seemed to have nothing to say to each other. Brucie once or twice jerked up her fork, to indicate that the food was good. Harriet searched her head for words to show that she recognised Brucie's courage, but her mind was so numbed by the falseness of her position as de Haas's guest that not even a reassuring glance was possible.

De Haas didn't seem bothered that his guests were so quiet. He brought in serving bowls, ladled out dainty portions, and took plates away. He listened to the scraping of silver across his porcelain and talked about the creation of each dish. Cooking and opera, he said, were the passions of his few leisure hours.

He watched them eat, but took little, beyond the fizzy white liquid which he sipped as he chatted. His smile, so horribly appropriate to a face whose naked bone created every contour, was fixed.

There was no reference to Robertie. For all Harriet knew, he could by now have collapsed, unconscious, on the lavatory floor. Nor was the subject of Ammu raised, until, as they lingered awkwardly over their coffee and little pieces of candied fruit, de Haas said: 'You will have perceived, Miss Weston ma'am, that I bear heavy burdens. One, of which you may not be aware, but which colours my perception of every aspect of life, is without glamour. I am diabetic.'

'That's tough,' said Brucie, not without sympathy.

Harriet threw a sharp glance at Brucie. 'The condition is common, and can be controlled.' Her comment, by contrast, was cold and hard.

'So it can, in one willing to live as bondsman to an illness. I refuse such submission; I am in disequilibrium; I rage against God.' He paused; his smile grew tighter. 'The role of Faust is forced upon me. In consequence I need constant medical attention, to keep at least my body within the bounds of its mortality. Your friend Dr Ammu Bai is – is she not? – a very accomplished high priest of the soul, and through that of the body, its creature. You see, my dear Mademoiselle Weston, that I follow Dr Bai in believing that healing must always start with the mind, and so ...'

'So!' Harriet's tone was still icy. 'So you think, do you, that your condition justifies the kidnap of Ammu, the exploitation of her uncle, the death of a child in Port Louis – you know that do you? – that a child died …'

'My dear, the death of any child is a cause of great personal distress, especially to women, and I pride myself on having a deeply feminine nature. However, one has to be objective. Nature appears profligate and insensitive until one studies the order behind it; baby birds are born in abundance so that cats shall not starve. We have so reduced our natural predators that the human population explosion is now the greatest threat to the survival of our species …'.

'Hold your horses,' said Brucie, her voice full of innocent surprise, 'are you trying to tell us you grabbed Ammu just because she's a doctor?'

De Haas nodded. 'Out of the mouths of babes …'

'But, for fuck's sake, how could we believe that when everybody knows you could buy the whole of Harley Street?'

De Haas smiled again. 'You have a crude mind, but one not without a certain power. I don't want Harley Street, my dear. It lacks the spiritual dimension. It has no capacity for transcendence. The crest of its ambition is to make money out of Arabian gentlemen with gonorrhea. Now, if you wanted Harley Street, and if I were so inclined, I could give it to you. But you have a better physician – God – who has bestowed on you something I would give my empire for – rude health.'

'Where is Ammu now?' Harriet butted in, trying to keep her voice neutral.

'I cannot speak for the lady. For all I know, she is preparing herself to meet you. I believe she might consider one hour after midnight tonight a suitable time.'

Harriet saw the knuckles of Brucie's hand whiten as her fist tightened, in silent excitement, crushing her table napkin.

De Haas was gazing at the same wrinkled linen with a slight frown of distaste, but his voice was as bland as ever. 'The first, purest hours of Sunday, the holy day, would, I am sure, suit us all. A light repast could be provided.'

'We'll be here, but won't need food or to see you, thanks,' said Brucie mildly. 'And now, are you going to open the gates?'

Harriet turned away when de Haas proferred his skeletal hand at the gate, but Brucie accepted it briefly. 'I need to talk to you some time about my bike,' she said cheerily, 'and thanks, you laid on a great breakfast.'

Brucie caught up with Harriet as she left the lane for the merciful ordinariness of the traffic of Highgate West Hill, cars loaded with Saturday purchases of food for the freezer. They still didn't talk: Harriet's head was whirling with thoughts too confused for language. Brucie, her arm slung heavily over Harriet's shoulder, sang a mournful song about Mad Bess of Bedlam. Harriet picked up the words:

> 'Poor Bess will return to the place whence she came,
> Since the world is so mad,
> She can hope for no cure;
> For love's a bauble, a swelling, a shame,
> Which maids do admire, wise women endure.
> Cold and hungry am I grown ....'

Saturday evening,
5 November

The ringing of a telephone somewhere below brought Harriet swirlingly to her senses. Whatever she had been dreaming had gone from her, but she felt her body gently let go of some wild excitement. Her arms were still wrapped around the hard little pillow on Ammu's bed.

Ammu! She sat up sharply. Ammu was the prisoner of one of the most powerful lords of the criminal underworld, a dangerous madman. Inside the bed on which she lay was a box of the tools of prostitution. How could her sleeping self have been so happy? 'You are an idiot,' she said to the pillow, giving it a little shake. Yet she was still smiling. 'Tonight, tonight, tonight,' she added, answering on the pillow's behalf.

She switched on the light to read her watch - eight o'clock. But in this world where night and day were exchanged, it was not morning; it was four hours to midnight, only two hundred and forty minutes until she and Brucie would be striding down Ladbroke Grove, looking for a cab to take them to Ammu at Highgate. And tonight they would wrench Ammu away from the appalling de Haas. Ammu would be free. And Ammu would know that Harriet had been faithful; had searched for and found her, had braved danger to rescue her. Then Ammu would discover, as Harriet herself had so recently discovered, that Harriet loved her. Harriet was possessed with an uncharacteristic desire to seize the pillow and dance it wildly, to the tune of the telephone's ring, round and round the little room.

But she didn't. Nurse-like, she ran through her checklist. Everything was ready. She had already been to the building society and extracted the further fifty pounds demanded by Brucie; she hardly cared that this left the account with less than one return fare to Mozambique: a single ticket was all she needed now. She had, after a fashion, washed, and put herself back into Brucie's clothes, steeling herself against the now rather revolting three-day old socks and underwear. She had borrowed and used what she earnestly hoped was Brucie's and not Sophie's toothbrush. She had massaged her toes, now complaining about being cramped into Brucie's boots. She had tidied her hair, combing it with her fingers and twisting it into a rough ponytail with a rubber band chosen from the seedy contents of the ashtray in Sophie's bathroom.

What remained to be done? She felt rather guilty that they had left Robertie locked in the lavatory at Highgate, but there was nothing to be done about that for the moment.

Next? She had still not telephoned her mother, but this was hardly the moment to deal with parental fuss. She had not yet retrieved her duffel bag from Sophie, but this was no time for complicated apologies about stolen letters; in any case, she was still bound by Brucie's injunction against speaking to Sophie.

All that remained to be done was to fulfil her promise to Dr Ramgulam. It must be perfectly possible to get up to Gunnersbury and back by midnight – but did tube trains still stop in the tunnel, for no apparent reason, for half an hour at a time? Harriet decided to call from one of the phone boxes near Holland Park, well out of reach of Sophie's ears.

Slightly subdued by her duty to phone Dr Ramgulam – an odd feeling, since what she had to say would surely interest the good doctor – and irritated to hear the house telephone once again start up its raucous call, she made her way down the stairs. It occurred to her that the phone had never rung before in Sophie's house, but this evening it rang incessantly.

Yet the normality of noise in a house, even of a ringing telephone, helped to make all of tonight's plan seem more real. It made everything a bit less crazy, even Sophie's house. It seemed so natural, somehow, for Harriet to be in the house that, standing on the doorstep, she automatically checked her pocket as if the house keys ought to be in it. No matter. She went out leaving the door on the latch.

Harriet chose her phone box with care, one of the old red ones, with a door, privacy, a bit of warmth. It smelled of stale tobacco and urine; it had a cracked Bakelite mouthpiece and a dial with letters as well as numbers faintly visible against the rubbing of thousands of fingers, but it gave the dialling tone; it worked. She had enough change – half a dozen tenpenny coins.

But there was no need to phone right away – there was plenty of time – she took a stroll round the park. She felt well, not at all tummyish or even, despite only three or so hours of sleep, tired. Now, she didn't at all mind her uncombed hair, filthy clothes, the boots half a size too short. Despite anxieties about the duffel bag, it was odd but nice to stalk along with arms swinging free as men's unencumbered arms swing. It was even odder to be able to let her mind ramble without any horrible doubts about Ammu piercing her thoughts like thorns. For the first time since her arrival in London, she found the place interesting, likable, unsinister. The lights along the avenue, haloed by fog, glimmered like phosphorescent sea creatures between the bare branches where perhaps some of the braver native birds were huddled against the cold.

Beyond lay the elegant stone facades of Holland Park, their windows darkened, where starlings and pigeons would be roosting under the eaves, borrowing a little warmth from the human gift of central heating.

Her boots rang clean as horses' hooves against the path. She was alone, apart from one small figure coming towards her. How odd this too felt; in Mauritius one was never alone in a park. The figure, a girl of about fourteen, drew nearer. She was singing, not a complaint above love, cruelty and death – of the sort Brucie's hard contralto had offered on Highgate Hill – but, in a clear, high, light tone, what sounded like a sprauncy little calypso. As the girl approached, the singing faded away – Harriet's ears strained to catch the last notes. The girl nodded silently. Harriet nodded. They passed.

Then behind Harriet, like the miracle of a blackbird's song, the next verse broke out, more confidently. In a rush, it came to Harriet: the words; the tune; it was that old Mauritian creole song. Her eyes suddenly filled with tears, and with a huge frog in her throat her croak joined the sweet voice behind her:

> *'Dimance bô matin, zène fille, nous va alle bazar;*
> *Ous a meté ous pti robe, zène fille, avec ous souliers;*
> *Mo a metè mo caneçon, zène fille, avec mo çapeau;*
> *Ous a passe par la porte, zène fille,*
> *Mo passe par la fenète …*
> *Batate av magnoc, zène fille, nous va alle manzé.'*

You have put on your little dress, young girl, with your shoes' … Such important shoes: to be worn on Sundays only, but to go to Mass, not to the market. And most definitely not with a companion who – for all the formality of long trousers and cap – has climbed out the window to meet you. 'Sweet potato,' Harriet intoned, 'sweet potato and tapioca we go to eat, zène fille in your pti robe.'

London fell away and Harriet was once again starting a new life in Mauritius.

The interviewer at the British Council, all those five years before, said Harriet was fortunate to be going to work somewhere as beautiful as Mauritius. Even so, she was not prepared for her first glimpse of the island, early that morning, with the light flooding in from the Chagos Archipelago. She had seen tropical islands from the air before, on the television screen. This was as vividly coloured but different: it stayed in view, grew larger; it was real. The Indian Ocean, deep and dark as a mass of military tanks, brushed itself in a line of frothy white against a wide, encircling coral reef. Within that enclosure, the little island floated in calm, milky-jade waters. Harriet watched as its features became clearer, its snowy sands, its glossy green plains rising to black mountains in the centre, their craggy outlines hinting at volcanoes.

On the ground, Mauritius sustained this delight. It was curious in an island so small that you could drive around it in half a day on the national road, a strip of patched tarmac paralleled by drunken telephone poles, with banana and pawpaw trees crowding the verges. Behind, on every stretch, were the same makeshift tiny houses with small, thin people in the yards eating, sleeping, talking in a strange language, or beavering away mending things which were already much mended. If you looked further inland, there was always the stretch of plain, silky with sugar cane, up to the black mountains. If you looked outward, the same clear sea ended everything up to the nearest landmass, the huge, lost island of Madagascar, a thousand miles to the west. It was hot – far too hot for Harriet – and sticky. The air smelled of steamy kerosene and molasses. And the noises were so different: voices, fast and high-pitched as the parrots that crowded every tree; even the wind made a faster, sharper sound, tearing through the spears of the sugar cane. But despite all this,

Mauritius resembled Palmers Green, an inward-looking preoccupied place, unnoticed by the world.

Harriet had little to do with the Mauritius the tourists knew. Though, like many people with long bones, she was a good swimmer, she only once hired flippers and a snorkel to explore the coral reefs. She learned nothing about scuba diving or windsurfing. She seldom lay on the beach, looking at the sky through the fronds of a coconut palm. At the insistence of colleagues, she visited their homes in the smarter quarters of Cuirpipe to meet a confusing assortment of relatives and eat from deliciously scented, beautifully presented pyramids of fruit and seafood followed by ferocious vindaloos and technicolour sweetmeats, but she rarely entered the compound of a tourist hotel. She felt no desire to dress herself in bermudas and gaily printed tops or take part in their discos or treasure hunts.

Mauritius was, to her, filled with glamour, but not that glamour. The glamour was not unconnected with the botanical gardens at Pamplemousses where there were water lilies with leaves ten feet across, and the heavy humid air vibrated against the chorus of a thousand frogs. It was more to do with the little houses, the temples, the solemn eyes of the small girl selling passion fruit at the roadside. In truth, it was to do with Ammu.

Harriet had stepped out of the plane into a wash of hot, moist air enclosing her like a womb. Melting tarmac made it a sticky walk to the little building bannered '*Bienvenue à Maurice*', where lines of small people were waving. The tide of moving bodies from the plane carried her into an echoing din of voices and the thumping of stamps on visas, and into the embrace of a reception committee from the Ministry of Health; introductions to half a dozen smiling people with long names and much to say about their ambition to improve standards in the nursing profession. Her luggage seized by eager hands; her passport removed from her and then returned; taxi drivers fended off like flies, and Harriet was in an air conditioned official car whizzing through a tunnel of leaves and drunken telephone poles to Port Louis and the little square hotel between a market and a mosque, where she pleaded for time to rest.

Harriet did not remember one name, one face. Only the telephone poles, and the boy who took her to the vast room, with a dark carpet, sticky in the humidity, and an air conditioner which would have drowned the din of all Palmers Green's pubs. It was, said the boy, the best room in the hotel.

At that point, Harriet had no idea whether or not she was glad to be where she was, wherever she was. Vague as a dream was her farewell at Heathrow, Mother bickering with Martin over a cafeteria table heaped with paper cups oozing instant coffee. She was wherever she was and in need of a wash, a rest, a chance to think. She would shower, hardening herself against the bathroom. But, after a few dousings with blood-temperature, blood-coloured water, and alarmed at the sound system from the local mosque which bounced the imam's whine off the cracked, white tiles, she emerged to face not the ordinary manageable mess of her luggage but, on that luggage, three cockroaches.

The size of chocolate bars, with stripes of red, green and yellow along their armoured bodies, they flicked long antennae, asking her in unison for real life chocolate bars. They could as well have been asking for her blood. She would have leapt onto the bed, if that weren't host to two more cockroaches. She stifled an urge to scream, wondering why the nerve which had carried her through her first dressing of a gangrenous wound failed her now.

She could have stood there, face to face with the cockroaches, draped in the bleach-clean towel, all day. But the door opened, and there was Ammu.

Harriet hardly took in the figure in the doorway. 'Uh' – gesturing towards the cockroaches – 'Uh, can you?'

Quick as the swish of a sari, the stranger was in the room, seizing half a dozen cockroaches in each hand and dropping them out of the window, which she then shut firmly.

'They fly in from the market down below,' she said in a voice with something of France, much of India, 'so keep the window shut and the air conditioner on.'

'Thank you.'

The stranger, perhaps forty, and dressed like a peasant, was small. She had the body of an adolescent and a delicately shaped face with big black eyes. Her smile was wide and innocent.

'Thank you,' said Harriet again.

The woman laughed. 'Europeans are fools to be afraid of them,' she said, her voice surprising deep and powerful to come from such narrow lungs. 'They only spread disease if you bring it in in the first place. They don't bite. They aren't poisonous. They're even quite friendly – look how they waved their little antennae. Does a dog greet you with so much charm? If you allow that their movements seem a bit spastic to human rhythms, they're beautiful.'

'Yes,' said Harriet, now feeling foolish, wondering who this person was, and if she ought to ask her to sit down.

But the stranger was already seated. She opened a bulging briefcase and took out a file of papers. She flicked on the lamp. (Harriet hadn't been able to fathom how to get the thing to work.) In leisurely fashion, she took out a sheet and began to study it.

Harriet stood awkwardly beside her bags, clutching the towel around her, and stared at the figure under the light. Was this the hotel manager? The other hotel people wore Western dress and the women, make-up. Was she someone from the Ministry of Health? All the other Ministry people smelled softly of deodorant; this woman smelled faintly of some cheap jasmine scent, but more strongly of the street. Her sari was worn, grubby at the hem. There were sweat stains under her arms and her sandalled feet were grey with dust. Yet she was obviously an educated woman. Perhaps she was someone from the university. Perhaps she was some kind of crook.

'It was very kind of you to deal with the ..., but I don't understand the context of your ...'

The woman nodded. 'I've come here,' she said, 'to ask you to bring your students to my clinics.'

'Your, um, clinics?'

'My clinics, people's clinics.'

'I see.' So that was it. The woman was selling something. Alone in a foreign country, Harriet felt exposed, nervous. 'I've just arrived. I'm not dressed. Perhaps you could leave me a brochure.'

The woman handed over the sheet of paper, softened by the heat of her hands. It was printed in washy purple, from a spirit duplicator. The heading, crudely hand-lettered, read

The Doctor Ammu Bai
Velopathic, Naturopathic, Homeopathic, Holopathic
Family of People's Health Clinics of Mauritius.

This woman, presumably, was the Doctor Ammu Bai. Where – if anywhere – did she qualify as a doctor? Harriet was too tired for all this. 'How interesting.' She folded the paper, and took a pace towards the door.

The woman did not take the hint. 'My clinics are in the villages, in the outbuildings of temples, some under verandahs of the houses of believers. They're all over the island, or will be soon.'

'I'll get in touch.' Harriet opened a suitcase and fumbled inside for a gown. 'I don't have my agenda yet. It's been nice meeting you, and thank you for dealing with the cockroaches.' Harriet's fingers found the gown, but she was reluctant to go into the bathroom, leaving her luggage exposed, to put it on. She draped it over her shoulders.

'You don't understand,' responded the woman hotly. 'I am not an ordinary connection. I have come to offer you knowledge you do not have and probably do not deserve – understanding of how our souls control our bodies.'

'I will follow it up, but I'm rather tired.'

The woman seemed not to have heard. 'I have many enemies,' she said. 'The Ministry is against me. They think health is given by a tablet or a scalpel; they think life is the gift of the government.'

'Yes, national health services are like that. They prefer things that are easy to administer.' Harriet wondered if this was the kind of Third World country where it might be dangerous to talk to someone opposed to the government.

'I had to bribe an airport clerk to get your flight details and hotel arrangements. No doubt by now he's sold to my enemies information that I have made contact with you.'

'I'm new here. I don't want to get involved in …'

'In what? In real people's health? You must understand that I can give people's bodies back to them – to themselves and their own culture. You don't value that?'

Harriet had done some homework. 'I understand that the government has clinics attached to every hospital,' she said cooly, 'and the primary health care service extends to each of the ninety-six villages.'

Dr Bai's small, powerful hands swept these words away. 'So it does. Men in white coats with little moustaches, who speak English – even if they learned it yesterday – to peasants who know only Tamil and Creole French. They shove a needle in their bottoms and a bag of antibiotics in their hands and charge five rupees and send them away. They don't understand them, respect them, or talk to them. They handle them like carcasses in the meat market.'

'Sounds like the British health service.'

'I don't doubt. Well, it's not what we want here. We have herbs that heal, but we teach people to despise them, to unlearn what their grandmothers knew. I am taking people back. I want our people to use the priests and the old women of the villages – people with knowledge that comes out of life – and be their own physicians.

'We have, in our tradition, good breast-feeding and weaning practices. But the Ministry teaches people to be slaves to everything that comes from the West, so the poor spend their little money on powdered baby foods from Europe. We have good food, healthy food, but the men in moustaches just watch while children spend their parents' small money on Coca Cola; and they tell Hindu mothers to feed their children on a food that's magic because Americans clog their arteries with it – slaughtered cow.'

'Perhaps they're undernourished.'

'Of course they are,' said the woman fiercely, 'when their mothers work ten hours a day making T-shirts for just enough money to buy chapattis reeking of chemicals.'

'You've raised rather a lot of issues, all at once.' Harriet's teaching experience could, it seemed, survive even a fourteen hour flight. Suddenly, in this strange country, where there were cockroaches and sweating carpets and people who paid no attention to a stranger's helpless nakedness, Harriet was involved. 'Dr Bai – you are Dr Bai?'

'Ammu.'

'I'm Harriet Weston, nurse tutor –'

'I know.'

'Would you like a cup of tea while I dress?'

'I'd prefer a drink. Have you tried our Mauritian rum?'

And that was the start of a process which led to Harriet's becoming Ammu's most faithful disciple – somebody who worked all day teaching student nurses and half the night doing what she saw as her real work, helping at Ammu's so-called clinics. A scientifically trained professional, she had watched, at first with horror, then with amazement and finally with wonder, to see very sick people made well through Ammu's manipulation of men with paint on their bodies, beetle-nut juice on their teeth and what she still saw as hocus pocus in their heads. But people had been cured, and Ammu had shown how this could be. And so Harriet had given herself for the first time in her life. She had become Ammu's – Ammu's follower, she thought; her slave, some people said, but then Ammu was surrounded by enemies.

Harriet brought herself up short. This was London. Her legs were blunt stumps clomping over the frozen path; her hands scorched stiff with cold fumbled at her cuff to give a glimpse at her watch: 9 p.m.; three hours until she was to meet Brucie, four hours to zero. She should phone Dr Ramgulam.

First she clambered down to the lavatories at Notting Hill tube station to thaw out her hands. Stiff and uncomfortable now in Brucie's clothes, she stared closely at the mirror reflection of a drawn, very tired face shadowed by a dusty red thatch of hair. She was almost as pale as Brucie, and her eyes had sunk into the contours they would take on in middle age; her body was not as confident as her mind about tonight. Now she understood her reluctance to telephone – Dr Ramgulam, too, might have doubts about this mission.

Now it seemed odd to Harriet that she had been, up till five minutes ago, so sure about their mission. Nobody else was. Even daredevil Brucie had become, after her first excitement, uneasy.

In the cold fluorescent light of the lavatory, Harriet stared at her pale, reflectionless eyes. Earlier that day, on their return from Highgate and de Haas's breakfast, Brucie's tawny eyes had been as opaque – weary, veiled, not wanting to hold Harriet's glance. 'It's all fine by me,' Brucie had at last said uncertainly. 'But just now I feel a bit shitty about Sophie.'

Then, Sophie hadn't seemed important. Now any uncertainty was disturbing. Why should Brucie feel 'shitty'? Sophie wanted Ammu to be free; she had herself put Harriet on the scent. Was it that Brucie realised that Harriet would immediately sweep Ammu off to Mozambique, as far as she could get her from Sophie's house, Sophie's dressing gown, Sophie's compunctions about peeping past the petticoat? Did Brucie sense that Harriet, too, had a private agenda, was not quite what she seemed? Harriet knew so little about her comrade in arms. It was so easy, when they were in action together, to treat Brucie like the magnificent simpleton she seemed so often to make herself out to be. 'We'll get the bike back, Brucie,' she had said – encouragingly, she thought then; patronisingly, she thought now.

'Sure.' And Brucie had lapsed into silence. Harriet looked forward to the day – she hoped very very soon – when Ammu would be free and they could, together, embrace Brucie, their special friend, and slowly, in the way of friendship, learn to respect her.

Harriet made her way to the telephone box.

The phone was answered at the first ring. 'Dr Ramgulam, sorry I haven't …'.

'Harriet!' Harriet jumped at the familiar bark. 'My dear, we were worried out of our tinies. Come home immediately, and let me tuck you up with a mug of cocoa; then you can relate your adventures.'

'Dr Ramgulam, I'm going to meet Ammu in four hours' time, tonight, 1 a.m.'

'I thought that was planned for last night, my dear, per kind favour of Tonton Robertie.'

'Brucie saw her. She was being taken away in a car. She *has* been kidnapped, and by de Haas.'

'How exciting! But then how do you get to meet her, my dear?'

Harriet's grip on the telephone receiver was a little shaky; this was not the time for Dr Ramgulam to play semantic games. 'De Haas has promised that Brucie and I will see her, alone, tonight,' she said severely. 'We're supposed to be going there to talk to her, but –' Harriet felt her earlier excitement rise again, '– we're going to rescue her. We're going to climb a tree to get her over the wall without touching it because the whole place is wired up with alarms.'

'This sounds very enterprising, my dear, and not a little confusing. One thing at a time. Pop up to Gunnersbury. We'll talk for an hour and then I'll drive you back in good time for your assignation. Only take twenty minutes that time of night.'

A worried glance at her watch, but Harriet agreed.

Dr Ramgulam listened closely while Harriet reported on the Purgatorial Fires, the invasion of Highgate, the breakfast with de Haas. Then she leaned back, and asked questions, which forced Harriet to tell the whole story over again.

'What do you think' she said, finally, and in a different, harder tone, 'de Haas expects to get out of this meeting?'

'Oh, I guess he thinks it'll help settle her down.'

'By domesticating her captivity?'

Harriet nodded.

'You don't think he would expect you to have marked out that very tree, that very spot to climb the wall, and have Oblomovs Numbers Three and Four waiting there, just to make sure nobody sprains an ankle?'

Harriet grimaced. 'Of course we'll be very secret about it and, when we move into action, very quick. He seems to think he's won us over somehow. he doesn't seem to suspect anything.'

'He has that high an opinion of his charms and that low an opinion of your intelligence?'

'Well, he is extremely vain, and he surrounds himself with sycophants, and he's hypochondriac and – well he's trusting in an odd sort of way, as if he thought he was invulnerable, like God.' Somehow, all this sounded very lame.

'Don't you think, my dear, that, before you talk to Ammu, you should talk to the police?'

Harriet started. 'Oh no, I can't. I promised Brucie.'

'Your promises to Brucie seem to be fairly tradeable commodities; is there any other reason?'

'Well,' Harriet shuffled. 'We can't, to be quite honest, be absolutely sure Ammu didn't go voluntarily to de Haas. I mean technically speaking. I mean, she didn't go freely of course, but it's possible she may have gone because she felt she had to do it, to protect Robertie.'

'Ye-es?' Dr Ramgulam prompted.

'Well, the police would take everything out of our hands, and Ammu's hands. They'd, well, see everything in black and white.'

'Ah, so you think, at least in the legal sense, Ammu may be guilty of something.'

'No! Certainly not. We just don't want the police meddling. Not at this stage, anyway. They'd be bound to mess everything up.'

'That's certainly possible. But would you and Brucie do better?'

'We might. Like I said, de Haas seems to trust us, up to a point.'

'Yes, my dear girl, he certainly trusts you to give him a little entertainment. Just put your scheme aside for one moment and think of him; think of what might be going on in his head. The man is posing –'

'Oh, he's quite insane.'

'That's not a very useful concept; we all follow different

logics. But think how convenient it is for him if you think him mad – not quite real – a character actor, not really dangerous. Think of the long, black cloak, the outspread hands, the performance over the food – pure theatre. And the arrangement itself ... why the middle of the night? If it is only to be domestic chat, why couldn't you come at 4 p.m., when the trains are running, for a cup of tea?'

'He wanted us to meet in the first hours of Sunday; he said it was a holy day.'

'I see. And you'll all pop down to early morning Mass afterwards?'

'Well ...'

'One a.m. indeed!' Dr Ramgulam scoffed. 'What a convenient time to kidnap you too, should he require a nurse as well as a doctor.'

'I had thought of that.' Harriet spoke quietly but firmly. 'Dr Ramgulam, if I can't free Ammu, I want to be in captivity with her.'

'And Brucie? What happens to her? Since he already has her bike, is she to be outrider to the ambulance crew? Does she want to be in captivity too?'

Harriet wriggled. She felt guilty about Brucie. 'Brucie wants to do it,' she mumbled.

'Although the woman seems to have a lot of initiative and a smaller measure of common sense, I suspect that your Brucie is also capable of foolish recklessness when her emotions are involved.'

'Which means?'

'I wonder if she doesn't have what my daughter would call "a thing" – about you.'

'Oh no, Brucie isn't like that, not at all. She likes adventure. She's amazingly brave, and so cool with it.'

'Very good.' Abruptly, Dr Ramgulam stood up, rattling the car keys in her pocket. 'All right then, my dear: yours and your Brucie's is the only show in town so we'd better let the curtain go up. But I like adventure too.

I'll come as well. I may not be able to run as fast as Brucie, but I can deliver a hefty swipe with my black bag.'

'No. You can't.' Harriet was irritated by Dr Ramgulam's jocular tone. 'We promised to go alone, and unarmed.'

'What a pity; I'd have enjoyed it. Then I'll go separately and wait, in the car, a few yards down the hill; speed up your escape.'

Harriet couldn't deny the good sense of this. 'Well, if you really want to ...'

It was well before eleven when they climbed into the car – just as well, in case of even thicker fog, a puncture, or some hold-up on the road. Harriet was subdued. Dr Ramgulam's fast and inattentive driving frightened her even when visibility was good; and, as the minutes ticked by, she was becoming uneasy about the rescue plan – too many people organising everything, too many questions looking for answers – Ammu seemed to be slipping out of sight behind a growing pile of arrangements.

They overtook a big red bus, its windows steamed up against the cold, the heads inside bowed in private thought. Harriet would far rather be on that bus, letting her mind sink into quiet, emptying itself of everything except her meeting, now little more than two hours ahead, with Ammu. But Dr Ramgulam, busy, managing, more involved by the minute, was determined, it seemed, to grind away at keeping conversation going.

'So it seems that Robertie's little business,' she barked loudly above the roar of the engine, 'has fallen victim to the merger virus, and become a hard-driven little cog in the de Haas machine.' She hurled the car around the corner. 'And Robertie feels the strain. He "gave" Ammu to de Haas, he says.' The car whipped along the north flank of Gunnersbury Park. 'I presume he means that he sold her. I wonder if that was to pay the "tax" on his pornography business?'

Dr Ramgulam charged into Gunnersbury Lane, into the stream of haloed headlights pouring out of the West End. She seemed not to notice Harriet's silence. 'I've been thinking a bit about pornography these past two days,' she said, 'although, regretfully, my own experience of it is rather limited. I've been trying to understand why it's so powerful; what it gives to the people it gives things to. Have you any ideas?'

Harriet's thoughts were elsewhere. She was now wondering if she ought to tell Brucie not to come; if it would be simpler, cleaner somehow, if she went to meet Ammu alone. 'No ideas,' she said.

Every light was against them, every intersection fuming with cars. The countdown had begun, though there was still masses of time, and absolutely no need to worry about the traffic. But Harriet now wanted this journey to be over, to allow her just twenty minutes to walk alone in the streets, to let her tongue and ears become very still, very new, for Ammu.

Dr Ramgulam, fingers drumming against the wheel, joined the queue at the first traffic lights. 'I used to have some theories when I was younger,' she said. 'As a student, I read Henry Miller – all that stylish erotica peppered with hints of dark things beyond what is permitted. It made me feel raffish and liberated; I had then no experience of sex with a partner.'

Harriet hated this kind of talk at any time. Right now it seemed particularly gross. 'Never heard of him,' she snapped, hoping to deaden this line of conversation.

'No, I suppose you haven't. Yours is a stern generation. But we all read Miller, in the sixties. I remember one image, from a book I'd borrowed (with many promises to keep it safe and not for long) from another student. A man and a woman were in a taxi, riding back and forth over, I think, Brooklyn Bridge. I fancy it was not long before dawn on a winter morning. She was sitting astride him, and her juices poured into his groin like "hot soup".' Dr Ramgulam chuckled. 'Clever that; real sex is seldom quite wet enough.'

Harriet stared ahead. Dr Ramgulam had turned the word 'wet' into an obscenity.

'I showed the passage to Ammu, just for a giggle. Ammu looked, grabbed the book and threw it into the fire. Then she turned on me like a wild cat. It wasn't a reaction I'd expected from someone with an uncle who took photographs which could not legally be sent through the mail.'

Harriet's heart fluttered. When Ammu was free, and they were in Mozambique, the memory of books like that, uncles like that, would slowly be buried by time and work.

'What Ammu did rather jolted me you know,' Dr Ramgulam said thoughtfully. 'She made such an issue out of what I saw as a harmless little game. At the time I told myself she was prudish – "frigid" was then the fashionable word.'

The lights turned green. Cars revved. Harriet was momentarily comforted to think that Ammu, too, had been a 'Sister Frigidaire'.

Dr Ramgulam inched the car forward, then blasted Harriet's little ease with: 'But now I think the opposite; perhaps sexual fantasy had too much power for her, roused memories, and feelings, she needed to crush.'

Harriet, desperately, tried to hang on to her own train of thought: how quiet it would be in Mozambique; how far from the corrupt, hateful past – there they would find peace in the midst of war. There was a moment's blissful silence.

But Dr Ramgulam went on: 'It was years later,' she said, 'that I came across real pornography; I mean images that go right out of the range of fun into cruelty and debasement, sometimes using animals, or children. If it hadn't been for Ammu, I wonder how I would have connected them with the mischievous erotic writing I had enjoyed?'

Harriet was yanked to attention. 'Please, Dr Ramgulam, this subject is disgusting.'

'Yes, isn't it. So difficult to treat coolly. Perhaps because pornography makes one feel guilty about one's own probably rather innocent fantasies. But for all that,' she added slowly, 'I must confess, my mouth still waters at the though of that hot soup.'

Harriet was silent.

'Thinking about the subject over the last two days, Harriet my dear, I discovered that that last sort, real hard porn, is still, to me, mysterious. Now I can, I think, understand how burglars become anally excited when they rob houses; I can certainly understand why murderers keep on bashing their victims long after they are dead, but the effect hard porn has on me is rather like the sight, say, of a dish of boiled sheep's eyes; it just makes me squeamish; it seems in such poor taste. Perhaps you are in the same position?'

Harriet's hope of some small private peace was now blown to the winds. 'I am not,' she said with real vehemence, 'I hate it. It makes me feel vile.'

'It does?' Dr Ramgulam was vague. 'Don't you find it curious that the human mind should have created for its pleasure something so – on the face of it – silly?'

'Silly! You think it merely "silly" when a child died in Port Louis because of pictures that Robertie …'

'The killing was an accident. You're talking about something different, about consequence, not intention. Your Christian religion distinguishes carefully between them –'

'– I'm not talking about something different. That man *intended* to abuse the child, and Robertie's pornography put him up to it.'

'Perhaps he didn't, Harriet my dear. Perhaps he

wanted to play with it, but be the big boy in the playground. And perhaps he wanted to revenge his childhood self for all the times he was the little one who got knocked around.'

Harriet was now thoroughly aroused. 'You sound like a criminal psychologist saying, "It's not my client's fault he murdered a dozen prostitutes; he had a domineering mother"!'

Dr Ramgulam tapped the wheel. 'I take your point, and I agree that we are always responsible for what we do, even when deeply wronged and mad with grief and pain. But you are still talking about consequences. Let's take a little moral holiday and try to find what he was seeking, the man who murdered the prostitutes, or the child. Yes, why did he want to buy Robertie's no doubt over-priced pictures in the first place?'

This argument was not of Harriet's seeking. It was certainly not what she wanted to give her mind to at this hour of all hours. And she knew she was being led by Dr Ramgulam, no doubt into some semantic trap. But she was too angry not to rise to the bait. 'His motives are not of the least interest. All that matters is that he made himself a beast.'

'Ah yes, he did. And, as Dr Johnson noted, that would have relieved him of the pain of being a man – unfair to beasts of course, who are seldom beastly, but there we go, burdened as we are with a sexist, racist and speciesist language.'

Harriet folded her arms and stared ahead. 'Twaddle!'

'You are no doubt aware, Harriet my dear,' Dr Ramgulam added thoughtfully. 'that there are many dark places in the human soul, any soul, even one you would see as great, say Ammu's.'

'Why Ammu? Are you suggesting that she had anything in common with the brute who bought Robertie's pictures?' Harriet snapped.

'No, at least not necessarily. I don't know what goes on in Ammu's mind. But I do see her as psychically somewhat fragile. How could she not be, growing up in a world moulded by Robertie and the egregious Du Deffand?'

'Fragile? Ammu is the strongest person I know!'

'Yes, that's what makes her so interesting. And it's interesting too that we both love her, and, I think, fail to understand her.' Dr Ramgulam paused, surveying yet another queue of cars at a red light. 'But I'll speak abstractly if you like. Now, a day or so ago, it struck me that pornography serves a purpose. Life is full of frustration, ego shrinking. Even sex is frustrating with all the relationship duties appended to it. Yet erotic passion, in its basis, is simple – powerful and mindless. It wipes out fearfulness, our sense of limitation. It makes the libido the centre of the world. It opens the gates to that delicious tide that rises and swamps us in pleasure. We want more, but often our fearfulness is stronger than our passion. So we design sexual fantasies to drug the fears and doubts that hold us back. Now, the character of these fantasies is, surely, dictated by the fears.'

'What are you saying?' Harriet struggled against surges of rage. 'That it's all right to turn your partner into a rubber doll?'

'No,' Dr Ramgulam was still calm, rational, 'I'm not justifying anything, just examining. You see, bad, cruel fantasies evoke our anger; but the fears that produce them might evoke pity. Anger, rejection, closes us to understanding; pity does not. If we look at the fears, perhaps we will understand the fantasies. Now, let me think.' She pulled up at the lights, parallel with a shiny new Porsche, music blaring through its open windows. To Harriet, this journey was as long as a plane flight to Mauritius.

'Freud says, Harriet dear, that the dark places in our minds are the source of our energy, and are churning with all the unexamined things in our lives – terrors, hungers, even our high ideals; all the monsters. Now perhaps if we look frankly at what we call deviant we may be seeing a little of the hidden side of ourselves.'

'Oh stuff!' Harriet rounded sharply, 'Have *you*, in your secret mind or anywhere else, ever wanted to abuse a child?'

'No; but I like to embrace my daughter; I certainly enjoyed suckling her ...'

Harriet found this disgusting: fortunately her mother never asked for more than the slightest peck on the cheek. 'That's not the same thing, for heavens sake!'

'No, women have so many more outlets for feelings, don't we? And don't we, with small children, have the enormous pleasure of having power over something that doesn't have power over us?'

'No.' Harriet was still staring at the offending Porsche. 'Just enormous responsibility.'

The driver caught her eye, leaned out of his open window, 'Your place or mine, girls?'

'Go to hell!' Harriet yelled.

With a squeal of tyres that rippled like a laugh, the Porsche shot ahead.

'He was only playing, Harriet.'

Harriet, bursting for air, loosened the seat belt. 'Maybe he is, but then, so are you. You say you want to understand pornography, but refuse to think about its effect on other people. Aren't the "consequences" just as much a part of understanding it as the "intentions" that priests, and psychologists, and thriller writers find so fascinating?' Harriet was now struggling with an urge to shake Dr Ramgulam. 'The child or woman tied up in those pictures could be you. Perhaps some man – any man, that fool in the Porsche, for instance – gobbles them up imagining that it's you, or me, or the woman of ninety some disgusting pervert wants to rape.'

Dr Ramgulam nodded. 'You may have a point, my dear. I am triple armoured: in middle age, middle class and my role in the National Health Service. I am amazed if anyone wants me for anything more intimate than a prescription. Yet I must insist that there is value in trying to understand in particular the sins we are not inclined to.'

Harriet was strangely excited and angered by Dr Ramgulam's bland tolerance. So much so that she deliberately flouted a taboo of polite discourse between white and black people. 'Does that mean you don't care about the consequences of racist pornography either?'

Dr Ramgulam's voice was as abstract as ever. 'I didn't say I don't care, but that I want to understand.' She paused, brows puckered. 'Yet I *do* understand racial pornography; it's the one sort that *does* hit me in the gut. How clever of you to raise that point. I'll have to think again.'

The Porsche, engine revving, was at the next lights, waiting for them. To Harriet's surprise, Dr Ramgulam ignored it, drove straight ahead. 'I remember a picture I saw once, a Victorian print,' she continued, 'it was a delicately executed etching of a line of Indian coolies under a white man's whip. It was made in British Guiana, I think.'

'Please, forget this,' said Harriet quickly. 'I shouldn't have raised that point.'

'No, no my dear, I'm glad you did. One forgets so much. That picture gave me, for a second, a surging sexual thrill of power. I wonder if I had deliberately forgotten that?'

Harriet stared ahead, mouth tight shut.

'Would the picture have had that effect on you?'

'No.'

'Is that because you are white and therefore not involved, innocent?'

'I don't want to know about this –'

'But I do. This is so much more interesting. Do you

think, perhaps, my dear, because I am black – in my subconscious mind even if my head feels as international as ICI – that my mind has in it a coolie, a victim? I rather like the idea; I hate thinking of myself as a yuppie.' Dr Ramgulam's car was now charging ahead, overtaking everything in sight.

'Yes,' Dr Ramgulam continued. 'I think you might have put us on to something. Because the victim doesn't believe in her innocence, does she? Society doesn't either, does it? Isn't that why so many rape cases fail in the courts? To some part of her mind the victim becomes the passive sexual partner, the lover, of the man with the whip, but not a free and equal partner; she sees herself as the guilty one, the one who has been defiled, the one who carries the stain of the sin, doesn't she?'

Harriet, still staring ahead, said stiffly, 'Every copy of that print should be rooted out and destroyed.'

'But even if it was,' Dr Ramgulam said excitedly, 'the woman under the white man's whip would not get back her innocence, would she? And what of Ammu? Perhaps she has been isolated by terrible things in her past that may still be in her present, more so if her debt to Robertie is not fully discharged.'

'She discharged it by throwing your Brooklyn Bridge book into the fire.'

Dr Ramgulam sighed. 'Yes, I suppose, in the end, that is the only thing to do.' She fell silent. Harriet looked at her watch. 'I'm sorry, Harriet. I underestimated you; that was patronising. I've been trying, in my clumsy way, to lead you to think something about Ammu.'

'I have thought it,' Harriet snapped. 'I understand how much she hates pornography. And well she might, with such an uncle.'

'Yes, she certainly hates pornography.'

Silence fell again. It gave Harriet no pleasure, but she recognised that she had, for the first time, won an argument with Dr Ramgulam.

They were in sight of the raised motorway, and within walking distance of Sophie's house, when Dr Ramgulam took up the subject again. 'Forgive me, Harriet, but I still think there is something missing in your perception, and that this might lead you to hurt Ammu.'

'Me! Hurt Ammu!' Harriet's tone was indignant, out of key with her feelings, because she was now rather sorry that she had, probably, hurt Dr Ramgulam.

She still felt sorry as she made her way to the steps of Sophie's house. She remembered the time, years ago, when she had stood by while Ammu demolished the arguments of some ministry official. Afterwards, Ammu had said, 'Don't be too impressed by that little victory; a fanatic will always win an argument, because conviction has so much more force than logic.'

Too bad. Dr Ramgulam had opened that can of worms and, as far as Harriet was concerned, she could do as she liked with whatever she found inside it.

Saturday midnight,
5 November

The last echoes of Dr Ramgulam's voice faded as Harriet came face to face with the silence at Sophie's front door. The dirty glazing now looked unfamiliar, sinister. In the street, cars passed, muffled by the fog, no people. Disembodied voices, music, boomed from a dozen invisible television sets. A cat, probably one of Sophie's, stared at her from behind the rubbish bins. With nearly an hour and a half to zero, she pressed lightly at the door she had left on the latch.

It was locked. Harriet had no key. And she was not supposed to talk to Sophie. Now uncertain about everything, she stepped back into the street, just in case Brucie's form might show at a window. Except for a pale glimmer through the glass of the street door, the house was in darkness. The front room had bay windows with curtains half drawn. The big room above, also in darkness, must be Sophie's bedroom, with Brucie's beyond; above were the two empty rooms, and then Ammu's at the top and the back.

Harriet crawled past the spiny hedge to peer in at the bay window: she could make out a big bed, a table with a basin and ewer on it, an armchair. It was neat, and bare, clearly unoccupied. A heavy screen, or something of the like, separated it from the room behind – the one she had tried to examine through the keyhole. Curious; that made four, with the one behind, possibly five, empty rooms in the house. There were seven bell buttons. Sophie was a landlady and certainly looked as if she needed money. Why did she have, as far as Harriet could tell, only one tenant? And why, exactly, was Harriet prohibited from speaking to her? Harriet felt her nervousness increase, with it the feeling that this house was not safe, that the bad thing that had happened to Ammu had started here.

So what! This was where Brucie had arranged to meet her. From here they were going to rescue Ammu. This was settled, final. She rang the bell. With luck, Brucie would answer, and she would find once again the good tough ally, the one person in this whole business who was what she seemed to be. Brucie had no diseased craving for Ammu like Sophie; she didn't slobber about her like Robertie; she did not envy her, like Dr Ramgulam. Brucie alone had no side. Brucie made her feel strong. After a minute, she rang again, willing Brucie to be there, come to the door.

Sophie's face, shut and angry, appeared in the frosted glass.

'So it's you.' Sophie let her slip in through the barely opened door. 'You been gone a long time.'

'Sophie, hello. Sorry to disturb you. Thanks: for letting me in, for everything.'

'No thanks to you –' Sophie spat out the words, 'you little fart.'

'Why, what's wrong?'

'Come with me.'

Once more Harriet followed Sophie down the hall that smelled of boiled cabbage into Sophie's den. Sophie flopped into the familiar chair. The cat on the mantelpiece grilled gently in the heat from the fire. Ammu's rum had joined half a dozen empty bottles under the coffee table. This time, Harriet had nothing to offer, and Sophie's glass was empty.

'So,' Sophie barely raised her eyes. 'What you been up to?'

Something was wrong. Harriet began nervously. 'I had lunch at Harry Wong's Fish Bar, when was it, yesterday?, day before? I thought the food quite good, especially the chips. Potatoes don't grow well in the tropics, they get squashy rather than fluffy if you mash them; I'd forgotten how good ... Mind you, the fish is fresher in Mauritius, and you can't believe how many varieties ...'

'I said "up to".'

'Did Brucie tell –?'

'Keep Brucie out of this.'

'We – I – went to the Purgatorial Fires, a men's club. It's in Docklands. Do you know it?'

While waiting for Sophie's reply (which didn't come) it occurred to Harriet that Sophie probably didn't; she never seemed to leave the house. So Harriet, very carefully, focusing on the complication of locked doors, the strobe lights, the press of people at the bar, gave an account – of sorts – of the place. Sophie stared at her slippers and said nothing. 'Then I met Ammu's Uncle Robertie. You know him I believe?'

'That's nothing to you,' Sophie muttered dully.

'Well.' Harriet racked her brains. 'He's a photographer. He has, um, international connections.' Sophie still said nothing. Stumblingly, Harriet described their meeting, trying to sound communicative without saying anything offensive to Sophie. It wasn't easy: even Robertie's contribution to Ammu's education was not a safe subject; it touched on a part of Ammu's life from which Sophie was excluded. About other things, too, she felt uneasy. What had Brucie, feeling 'shitty', reported to Sophie? Had she admitted that she exceeded her brief? And then, if Brucie had told the whole story, what would Sophie make of Harriet's half one?

As she struggled on, Harriet's discomfort increased.

She was not telling lies, but she felt like a liar. She was *not* Sophie's friend. What had come out of Harriet's mouth, unbidden, when her tired head was buried in Brucie's shoulder, showed that she intended to oust Sophie from Ammu's life. Perhaps Sophie sensed this. Perhaps Brucie had said as much. How much had Brucie said?

And then perhaps, like Harriet, Sophie was dissembling, maybe, like Harriet, because there seemed to be some safety in it. Sophie's sullen silence gave no clue, so Harriet dribbled out more small talk about Robertie, about the club. She didn't mention Highgate; she didn't mention breakfast. She didn't mention de Haas.

At each pause, Sophie gave a brisk nod: more was due, and more.

'I really didn't understand what was going on,' Harriet said desperately. 'I'm sure you'd get a much better idea if you'd just talk to Brucie.' Harriet glanced quickly at her watch – 11.45, still time. 'Would you like something to drink? If there's anywhere open at this time?' Sophie nodded. 'I'll pop out, get a bottle.'

Harriet escaped with relief to the same seedy bottle shop on the corner, where, as Sophie had promised, two knocks at the side door admitted her entrance. She dithered over the various rums, then chose scotch. The stuff was a frightening price: the 'after-hours mark-up' they explained. Harriet swallowed hard, and paid. With the bottle clunking against Brucie's jeans, she marched back through the empty streets.

In Mauritius at this time, the second-shift people, released from the factories at ten, would still be swarming over the market, while vendors with sweating faces yelled their bid prices, and shouts rang out from a dozen card games, enticing the hopeful to take their chance to quadruple a day's earned rupees. Everybody would be bursting with the joy of a night of freedom, before the factory bells rang once more. Harriet was still getting used to a society of people with veiled, suspicious postures and eyes in deep shadow, people like Sophie.

Tomorrow, when Ammu was free, Harriet would tell Sophie the whole story, but, for tonight, discretion would, she decided, be the better part of valour. In the half hour that remained, she would do no more than try to get past Sophie's hostility to find out why Ammu had come to Sophie's house, how she had, from there, fallen into the hands of de Haas. Perhaps the drink would help melt Sophie; perhaps this time Harriet would be able to listen coolly to talk about Ammu's arms around Sophie, find out what lay behind.

The door was still on the latch. Harriet let herself in. Sophie, cigarette threatening to drop more ash on the carpet, hadn't moved. 'You took a hellava time about it,' she muttered. Harriet, exchanging a glance with the cat on the mantelpiece, put the bottle on Sophie's coffee table.

Then she turned to sit. Ammu's letters, still tied with their silk ribbon, were on her chair.

Harriet swallowed. This she was not prepared for. She picked up the bundle, stared at it, while her fingers looped themselves around the ribbon; then she placed it carefully on the floor beside her.

'Why didn't you get rum? Scared it'd turn me maudlin about the woman?'

Harriet shook her head. 'I didn't think you were maudlin last night. I know you love Ammu. I, ah, respect that.'

'You sure have a funny way of showing it.'

'Sophie, I'm sorry about these, these –. It was a misunderstanding.'

' "Misunderstanding?" Come on. It was another way of showing what a stinking crawler you are. Fling your arms around Brucie, did you? Buy me off with a bottle of scotch, will you?'

As she had done just twenty-four hours earlier, Sophie

tore open the bottle, sniffed it, said 'cats' piss'. But then, greedily, she slopped some into one of the glasses on the coffee table and gulped it down. Harriet's hopes rose slightly. As if standing by a bedside, she waited for the drug to take effect. After all, this was one drug, a painkiller, Ammu believed in, because people prescribed it for themselves.

' "Misunderstanding?" Piss on your misunderstanding.' Sophie lifted her head, revealing the eyes, so startlingly alive in the pale mask of her face. 'Those letters sat safe in my dressing gown for six weeks. I never laid a bloody finger. They were not mine – get it – they were part of the woman I love. They were something I knew she'd come back for if I kept them safe. And now you – with your itchy little paws – you've as good as burnt them to a heap of bloody ashes.'

Harriet hung her head. 'I'm terribly sorry. I didn't know then that you were going to help me. I regretted it immediately. I wanted to put them back.'

'So if I was daft enough to help you, it was to help you do what? Help you get Ammu in a worse mess! Here, gi'me'. Struggling out of her seat, Sophie grabbed the letters and violently tore off the ribbon. Ripping apart the envelope with the stamp from Swaziland, she waved de Haas's letter at Harriet. 'Since you thieved the letters, why didn't you bloody use what they told you? And you supposed to be an intellectual, someone who can read French on wine bottle labels, a bloody nurse tutor no less.'

Harriet was stung by the unfairness of this: she and Brucie had, after all, done very well out of their first night of investigation. 'I don't know what you mean. What could I have used in them?'

Sophie thrust de Haas's letter under her nose. 'Who do you think wrote this? Whose ugly scribble is that, there at the bottom?'

'Yves de Wet de Haas.'

'Ah, right first time. Well, aren't you going to read me the letter, in English?'

Harriet translated:

> '...I agree with you that he has enemies: he is himself the chief of them; you might ask yourself if you are not the second. I shall have completed my business and will be in London when this communication arrives, and ready to receive you. Everything at issue is negotiable. I wish you to have this message in my own hand.'

Harriet's voice trailed away. All this sounded so, some-how, civilised, in English, like a letter from a family doctor or lawyer. Anyway, Ammu was always going on about enemies. What should Harriet have seen in it that had eluded her?

'And what did'ya make of that?' Sophie thundered.

'Well, I found it all very worrying. I suspected him immediately.'

' "Worrying!" Hell's sake, you don't have to act so wet. You knew what was in that letter. So why didn't you give Brucie the tip-off? You knew the man that'd got hold of Ammu was de Haas; everybody knows de Haas is a piranha, yet you let that fool Brucie barge into his house like a mad bull, yelling for Ammu. What in God's bloody name do you think you are? Do you think you can beat de Haas? Do you think you can make him give her up? Do you think you can manage this bloody world like it was a bunch of student nurses?'

Harriet shifted in her seat. What had she done? She didn't understand. How had she made things worse? 'It all happened so fast.' Harriet looked up. 'I didn't realise for ages one of the men at the house was de Haas. I thought they were both minders; they didn't look like anyone important. But I didn't need the letter to know the trouble was serious. Robertie as good as told me. Really, the letters proved not to be important.' She paused. 'All I want is to get Ammu out of there.'

'What we want doesn't prove a bloody thing. It's what we do that counts. What you've done shows you're a nit as well as a crawler. You've really done her in. You know that?'

'I don't understand what you mean,' Harriet snapped. 'What's gone wrong?'

'He'll kill her now. You know that?'

Harriet's stomach lurched. 'Oh God! Why? He only wants her because she's a doctor. At least that's what he said.' Harriet paused. 'I don't really understand why he's holding her.'

'Why do you have to understand? With de Haas, you don't need to know what's in his head; you just feel it like you feel a migraine coming on. Can't you feel it?'

Harriet shook her head slowly. 'I didn't know what to think. I thought, somehow, he sort of trusted us; saw us as harmless, I mean.'

'Harmless? When you've busted them?'

'No, we haven't; that's not what it's about. Look, I know Brucie has filled you in on what happened last night. She told you, didn't she, that de Haas wants a doctor? We reckon Robertie sort of sold Ammu to de Haas to pay his debts. But de Haas is going to let us talk to her; he said so. And we've got a plan; did Brucie tell you?'

Sophie shook her head. Harriet took this to mean 'yes'.

'She told you we're going back to Highgate tonight? We're going to get Ammu out, or, or … I'll go to the police.'

Sophie rocked her head slowly from side to side. 'I wouldn't think even Brucie was that much of a fool. I wouldn't even expect to see her tonight if I was you. I'd just be smart, and go back to Mauritius tomorrow. I certainly wouldn't talk about fuzz and stuff, that's if I didn't want a postcard from de Haas on holiday in the Caymans and another one from Robertie in Dartmoor, while the girls at Holloway throw dice to choose who's gonna be first to jump on Ammu –'

'Ammu's done nothing!'

'You think that's what the police would think, while de Haas's slaves were handing them chippings off Emperor Bokassa's spare diamonds? D'ya think that's how a great British jury would see it, deciding between a little female wog – who'll go to her death still covering up for Robertie – and the biggest law sharks in Lincoln's Inn? That what you think?'

Harriet twisted and turned in her seat. There were blank walls everywhere she looked. She felt desperately in need of help. It was impossible to communicate with Sophie, someone determined to rubbish everything she said and did. She had quarrelled with the good Dr Ramgulam. She needed Brucie. But where was Brucie, and what was this Sophie was saying about not expecting her to turn up? And why had Dr Ramgulam hinted that Harriet was hurting Ammu? Harriet couldn't make sense of it. How could she hurt Ammu when she meant so well, had done so well in finding her, finding de Haas?

Sophie still stared. Her hostility was palpable and slow, making Harriet desperate to get away, get upstairs, above all get hold of Brucie. But she sat there, in near total silence, while the cat on the mantelpiece stared at her and Sophie knocked back a second and then a third glass of whisky.

When Harriet finally found herself in the bathroom, she was leaning over the basin, being sick. Where now was her bold vision of rushing the house with Brucie and freeing Ammu? Where now was Ammu, in what new trouble?

After cleaning up the still recognisable fragments of the breakfast provided by de Haas, she tried, laboriously, to gather her thoughts. It was five past twelve; Brucie had not shown. Ammu's letters (apart from de Haas's, last seen as a crumpled ball in Sophie's fist) were still on the chair in Sophie's den; the duffel bag was wherever it was; Ammu was somewhere, perhaps back at the house in Highgate waiting for Harriet, and in danger of her life. Where was Brucie?

It was only just past midnight; they were not due at Highgate for another hour. Harriet decided to wait another five minutes before knocking again on Brucie's door. If she had been able to think of any word that could mollify Sophie, she would have said it. She felt sick, stupid, miserable, frightened, and terribly alone.

Early morning,
Sunday 6 November

After waiting another five minutes on the stairs at the turn just above Brucie's room, Harriet made her way down, to knock again at the door of the room she knew well to be empty. The house was deathly quiet. Something loose rattled on the roof. Beyond, occasional cars rasped through empty streets, echoing the snores of the city's seven million sleepers.

'Brucie,' she called in a voice that carried only a few inches. 'Brucie, we're going to be late.'

Silence. No answer from Brucie, no movement from Sophie, no glimpse of the cats. She waited an interminable sixty seconds longer, then knocked.

Did she hear something? She inched the door open into darkness, silence. This house was horribly full of empty rooms.

'Brucie,' she whispered, just in case.

She flicked on the light, and went in – no Brucie, but this room was not empty at all. Crammed and disorderly as a junkshop, the place was a tip: the bed was a huddle of grubby blankets; chests spilled clothes from their half-open drawers; more clothes, rumpled pages of magazines, mugs of slimy coffee and bits of pitta bread littered battered cane and wickerwork chairs and tables, and spread over the floor.

Harriet, suddenly feeling more in command of herself,

smiled. She could have guessed Brucie would live like this. Rather fondly, she tutted her nurse's disapproval of such disrespect for food when a quarter of the world was hungry, and began to scoop up bits of the bread.

Automatically, she reached out to a scrap of magazine paper for something relatively clean to wrap them in. Her eye fell on a picture, a colour photograph, of a young woman bound in chains so tight that her flesh bulged over them. Though the woman must have been in pain under such constriction, her face craned up towards the camera with a leering, ogling, mocking, simpering smile. Shock, of the sort Harriet would feel if she came in the street upon an old man knocked down by a car and bleeding from the head, washed over her. But such shock would quickly be followed by action automatic to a trained nurse. This shock offered no such relief. Harriet turned away. What could anyone want with such pictures? What could they be doing here in Brucie's room?

Then she looked again. Had she seen what she thought she saw? The woman was wearing tight black leather knickers slit at the crotch. Her labia, swollen and squeezed into the slit, seemed to be thickly coated in lubricant jelly. Harriet kicked some clothes over the thing. She looked up blindly. But her eye strayed; pictures of the same sort were strewn all over the floor. The paper had a used, well-thumbed look, Could Brucie *enjoy* something like this? Did she do this sort of thing? It was appalling. Harriet knew lonely and envious old men slavered over such things, but Harriet couldn't square it with the Brucie she knew, someone so kind, so efficient, such a friend; a breath of sanity. 'Oh God!' Her fists, still wrapped about bits of pitta bread, bunched over her eyes, and Harriet stood in the middle of the room overwhelmed with despair: this was what was inside the head of the one person she thought she could trust!

Ammu was trapped in the poisonous swamp of

Robertie's weakness, de Haas's cruelty, and, if Sophie was to be believed, she was now in danger of her life. Harriet's attempts to rescue her had, again according to Sophie, only increased the danger because Harriet had encouraged Brucie, a foolish innocent, to barge like a bullock into a family shame Ammu was struggling to assuage. Anyway Harriet was, in the view of Dr Ramgulam, too insensitive to do anything but hurt Ammu.

Harriet had dreamed that, tonight, she and Brucie would again enter Ammu's prison, but, delicate as thieving cats, they would steal her away, take her back into the ordinary, sane world, where she would see that nothing she could do would save Robertie.

But there was no ordinary sane world. And there was nobody, but nobody, she could trust. Brucie, the one ray of light in all this swirling madness, had something horrible inside her that connected her with Robertie. Harriet scrunched the bread, now slightly softened by her hands, into crumbly balls. Perhaps it was not only inside Brucie's head; perhaps she also dealt in these things, was just another, more charming, Robertie. Perhaps – oh God – she was even part of the plot, working for de Haas, playing a scripted role in some game of taunting Ammu, teasing her spirit to breaking point, forcing Ammu to watch Harriet's frantic attempts to help.

Kicking at yet another heap of things on the floor, Harriet trod on something squidgy. She stepped back sharply to see a tube, its white paste squirted over the floor. There was no cap. Cautiously, as if touching one of the unclean things in the box under Ammu's bed, she picked it up: Hydrocortizone ointment, presumably prescribed by some doctor for her eczema. Ammu would not approve of Brucie putting poisonous chemicals on her face.

Harriet put the flattened tube on the dresser. Now she

thought of Brucie standing in the middle of the courtyard, her spots red as wounds in a ghostly face, moaning, 'It's not the bike; it's what the fuck they want with us.' Brucie muttering 'Could be I been clever enough to get us killed.' Brucie had been afraid; Brucie had blamed herself for their failure.

Harriet couldn't disbelieve in this Brucie. Brucie was her friend, her one sane ally. She told herself firmly to forget the pictures. For all she knew, somebody might have dumped these things in Brucie's room and, even now, be preventing Brucie from getting to her.

Who? Sophie? Sophie was filthy minded, a broken thing, far from sane. But Sophie loved Ammu. That was no act. Why did everything that seemed good have something horrible attached to it? And which was real? Harriet threshed about in her mind for some point of sanity.

Dr Ramgulam – at their first meeting, the wise woman had spoken. If Harriet now had orders they came from Dr Ramgulam: 'If I was still a Hindu or Christian or anything, I'd say, do what your heart tells you. I'll pray for you.'

'All right, Jasbir Ramgulam,' Harriet said out loud. 'My heart knows what to do. I am Ammu's lieutenant in medicine; and I'm also her lieutenant in war. Tonight, it's war.' As if Dr Ramgulam's words had injected her with some powerful drug, she felt, immediately, a different person. She knew exactly what to do.

First, appease the gods. She marched to the window, and threw up the sash. 'Eat this at dawn, you sparrows and pigeons,' she called into the darkness, spreading the pitta bread on the sill, 'but only if I have freed my Ammu. Otherwise, let it grow tentacles of mould to spread and consume this vile room.' She shut the window, shutting out, also, the thought that this was the kind of magic Ammu had banned from the clinics. Too bad, Harriet was surrounded by evil and needed cunning.

Next, to square it with, or confuse, Brucie. It was well after midnight; she had to move quickly. She dashed upstairs, not bothering, now, to be quiet, and scrabbled about in Ammu's little escritoire for pen and notepad, neither of which were to be found. She tore out a piece of the lining of the drawers, then ran down the stairs back to Brucie's room, where she found a stubby and much-chewed biro in a tooth mug. She thought for another second, then wrote: 'Disappointed you didn't make it. If you do truly care about Ammu Bai, you will know what to do.' She spiked the note over one of the handles of a drawer.

Then she left the house, pulling the lumpish front door shut and locked behind her. She never wanted to enter that house again. Duffel bag, money, passport, even Ammu's letters, seemed nothing.

Almost immediately, a faint puttering sounded some-where close, and a cab, its light glimmering, appeared, stopped. At last, a good omen! She leapt in, shouted the address. The driver, cap pulled low over his ears, nodded and rushed her into a thick white blanket of fog. She recognised nothing but the faintly glowing signs along the Westway, until the cab slowed and its lights dimly illuminated the crumbling brick walls surrounding the house in Highgate. A moment of confusion, doubt about having come to the right place; another of shock when she saw the 'extras' on the taxi's meter. Then the cab had swung round in the narrow lane, its wheels crunching through iced puddles, and was gone.

Harriet stood before the now wide open gate. She was a little shaky, but her stomach was quiet. She was only twenty-five minutes behind schedule. But she was alone.

The place was different without Brucie, vacant, as if nothing could ever happen here. Streetlight filtered through the foggy trees onto white walls, dark holes of windows. The car was not there. There was no sign of Brucie's bike. All the doors were shut tight. A bluish light flickered somewhere inside the house (not Ammu's cellar), but a general darkness and desolateness hung over the building. What was she supposed to do? Ring the doorbell? Have de Haas play butler this time and usher her in?

Boots ringing against the flagstones, she marched round to the south side and tried Robertie's door. It was, as before, unlocked; his room dark and empty. The boiler hummed. So far, so good. She would find her own way to Ammu.

Panting hard, Harriet stood in Robertie's room, catching her breath, getting used to the darkness. The lacquer table glimmered faintly; the rug she had pulled from the window was back in position, the futon neatly folded, the room sweet-smelling and immaculately tidy. She checked the bathroom, noting a bottle (presumably the Panadol) on the washbasin, the lavatory (good, no sign of Robertie's unconscious body). She touched the latch of the door between Robertie's room and the main house: it moved; the broken chain had not been replaced. She pushed the door a little wider. There was a sound from somewhere in the house, muffled, but definitely a voice, a female voice.

The library was longer, the hall bigger, and, in the thin trickle of streetlight, gloomier, than she remembered. She could detect no sign of movement from upstairs, anywhere, just the muffled drone, ahead, of the voice, which now sounded like a child. The lances were back on the wall. She hesitated, then carefully took one down and heaved it onto her shoulder. This seemed to clear her ears. Now she could surely hear the titter of children's laughter – what could children, laughter, have to do with such a place?

On tiptoe, ends of the lance rocking before and behind

her, she approached the dining room and put her ear to the door. Yes, now definitely a woman's voice. A voice terribly like Ammu's! Harriet booted the door open. The table, now bare of its cloth, reflected the pale light, with Harriet's form in silhouette, from the hall. But more strongly, its polished surface flamed and flickered with the reflections of images from a television screen on the sideboard where the silver tureens had been.

On the screen, seated in a throne-like wing chair, was a young long-haired woman, holding in her lap a little naked boy. The child was crying, and seemed slightly under-weight, but otherwise looked quite healthy. His feet scrabbled against the slippery silk of her sari. Harriet stared. The woman was strikingly like Ammu ... she was Ammu! It was a younger Ammu, clearly herself, but with less defined, softer features, a fuller neck, and a different way of holding her head. The eyes had little of that look of going right inside another person's skull that was the most striking thing about the Ammu Harriet knew. This Ammu had a forced, movie-star smile, reaching no further than the edges of a straining mouth. This Ammu was wearing a sari, but that too was different, fluffy and new, with an intricate pattern of gold woven into the silk, a sari that would have cost as much as a crate of vaccines. Behind the crying of the child, she could hear the tuning up of a sitar – no, as the volume rose, Harriet realised that it was some electronic instrument. A faint drumming started up, spread, and tangled with the electronic whine. The child stiffened.

Ammu's image, still smiling, reached out a hand, placed it under the boy's genitals, and spread them out to view.

Doctors and nurses are required to do very intimate things with people's bodies, and they (even Harriet) quickly learn how to do this with remoteness and respect. This did not seem like a medical action. There was something out of place. Surely not possible; it was no doubt the dirty mind of the camera. For all that, Harriet jerked forward to switch off the set. From the rumbling and clunking which followed she realised that she had been seeing a video film.

What did this film mean? Why had it been made? Why was it running with nobody watching it? If Ammu was here, and had turned it on, where was she now? Was de Haas here, his car hidden away with Brucie's bike? Was he even now, from some secret place, watching her?

Harriet had come, at de Haas's invitation, to meet and talk with Ammu. She had rights in the house. Reminding herself of this, she marched back into the hall, checking out its dark corners, felt her way round the library, wrenched open the door into the kitchen, where the roar of the boiler shocked her into a quickly stifled yelp. Frequently, she glanced behind her. Always, she was careful to stand with her back close to a wall. She didn't call out for Ammu; not exactly because she didn't want to break cover – anyone who was interested to know would already know she was here – but because she didn't want to break something else. What? It couldn't be Ammu's privacy; that she was already invading. Although she felt this to be a wicked place, she was acting a little like someone in church, coming up to the Sacrament, then waiting for it to reach down to her; or, like someone at a seance, bidding the spirit, getting into its range, but not seizing it by the crop.

Harriet shook herself. She was shaky in a way that could perhaps be explained by several days with too little sleep and food; she was upset and perhaps unbalanced by Brucie's magazines and then her reaction to the video. She knew what to do. For now, she would act; she could think later. She advanced towards the cellar steps. Check the cellar. Then she would tackle the unknown territory of the upper floors where de Haas and his henchman had been; where – although she hated the thought of Ammu being anywhere near those men's bedrooms – Ammu must have been before they took her away in their car.

Though she still felt no fear, her knees shook dangerously as she crept down the steps, the point of the lance knocking against the low ceiling, bringing showers of dust and plaster onto her head. Drenched in sweat, her clothes felt icy cold and clammy. She tried to cut the video out of her mind, telling herself that Brucie's magazines must have distorted her perception for her to find herself so upset, so out of control. Dozens, perhaps hundreds of times, she had seen Ammu hold in her arms a naked child. She had seen her examine the genitals of boys, girls (especially for herpes), old men with discoloured, swollen scrotums, prostitutes riddled with syphilis. None of that had bothered her. This was nothing; only her imagination, diseased by Brucie's room. For all that, the lance now seemed the instrument of a different kind of war, and she laid it down, as Brucie had done that morning, this time on top of a spiderwebby crate of wines.

The wine cellar, chapel, stockroom, Ammu's room – all were empty. The sprig of ivy was still in the plastic mug by the mattress. The sari, smelling faintly of jasmine, was still in the tea chest. The air was fresher, cooler, than in the ferociously heated body of the house. Everything here seemed calm, a gentle refuge for the household gods. But not, at this moment, for Ammu.

She made her way back, fighting off disappointment. She had felt Ammu's presence so strongly in that monkish room. That was, she now realised, where her mind had pictured Ammu being, Ammu waiting, Ammu even rather pleased to see her alone, Ammu seeing Harriet as her one saviour. Now, feeling more vulnerable, she paused beside the lance. But no point: she had no skill in the use of any weapon, least of all something so theatrical.

She paused again in the hall, sizing up the wide staircase that divided into two at the first landing. Brucie had heard the men moving in the rooms on the south side, over Robertie's quarters, so she would try the other. She glanced quickly behind. As she was darting up the first steps, she heard a call from the room with the television. She stopped to listen, turned.

'Harriet?'

'Ammu!' Harriet's voice shot out from her like a trumpet. 'Ammu?'

The door of the dining room opened wide, and there stood the most beautiful woman in all the world. The video, everything, fell away.

'Ammu! Ammu! Oh my darling.' Harriet leapt down the steps and flung herself at Ammu. She felt Ammu's arms grip hard around her back. It was the first time the arms that had held so lovingly so many sick and broken people had ever embraced Harriet.

Harriet, deprived of speech by a huge lump in her throat, patted all over Ammu's head and shoulders and arms and back, as if to make sure all of her was there and still joined up. She lifted Ammu up into the air, like a child, then lowered her to her feet again, and buried her face in Ammu's neck. The scent of jasmine brought a great rush of tears, soaking Ammu's throat. She wiped them away with a finger, tracing tenderly the sinews.

Ammu shifted. Speech returned, awkwardly, to Harriet. She moaned 'Oh Ammu, thank God I've found you.' She sank her lips in the wild untidy black hair that was instantly wet with her tears. 'I've been so frightened for you. When I didn't see you tonight, I thought something terrible had happened. I thought somebody was going to murder you.' She seized one of the little hands that had been so slandered in her sick mind's reading of the film and covered it with kisses. 'Oh, Ammu, I've been thinking such mad terrible things.' Once more, she inhaled the innocence of jasmine. 'Ammu, I love you. I love you for ever, for all my life. I've always loved you;

I just didn't know till now. Oh Ammu, thank God you're safe. We'll never be apart again.' Ammu's bones, crushed in Harriet's embrace, felt fragile as those of a little bird.

Checking quickly for any signs of de Haas, she pressed her lips to Ammu's ear and whispered harshly, 'I'm going to get you out of here, away from this terrible madman. I'm taking you somewhere safe.' She moved her head just for another quick look round and a quick breath, then pressed hard against Ammu's ear, whispering, 'There's a place where we can get over the wall; where a tree forks close to it; Dr Ramgulam is waiting, in her car, just down the road. She knows all about it. And she's getting tickets in the morning for the first flight to Mozambique. Just tell me, quietly, quickly now, where's de Haas? How do we slip out of the house? Through Robertie's room?'

But Ammu's hard little palms were pushing at Harriet's chest. 'This doesn't sound like you, Harriet. What's come over you?' Her voice was quiet, formal.

'I was a fool. Like I said, I didn't know, I didn't know how much I loved you. I've always loved you; you are my life. We'll talk about it all later. Just tell me how we get out of the house.'

'Harriet, listen for a moment.' Ammu spoke carefully. 'There is something important you have to know.' The arms that had held so many sick people were no longer holding hard to Harriet's back.

'Why? What's wrong?' Harriet's heart sank at Ammu's tone. Ammu was leading her into the dining room. 'No, I don't want us to be in here. I want to get you out, and away, now. This house isn't safe. It's a horrible place, that room especially, an evil place.'

'Come on. It's only a house. Nobody will bother us.'

Harriet followed Ammu into the room. Now she could take in details. With a shock, she realised that Ammu looked terribly tired and strained, much older. There were lines around the wonderful eyes, and shadows deep as bruises under them. Ammu, always so slender, was now painfully thin, frail as a famine victim. Ammu, who was always exploding with energy, was quiet, too quiet. But she was, if anything, more beautiful than ever. Harriet's whole soul rose up to seize Ammu, carry her out, carry her away from all this horror and to safety. Something was very wrong.

Ammu was up at the sideboard, fiddling, inexpertly, with the video machine.

'Ammu, I saw that before. I don't want to see any more.'

'You must. I've put it on for you.' After several minutes of getting nothing from the machine but a noise like fire guzzling sugar cane, Ammu managed to rewind and start up the tape.

'We made this, Robertie and me,' she said. 'It was a sales promotion.'

The film began with the camera panning over a line of perhaps twenty children, some as young as four or five, all of them thin-limbed and slightly swollen-bellied, all naked. A few smiled awkwardly as the camera caught their eyes; one drew a thick plait of hair across her face in a gesture that was perhaps withdrawal, perhaps coyness; others hunched their shoulders or turned away their heads. At the end of the line stood the figure of Ammu, in the expensive sari, looking tall, and very clothed. The camera paused at the Ammu figure, which stepped forward, scooped a small boy up into her arms, and prepared to speak.

'Ammu, I can't ...' Harriet leapt across the room and switched off the set. ' ... look at it. I don't want to know about these – these lies about you. Ammu, I can't ... I don't understand.'

'I'm trying to make you understand. Watch it. I'm trying to explain about Mozambique.'

'What's this got to do with Mozambique?'

'You must go by yourself, Harriet.'

'But why? I can't. I could never do it, not in a million years. You know the clinics need you. It's only because of you. You said in your letter, you said ...' And, with the force of a horror movie, it shot into Harriet's mind that, without Ammu, she would lose faith in the clinics, in the vain and often stupid healers whose lack was made good by medicine or advice administered discreetly by Ammu, though the holy men's cures were what Ammu and the people boasted of.

Ammu, very slowly and patiently, as if talking to an idiot, said: 'Harriet, the past is never over. I thought it could be, but it is a snake that will lie quiet after you feed it, but come back hungrier and more demanding for its next meal. This is justice, Harriet.'

Harriet shook her head. 'Ammu, whatever Robertie has done has nothing to do with –'

'I'm talking about myself. Remember your room at the Ambassador Hotel in Port Louis?'

'The cockroaches?' Harriet seized on this with relief. 'You saved me from them.'

'I'd been there before, to certify the death of a Mauritian child –'.

'Oh God, Ammu. Dr Ramgulam told me.'

A slight frown crossed Ammu's brow. 'Then you know?'

'Yes, I know, and I know it's not your past. Ammu, you can't think you have to pay for what Robertie has done. That's not justice. I mean, any court of law ...'.

Ammu pressed her palms together in the graceful Indian gesture of respect. 'No, you don't know,' she said slowly. 'I wish it wasn't necessary to cause you this pain.'

Harriet's head was wild with confusion. 'Ammu, forget all this. Ammu, I don't want to go to Mozambique if I can't go with you. I don't want to go anywhere if I can't go with you.'

Ammu breathed into her palms, still folded before her

mouth. 'I believe that you, Harriet, have an innocent, unspoiled past,' she said softly. 'I don't know why people see innocence as something yielding, pliable. It is hard. It is what the Judgment is.'

'Ammu don't' – once more Harriet's arms reached out – 'Please.' Ammu didn't move. 'This is, this is talking riddles like a temple priest. This is rabbiting. I love you, Ammu; I love you and want to work with you, all my life, all my life with you in your wonderful work. You have done such wonderful work. You give people back to themselves; you said this yourself. Ammu, you are the only doctor I … I believe in.'

Ammu did not respond. Stumbling uncertainly, like a very old woman, she made her way to what seemed to be a bookshelf, pulling away a facade to reveal dozens and dozens of bottles. 'Will you join me in a drink?' Her voice was dull. 'There are several interesting liqueurs.' When Harriet didn't reply, Ammu selected a bottle of something the colour of meths, and a tiny glass. The stuff poured thickly, like oil.

Ammu turned to Harriet, twisting the glass in her hand, showing the engraving on its little bowl, the fine twisted threads inside the narrow stem. 'A Victorian glass; amazing, isn't it, that the people who were murdering India could make something so spiritual, and perhaps use it to toast the massacre of another bunch of coolies. Don't drop it.'

Harriet took it. She watched as Ammu slopped a large quantity of rum into a tumbler. Leaning against the sham bookshelf, Ammu said: 'It's the end for us, Harriet. Or rather, it's the end for me, the beginning for you. You have great courage, yet you understand the fears, even the cowardice, of the sick. Anyone working with you can understand why nurses – the people who do the caring, who lay on hands – are more valuable than doctors. Once out of my shadow, you will become a great nurse, you will keep alive a tradition begun by some very great English women.'

It was years since Ammu's theatricality had discomforted Harriet. 'I've always loathed Florence Nightingale and all her ilk,' she said sourly.

Ammu waved this aside. 'That's because she bequeathed her ideals to you. You didn't learn to value a fortune inherited so young.' She pointed to the now blank screen. 'I did that to fund my training. The scholarship I boasted about was a fiction.'

'What? Dr Ramgulam said ...'

'Jasbir is very clever, but an innocent, like you. My grades weren't good enough, nowhere near. I was always a mediocre student, but I thought the money was owed to me; I hadn't had the schooling the white students took for granted, like all their advantages.' Ammu was now smiling faintly. 'Liverpool only accepted me because they wanted to make some gesture towards the poor benighted creatures of the Third World. Serve them right if they got me! I wanted to take their training, while I hated them for their stench of privilege. It gave me satisfaction, then, to pay with dirty money for what they got free.'

Like the blocks of a child's jigsaw puzzle, bits of pictures began to clonk together in Harriet's mind, making the image of a monster. 'I don't know what you're talking about,' she whispered. 'I don't need to know if you've done anything you regret. Everything will be new in Mozambique.'

'That's not all, Harriet. It began when I was eight years old. I used to sell Robertie's grainy old black and white photographs at the posh beaches and barbecues. There weren't many outlets. Tourism was then in its infancy in Mauritius. But a little girl without a word of English or German got much better prices than any man could. And I always knew who'd buy – from the way he looked at me.

'And so it went, on and off, through my youth. And

then there was medical school. I was starting then to see the evil of it, but I was too full of hate to understand. We think, you see, even if we are engaged in it, that evil is something outside of us. But it's in us; we give it its force, all of us, even good people like you. Le Maréchal gets his power from ordinary, small people like Robertie and me.'

Ammu finished the rum, and poured herself another. Harriet sat, open-mouthed, like a concussion case.

'After medical school I needed money for the clinics. Children were dying because their parents were illiterate. You know that? Such children were not listed in the registry of births and therefore, to the Ministry of Health, they did not exist, even when tuberculosis raged through the villages and children with blood on their handkerchiefs were selling mangoes in the market. I thought I could do enough good with the money to cancel out the way I got it. The Gita teaches that all sin can be absolved, even, with huge effort, in one lifetime. Funny, I thought the great teachers were familiar with every kind of sin.'

Harriet shook herself. 'No, I don't believe this. Please, Ammu, please, I love you. Forget all this. It's nothing to do with us. It's some dreadful nightmare made by this evil house.' The glass, its contents untasted, fell from Harriet's hand. The purple stuff spread stickily over the soft grey silk of the carpet. With the heel of Brucie's boot, Harriet crushed the finely blown glass and ground its fragments, soft as coriander stems, into the carpet.

'Don't do something like that in Mozambique,' said Ammu vaguely, 'people with no shoes may walk where you have been.'

'Ammu, leave all this alone. We'll take the first flight to Maputo. The health services have broken down. The people need us there. You said so.'

'Harriet, my poor child, you still don't understand. I can't go, and I don't want to go. I want to be here. I cannot pay my debts; so I have declared myself bankrupt.

I have no secrets here. I feel free. For the first time in my life, I feel free.'

'But what about the people? What about me?'

'You have your freedom too. I'm giving it back to you. I wish I could pay for what I have taken from you, but' – she gave a ghostly smile – 'you are obliged to absolve a bankrupt.'

'But, I … I still don't understand …'

'You will tomorrow. Tomorrow you will understand very well. Tomorrow you will feel defiled by me. This, I think, is the worst thing I have done to you. It is of no value to say it, but I regret that very much.'

'Ammu, I still can't see …'

The ghostly smile again. 'Remember something? "I am, as I explained on your three previous visits, interested to see your clinics, of which I have heard reports. Thereafter I will be in a position to make a judgment about involving my students." Does that mean anything to you?'

Harriet nodded. 'It comes from my first letter to you. You brought that letter to England.'

'Yes, I did. And now, at last, you are in a position to make a judgment, not about the clinics, for those, I believe, you have already judged to be valuable, but about me.'

'But Ammu, I didn't know *anything* when I wrote that letter. I was somebody else then …'

'True. But you can see why I can't go. I've just explained it to you. And it was clear in my letter, a very belated answer, perhaps, to the first letter you ever wrote me.'

'No it wasn't clear,' Harriet wailed, 'you just told me to come to England. And I came.'

'My second letter. You ought to have respected my wish to be left alone. But I understand. I know you mean well.'

'What second letter?'

'The one I gave to your mother; I found her very charming; you're fortunate to have such a mother.'

'Oh my God!' Harriet's head sank into her hands. 'I haven't been in touch with my mother. So your letter's in Palmers Green, unopened, like my letter to you at Camden Town.'

They talked for, at most, another ten minutes. Gradually, it sank into Harriet's frenzied consciousness that Ammu really was not going to go to Guija, that Ammu was cutting Harriet out of her life. All the details Ammu lavished on her – about the considerable sums of money extorted with Ammu's particular brand of menaces from half a dozen charities and now placed on deposit in Harriet's name; about the welcome, and protection, the embattled Mozambique Government had promised Ammu; about their embarrassment when she sent a message saying that she would like to have discussions with the local witch doctors and birth attendants and to involve them in the clinics – all these things washed over Harriet's brain but failed to enter.

Only when she heard a name from another world did Harriet's brain start into life. 'What was that about Sophie?'

'There's some money for her at the Midland Bank, the branch in Highgate Village. Not much; it was all that belonged to me and not to the clinics.'

'But why?' A stab of inappropriate jealousy ran through Harriet. 'Why are you giving her your money?'

'Not because I think it'll do her much good. Her life, like mine, is poisoned. I suppose I would like her to think of me with fondness. I wish it was enough to free her from her prison.'

The jealousy faded. 'But Ammu, she loves you. She loves you madly. She's going to pieces without you. How can you be so cruel to her, even if you don't care about me?'

Ammu smiled wryly, and the wonderful eyes flickered

with something of their old light. 'I loved her too,' she said. 'Tell her my nights with her were the last sweetness I have known.'

'All right.' Harriet bit on her lip. 'I'll tell her.'

'I cared much for you, too, Harriet, and admired you. I so often wished I could take on some of your self-possession, often envied your steady power. I didn't know you loved me.'

'I would have done anything for you.'

The wry smile again. 'That much I did know. But it's no help now. The circle has closed. The only thing left for me is to betray no one else, including the one person who has stood by me all my life. And this way, at least, I shall not betray you.'

'But Ammu what are you going to do about de Haas? He's the most awful person I've ever met. He's mad; no, he's not mad; he's not human; he's possessed. You know what he does? He doesn't only deal in Robertie's pictures. He sells guns to make people in Mozambique kill each other. He's a ... he's a ... you can't know what he is.'

'I do, and I'm going to stay with him. He needs what I can do for him.'

'Oh God no! I mean, I know he's diabetic, but, but, you couldn't go with him? You couldn't ...?'

'I am going with him. All the way. He and I are joined for ever.'

A dark cloud of something like unconsciousness blanked out Harriet's mind. She was hardly aware of Ammu leading her towards the door, dismissing her. Harriet stumbled, like one blind, into the hall.

She stood there, gradually becoming aware of the sound of wailing, long cries, rising to a howl and then falling, agonisingly slowly, away. It was the familiar, dreadful sounds of female grief that followed every funeral procession in Mauritius. But she knew she could not go back into the room, because Ammu was no longer in her world.

A tall figure was coming down the stairs. She opened her eyes on Monsieur Yves de Wet de Haas in a dark red, silk dressing gown, an ivory-stemmed cigarette holder between his ivory-coloured lips. He paused. Stiffly, as suited to an invalid, he bowed low. She stood aside to let him into the dining room. His voice growled softly. The wailing grew fainter, died away.

In Robertie's room, she stopped again. Something was different. The boiler hummed; the ticking of its clock echoed through the kitchen wall. On the hill beyond the wild garden, the first traffic was groaning, engines heavy with full choke. But there was something else, something like a heartbeat. She couldn't talk, least of all to Robertie. Well then, he was alive. That was all she could be bothered to note about him, or anyone else in the world. She made her way straight towards the door.

'Harriet!' A harsh whisper, not Robertie. Harriet was puzzled, irritated. 'Harriet, why have you left Ammu inside? Let's get back, grab her, and run like fucking blazes.'

'Oh, Brucie!' Once again, Harriet fell into a pair of arms, but this press of powerful muscles squashed her nose flat against a hard leather jacket, shoving into her nostrils the scent not of jasmine but of cigarettes, hash and coconut oil.

'Hey, what's all this about; what's wrong kid?'

'Oh my God, Brucie ...' and Harriet was weeping and weeping and still weeping half the way down Highgate West Hill, and weeping more all the way back to Ladbroke Grove in the wild drive in Dr Ramgulam's car.

Dr Ramgulam, sitting there, bolt upright under her seatbelt, with the engine running, took off as soon as they were inside the car. Asking nothing, saying nothing, she roared, at motorway speed, through the empty streets, stopped right outside Sophie's door. When Brucie got out, and stood silently holding the door for Harriet, Dr Ramgulam turned, put a hand softly on Harriet's arm, spoke for the first time: 'Come to my house, my dear, if you like.'

When Harriet shook her head, Jasbir Ramgulam smiled sadly. 'Perhaps we can still help Ammu, my dear girl. Think of that tomorrow. I'll be waiting by the phone.'

It was left to Brucie to thank Dr Ramgulam, tell her that they would explain everything on the morrow, and lead Harriet, now almost senseless with weeping, up the five cracked steps to Sophie's house.

Sunday, 6 November

Another foggy, watery day advanced while Harriet, painfully slowly, unravelled what had happened between her and Ammu.

Brucie listened. Sitting on the little chair in Ammu's room, with her elbows on her knees, she held her head so low in her hands that all Harriet could see of it was through the sprigs of wiry black hair that sprang up between her outstretched fingers. Brucie said very little, just occasionally: 'A-huh', 'Oh shit', 'Jesus wept', and then, 'Hell, kid, you must have a stone like Ayers Rock.'

In the many long pauses, Harriet found herself examining the springy black hairs, astonished that each had its separate source of life in a follicle in the skin that glimmered dead white under the overhead light; each one making its own way in its world of Brucie's skull, yet each growing at the same rate as its neighbours, as if in agreement that they would, together, confront the barber's shears. Ammu had wanted freedom for every follicle on every head, every fragment of life on earth, yet she had mutilated the freedom of a generation of children, and then given up her own – to de Haas.

Otherwise, Harriet was hardly aware of Brucie. She was mildly discomforted by the smell of the clothes she and Brucie had now been wearing for almost four days and nights, but Brucie, the room, the light, herself, even what she was saying, seemed to be part of something unrolling in slow motion behind the screen in an operating theatre.

None the less, the nurse in her, now almost a separate consciousness, noted that her sore eyes and throat, though probably no more than a reaction to all that pointless weeping on the journey back from Highgate, could well be early symptoms of a cold.

But, from time to time, a few things moved up close and stayed in view. Ammu, the wonderful doctor who had healed so many children and was adored by them, was Robertie's partner in a vice so horrifying that Harriet's mind had no adequate name for it. She had been his associate since she was eight years old. Ammu's mind could have no true name for anything, having been poisoned from the dawn of the age of reason. The Ammu Harriet loved and had admired more than any other being, was a fraud. This Dr Ramgulam had hinted at. Children ran out of the shanties calling after an Ammu-doctor who would defile, destroy them.

'A child died in Port Louis,' she said almost dreamily. 'It was a boy, I think. I don't know why I think it was a boy, Dr Ramgulam didn't say exactly; perhaps I couldn't bear it if it was a girl. Why should that be? Perhaps, if it was a girl, it would be as if Ammu had made it happen to herself, or to me?'

Brucie grunted. Silence rolled like an echo through the room.

'A man killed the child doing to him the things he saw in Robertie's photographs – Ammu's photographs. When the hotel management found him, they called Ammu to certify the death. I suppose they didn't dare call a proper doctor. The prosecution did though: Dr Ramgulam was the state's medical witness at the trial.'

She leaned forward, taking up the same position as Brucie, then turned her head against the smell of her underarms. She wasn't being quite fair. The death was an

accident. 'Perhaps the man wanted to play,' Dr
Ramgulam had said. And, earlier, 'Robertie doesn't have
the stomach for real crime.'

What poison was now spreading through Harriet's
mind? At the house in Highgate, Ammu had forced
Harriet to look into the face of the worst of herself. Harriet
had, at the time, been unable to see; now she not only saw,
but strained her vision to make out things that were even
more dreadful.

Why? Was it because the real worst was something that
was not even, in the legal sense, criminal, but just stupid,
vapid, banal, waste – what Brucie would call 'naf' and Dr
Ramgulam 'a dish of boiled sheep's eyes'? Was it because
that worst offered so little relief in moral outrage? Or that
it made such mock of what Harriet had called 'love' that
she now wanted to scratch the very word out of the body of
the language?

'The worst,' she muttered aloud, 'is that Ammu just
gave herself to de Haas.' The almost-touch of a red silk
gown as de Haas, smooth as the ghost of a Persian prince,
moved in to take Harriet's place in the dining room,
passed across her brain, sending a shudder through her
stomach already wrenched with nausea. Could there be
worse than this, this thing so much deader than death?

Brucie grunted. Something on the roof rattled softly.

Harriet struggled with sanity. Ammu had the right to
choose any lover she wanted, even de Haas. There was no
evidence that Ammu did anything more than recruit
Robertie's models. There was also no evidence that she
had done anything at all in the past fifteen years or longer
except give Robertie money; there was certainly nothing
to suggest that this thing was going on while Harriet was
working with Ammu, listening, late into the night, to
Ammu's talk about schistosomiasis, rubella, schizophrenia, and loving her in blind devotion.

'You could help Ammu more if you admired her less.'

Dr Ramgulam's words could not have changed anything, even if they had been said five years earlier; the mould had been set years and years before.

'We must never tell Dr Ramgulam about this,' Harriet said inconsequentially. 'Her uneasy feelings about Ammu were too close. She knew so much without knowing, yet she had so much sympathy with Ammu's pain. If she knew Ammu had gone to de Haas, it would be more than she could bear.'

'Do you know –' a harsh croak, the true negative of a laugh, scratched through Harriet's throat '– Dr Ramgulam was afraid I would hurt Ammu. I, me, hurt Ammu!' Dr Ramgulam's philosophy, cemented with charity, now seemed to Harriet no more than the babblings of a well-fed child.

'Won't breathe a word to her, promise,' said Brucie.

The silences between Harriet's half-sentences got longer and longer. Was she dropping off; or was she slipping out of her head into some dark chasm?

Across the room there came a movement. Brucie, joints creaking, got to her feet. Her hair, still tousled by her fingers, stood out in little spikes. 'I'll fix us a drink,' she said, 'a stiff one, to knock you out. You must be knackered to the jaws.'

Harriet listened to the padding down the stairs, right down to the kitchen: boots that could crash like a cane mill, or take the footfall of a pilgrim at Cavadee. The thought of cocoa strayed into her mind, bringing a thin flicker of comfort, but Brucie would probably, right now, be lifting the remains of the scotch Harriet had bought for Sophie the previous evening.

Sophie: the figure of Sophie, grim and hating, sprang into Harriet's mind: the crushed face, the sagging belly, the slow, heavy, springless walk that put Harriet in mind of a geriatric ward; the family of unpurring, staring cats.

Oh God, poor Sophie – Harriet's hands pressed against

her temples – Sophie needed Ammu. Sophie said Ammu had given her life. Sophie was a wreck. How could anyone want her? Yet Ammu had not found her useless, worthless; Ammu said Sophie had given her the last sweetness she would ever know. Given it, but it was no use, no use to Ammu, no use to Sophie; because Ammu had given Sophie life, and then taken it away again. Sophie had said it. Nothing could now be of any use to either of them. Harriet's head buried itself in her hands while new tears welled up, for Sophie.

Was she asleep when Brucie returned? She was still sitting on the edge of the bed, hot tears oozing between her fingers.

'I never thought of you as a crying lady, y'know,' Brucie said, almost cheerfully, dumping two grubby tumblers and a shining new bottle of Espirit de Maurice on the escritoire. She pushed aside stems of the dead begonia which had gone rather soggy since Harriet had tried to revive it with a tooth mug of tap water. 'You were always so much the nurse, the professional who can look right on at any old crap. I thought, nothing really gets at that bird. She's an armadillo. She's still be binding up wounds while we all shiver in the queue for the Last Trump.'

'Brucie – how did you get that brand of rum?'

'Shit. I scoured bloody London. Finally found it at Brixton market, only market in town for my money.'

Slowly Harriet took this in. Brucie had wanted to get a welcome home present for Ammu. It was a beautiful, generous, stupid gesture. Harriet wanted to thank her. Instead, she broke out into a loud howl, an echo of the terrible cries of Ammu from the dining room.

'Aw, c'mon now. Somebody'll think I'm skinning a cat. Shit's sake there's enough cats round here I could so easily do it to.'

Then they had the tumblers in their hands, and Brucie was on the bed beside Harriet with an arm slung heavily over her shoulder. Harriet choked on her first mouthful. Brucie thumped her on the back until she was breathless.

'Listen, kid,' Brucie said, 'it's not something you want right now, but I need to fill you in on how I got in a mess tonight, why I got late. Sophie's in shit. We got her in it. I'm sure you're up to the gills with this sick stuff, but you gotta know ...'

Emphasising her points with a finger tapping against Harriet's knee, Brucie quickly explained how Harriet's irruption into their lives had knocked away the few props of Sophie's rickety cohesion.

'Basically, you see, it was them letters opened her up. They told her de Haas was on to Ammu. And Sophie thinks de Haas is Dracula in person. Get it?'

Harriet nodded. Sophie had said as much to her.

'And you know Ammu disappeared round the time he wanted to meet her in London, yeah?' Brucie, speaking slowly as ever, paused to lift a spot of dirt from Harriet's polo neck. 'Well Sophie reckoned Ammu went to tell him she was gonna spill the beans all over his whole bloody empire.'

'Sophie got it wrong then, didn't she?' said Harriet, scarcely bothering to veil the bitterness in her voice.

'Well, maybe,' said Brucie vaguely, 'but when I told her we was going up to Highgate to spring Ammu, she couldn't handle it. She was near raving. First she was yelling all over the house for us to cool it or de Haas would murder Ammu. Then she said she'd just murder him instead. Chrissake, I near gave her Ammu's bottle of rum just to shut her up with a drink; it's easier those times; she's so much more sober when she's drunk.'

'Then you'd better take her the bottle now; put her out of her misery,' said Harriet brutally.

Brucie, ignoring the interruption, continued in the same monotonous drone, 'She got it into her head to phone de Haas. I tried to stop her, but she's got muscle like you wouldn't credit. So she got on to the phone and rang the fucker. She told him if he touched Ammu he'd have to take her too, because she'd be doing him in straight.' Brucie, brows furrowed, picked another spot off the sweater. 'I reckon he said "Fine. Just wait by the phone while I send an Oblomov to slit your throat." Someone was trying to phone her back all last night: probably to fix an appointment for it. De Haas won't take neck, you know, from people that's just scum to him.'

Brucie frowned harder, as if dealing with a mathematical puzzle. 'Maybe Ammu didn't put it that clear to you at the house last night, kid, but she's *got* to stay with de Haas. Otherwise it's shit creek for Sophie, and, of course, for Robertie. He'd have Sophie's guts for garters on one leg, Robertie's on t'other, and Ammu still having to stand there giving him insulin injections.'

Brucie paused again. Harriet was shaking her head, not speaking. She didn't have the energy to explain that what she had seen between Ammu and de Haas had suggested a relationship of a very different kind.

Brucie seemed not to understand. 'But later, y'know,' she added, 'after I stood you up and you went off to do the job anyway and while I was marching up and down, I thought, "Why'm I so dead stupid? We can *all* run – Ammu and you and me and Sophie and Robertie. We can grab Ammu and all run like the bloody clappers."'

Harriet's laugh came out like a bark.

Brucie squinted hard at her. 'I thought, "What's stopping us all just going to Gweejee-what's-its-name?" It could'a worked, you know. I could do a job for you. Told you I used to be in the St John's; you can't tell me a fucking thing about triangular bandages. Now Sophie, she can be kind of motherly when it's anything around Ammu, though, God knows, she wouldn't move an inch without those damn cats. But, best of all, de Haas wouldn't come near the place. He only plays his wars from the other end of a modem.'

Brucie thought for a second, then added: 'I thought, too, if it's okay with you, we could take that old fart Robertie as well. Now that poor bugger, he's in crap deeper than a pig, but nobody 'cept Ammu gives a monkeys.'

Gwee-jee, Robertie, Sophie – all this was meaningless because there was no Ammu to save. Harriet drank the rum as Brucie's words rolled around her head. Brucie refilled her glass and she drank more. 'Brucie,' she said, after a while, 'why do you have those awful pictures in your room?'

'Pictures?' Brucie's face fell. 'Oh, you mean the dames. You saw them, did you? That's bad news.' Letting out a soft whistle through her teeth, Brucie withdrew her arm from Harriet's shoulder, her hand from Harriet's knee. 'Why do I have them? Well, I sell them.'

Harriet didn't respond.

'But, okay, I use them too, and you don't like that, yes?' Brucie was speaking more slowly than ever. 'Okay. Well, I dunno why. They're a laugh, I guess. They turn me on. They make me feel – uh – like I was a seriously bad girl, like I was a big number.'

'Why?' Harriet looked up at the pale cheek spattered with spots, half turned away from her like a child anticipating a blow. 'I mean how? They're so cruel.'

'Uh, well, it's sort of like their insides were outside; like there was more of them you could jump on. Like they was seeing you as some big Sex Pistol. It's not real cruel, real dames. It's not real anything. It's only a joke.'

Brucie scratched at a spot on her chin. 'I'm sorry,' she said.

'All right. Thanks. Don't tell me any more.'

They sat for a minute, looking away from each other, till Brucie rounded sharply, 'Ammu never did nothing like that!' she said fiercely. 'Ammu never did nothing cheap. She just got thrown in a filthy hole.'

'Ammu did something far worse than cheap.' Harriet stared ahead. 'Sex is disgusting. It makes people do filthy things.' The appalling thought sprang into her mind that Ammu might have enjoyed what she did for Robertie; maybe it made her feel like a big number. Dr Ramgulam had hinted that Ammu liked to be a big number.

'Harriet? Y'know, I don't think that Ammu ...' Brucie was feeling her way, '... has done something so very very very bad. I mean, it's terrible all right, but not so you can't bear even to think about it.' Brucie tapped the spot on her chin, as if to put back the scab she had lifted. 'What I'm getting at is it almost seems like you'd hate her less if she'd killed that little boy in St Louis herself, to grab his money or something. I'm not sure that's right. After all, y'know, she tried so bloody hard to get it on the level. She did so much good, in Mauritius and such.'

'So?' Harriet's voice was icy.

'If she was trying to pay it all back, like with healing ten or a hundred times as many kids as she hurt, it could've seemed even harder for her with you around, y'know, the way you were thinking.'

'I didn't think at all. I didn't know anything! I was a naive, blind, deceived fool.'

'I mean, you set such helluva high standards around sex and stuff.'

'I do not! I don't know anything about it. Unlike Dr Ramgulam, I don't want to.'

'Yeah, sure.' Brucie was still fiddling with the spot, Harriet, aware of this from the corner of her eye, resisted the urge to slap down her hand. 'I know what you mean. I get up to the vomits sometimes when some fucker makes a pass; can't bear to think that what's going on in his head isn't a thousand miles from what goes on in mine. I just think it might be nice for Ammu if you said you loved her.'

'I did,' Harriet said grimly, 'but I don't love her now. And so what: she never loved me anyhow. She loved Sophie before and now it's de Haas. Doesn't she have exquisite taste!' Harriet took a gulp of rum. 'Ammu finds me cold, hard – stupid in the way Dr Ramgulam finds her daughter stupid. Well, that's what I am. I've been stupid enough about her. Dr Ramgulam said I admired her too much, as if that made a wall between her and me. It certainly made a wall between me and my reason. Anyway, all that's over. Love! It's so much idiocy. Everything's idiocy.'

'Yeah,' Brucie was still vague. 'Love and stuff, it's not the most important thing. You must've meant a lot to Ammu that she wanted to go to Gweejee with you. Shame, hey; she could've told those silly farts to stop killing each other, doing the South African special branch's work for them; she could've done that. It's like she's got enough shit in her to see everybody else's shit for what it is – last night's dinner. Don't ya think? ... D'you like poetry?'

Harriet had had enough of Brucie's poetry. 'I learned all I need at school.'

'Not this number, I bet:

> A woman can be proud and stiff
> When on love intent
> But love has pitched his mansion
> In the place of excrement.
> For nothing can be whole or sole
> That has not been rent.'

Harriet was irritated. 'Surely it should be "rented", as in "hired" or "loaned".'

'No, you sausage; he means "rent", as in "torn" or "ripped", like Ammu's been torn by her godawful life. Anyway, you couldn't stick in a word that'd have to rhyme with "excremented".'

Harriet spluttered. 'I think your poem, or your rum, has excremented my brains.'

Brucie's arm was instantly back on Harriet's shoulder. 'Well, let them go. Brains, love, who needs 'em. Let's excrement them right now. You're the teacher; give the word.'

Brucie's arm was comfortable. Harriet felt herself soften. 'Oh Brucie, you just don't know how miserable I am.'

'I guess not.' The furrow was deep on Brucie's brow. 'How about another poem?'

Harriet turned her tear-swollen face to Brucie. 'I'm thirty-five Brucie, you know that?' Brucie nodded. 'And I've never had sex with anyone.'

'Not with a bloke? That's pretty smart going.'

'I think there is a lack in me; I think people can sense it. The students call me Sister Frigidaire,' she wailed.

Brucie laughed, quickly converted it into a cough. 'Well, call them something back. Call them Misses Hoovers, y'know, mouths full of dust.' Brucie was getting quite agitated; perhaps she was sorry she had laughed. 'Anyhow, you can tell them from me nobody has to do nothing they don't want to do.'

Harriet was hurt. It had cost her something to tell Brucie of this humiliation. She said nothing.

'Now me,' Brucie continued at a pace that, for Brucie, was rattling, 'I do sex, but not relationships; can't bear that mooning and crying and stuff. To me it seems kinda clean that way. I don't care who says it's a lack in me.'

Harriet was still quiet.

'Yeah,' Brucie continued, 'I'd rather cry over a poem than some woman, any day. Want one about a fieldmouse that's huddling out of its brains in fright when they've reaped a cornfield and smashed up its house? Now, that's a real problem, none of this stuff about ''my lady turned her velvet eyes on some other bloke''.'

An awkward, wry smile broke over Harriet's face. 'I remember that mouse, Robbie Burns isn't it?'

'Yeah, that's a heap better. Now let's see … "Ah, wee, sleekit, cowrin, timorous beastie …".' She paused, 'Shit – I mean excremented – no, it's too damn sad; we'd both be howling. Have this instead.' Sitting up straight, and tapping out the rhythm with a foot, Brucie chanted briskly:

'There was a bloody sparrow,
Flew up a bloody spout.
Came a bloody thunder storm –
Blew the bugger out.'

Harriet laughed until she almost fell off the bed.

'Hey, watch it, it's not that funny! Shit, kid, you're crying again.' And Brucie, leaning forward, kissed Harriet, softly, then again softly, and then, when Harriet kissed her back, flung her arms around her, and kissed her fiercely on the mouth.

'Oh, no!' A surge like a long knife ran through Harriet's belly. She pushed Brucie away.

'Let me, Harriet; maybe it'll help you forget.' Brucie's words came thickly out of swollen lips. 'And I'd like it a lot.' Her mouth fallen open with concentration, she fingered the rough ginger hair that had strayed over Harriet's face, glued to it with tears. Strand by strand, she tucked it back into the tangle on top of Harriet's head, and then began to fluff it into an enormous Afro.

Harriet looked up at her with a serious face.

'You got nice eyes,' Brucie whispered, 'they're so blue and pale you can't believe they look at ordinary things, like they was made to look into the stars. I dunno what colour a fieldmouse's eyes are, but they could be this blue, easy.'

'They're black.' Sophie had thought that Ammu's eyes

soaked things in, because they were so black. Sophie knew all the time that something dangerous, dreadful, was happening to Ammu. Maybe she could look at her eyes and see a little frightened animal. Harriet had not looked at Ammu's eyes in that way; she had looked only to know the sparks that flashed out of them. Ammu was always fighting. Her eyes were always fighting. 'What do you think she is trying to shout down?' Dr Ramgulam had said. Now that Harriet knew, she couldn't bear to think about Ammu's eyes.

'Surely people must have told you you got nice eyes?' Brucie's gentle fingers were still combing her hair.

'Martin did – he was my fiancé – that was ages ago, before it all fizzled out. He said they were diamonds. He wanted to put them in a ring for people to find two thousand years later. He used to dig up Roman rings, you see. He liked that sort of thing.' Ammu, on the other hand, had found Harriet's eyes disconcerting. She said they were like glass. Perhaps, Harriet thought, Ammu was right: she had looked at Ammu with blind eyes.

Brucie took the tumbler out of Harriet's hand and refilled it. Harriet drank the lot, this time without choking. She could feel her movements, her heartbeat, slowing. She was very miserable and very tired, and she must be getting drunk. Brucie had three eyes, one in the middle.

'You've got nice eyes too Brucie. But I can't work out what colour they are.'

'They're yellow, like a cat's, for seeing in the dark.'

'What do you see, when you look in the dark?'

'I see one very unhappy lady. It breaks me up.'

Harriet, the room beginning to turn around her, leaned heavily against Brucie. 'Are you going to kiss her again?'

'I sure want to. But I need to be sure too that it's okay with you. You're in a real bad space, and I just wanna find some way to get there. I'd like to hold you.'

'Hold me.' Clumsily, like whales stranded by the tide,

they rolled together on the bed. Ammu's tightly-drawn cotton counterpane tangled in the sticky leather of their clothes. Almost smiling to think that this was the second time she'd been in a bed with Brucie with her boots on, dimly conscious of the gas fire hissing hotly beside them, and the bright overhead light, Harriet buried her head in Brucie's shoulder and passed out.

'Hey, c'mon now, show a bit of respect,' Brucie was muttering.

Harriet came to, into the glare of a burning light, spitting gas, and a splitting headache, while her lips, dry and cracked and sore from too much of winter and weeping, were inside Brucie's jacket, mouthing the fabric of her shirt, searching for her breasts. At the centre of all this was a terrific commotion in the groin.

'Brucie, I don't know what to do. You'll have to show me.'

'How should I know? I've never been with you before. It's you, you'll have to show me. Promise? Like say, "one millimetre to the left," that sort of thing.'

To the left of what? Harriet's agitation was everywhere.

So Brucie's big clumsy hand, undirected but cunning as a little mouse, moved down towards the dozens of zips and buttons that protected Harriet from the world.

Sunday night,
6 November

The sun's first rays slid down the mountains to the milky-jade sea. Ripples rolled through Harriet's hair, lapping at her cheeks, nudging her further and further out, as she floated in the swell closer and closer to the outer reefs. On the far side, she could hear the Indian Ocean, booming, hurling the pain and anger of Mozambique against the gentle coral.

From the shore side, a dark speck emerged. Rising and dipping like a porpoise, Brucie was swimming up towards her, flippers, snorkel and sleek dark head breaking through the waters. Brucie approached, slowed, swam close enough for Harriet to reach out a hand and touch her cheek.

Harriet felt the little hairs, softer than the softest fronds of seaweed, the outlines of her spots. Brucie should take off her goggles; the salts of this pure sea would help her eczema. Treading water carefully, she turned to Brucie, took the goggles in both hands. They were stuck to Brucie's face. She pulled hard, harder – they came away. But the face came away with them, and Harriet was looking into a skull and its naked organs. The tongue moved. Ammu's voice rolled out, as if from the void of the darkened dining room, said 'Harriet?'

Harriet screamed, lost her balance. The water rose up and swallowed her, pressing her down to where it was wild and dark and churning and heavy like molten lead, crushing her legs, her pelvis, her chest, and pressing at a raw, wounded place between her legs.

'Brucie! Brucie!' Harriet was on the floor threshing in a tangle of blankets. Ammu's room; Sophie's house! She kicked free of the bedclothes, leapt to the door. Flinging it wide she yelled 'Brucie! Where are you?'

Cars were growling in the street below, and through the wall came the drone of a television. Somewhere, a dog was barking. The loose thing on the roof rattled. It was again thick night, about half past five. In Mauritius the sun would be preparing to drop into the sea. 'Brucie?'

Brucie was not in her room.

'Brucie?' Whispering now, Harriet checked the bathroom, the kitchen, peered out through the front door.

'Brucie's gone.' It was Sophie, calling from her den.

Harriet couldn't talk to Sophie. She padded back towards the stairs.

'Harriet?'

Harriet pretended not to hear.

Sophie's voice followed her. 'Harriet, Brucie's out on a job. She said to tell you. She'll be back around midnight.'

Harriet crawled up the stairs. She didn't know Brucie had a job. She didn't know anything about Brucie. She was a nurse, someone who was supposed to be able to look at people, get their measure. Yet she had been duped like a child by Ammu, and had lain in the arms of a woman who had horrible pictures strewn over the floor of her room. Worse – she had done with this person that thing she thought she could never do. Worst of all, even now, in her legs and in her groin, and gripping her stomach in spasms, was a funny watery soft feeling which made her feel quite sick. What on earth had she been possessed by?

What had she done? Brucie coming so close at her, her face so near that Harriet's eyes couldn't hold the soft dun-coloured eyes; Brucie's kisses wet all over her head and throat; then her lips slithering down Harriet's breasts, stomach, leaving a squiggly track like a snail; then making her start with fear, cry 'No! No!' when they began to mouth tiny kisses in Harriet's dense pubic fleece; Harriet roughly pushing Brucie's head away against stabs of desire so sharp she couldn't breathe for the shock of them. Where had she been? What had she done? What was she?

Though hardly able to bear the sight of her reflection in the glass of the landing window, she forced herself to stand still for a moment, look hard at the cold, forbidding, scrawny figure with a madwoman's tangled hair: horrible; disgusting; something wrenched from mother, father, home, self.

Tugging at the wild hair, as Freni, sitting by the roadside had yanked at her last poor tufts, she let her feet take her back into Brucie's room. Why did she want to see Brucie again? To tell her 'No, no, it never happened'? Or was it just to torture herself by looking again into that spotty face to feel the warmth that had made her own hard face melt?

She closed the door and felt the stillness, and the smells, of Brucie round her. Even the room was making her feel soft. She snapped on the light and was surrounded by clothes, coffee mugs, ordinary junk. But where were the magazines? Out of nowhere came a dislocating stab of tenderness for this messy coot's nest, even for the heaps of clothes acrid with the smell of cigarettes and London sweat.

She picked up a pair of striped pyjamas, the legs crumpled like two concertinas, the waist cord frayed and lumpy with ancient knots. She sniffed them; again cigarettes, sweat, plus coconut oil. On impulse, she hugged them tight to her chest. Then she shook them out, folded them and laid them neatly on a pillow, where they stayed, square as saluting soldiers in a carnage of rucked up blankets. Oh Brucie! Where now was the old Brucie, ally, friend, sanity?

Where? Stupid to ask. Brucie was out, selling narcotics, the Brucie who kept heaps of disgusting pictures, whose filthy body had rolled all over Harriet's filthy body. Harriet was fretting to do something, but it was not to see Brucie. It was something else, something terribly important. The business of Ammu was not yet resolved. She should get out of Brucie's room and think.

Turning away from the ridiculous pyjamas, Harriet became aware that the room was different. Something was missing: the magazines? Yes, they were gone, definitely nowhere on the floor. On the dresser was a neat pile of paper: a detective story by someone called Katherine Forrest, a copy of *Catch 22* with curvature of the spine, a scattering of Tom Sharpes, and a very old and worn copy of *The Albatross Book of Verse* stamped 'Limehouse Secondary Modern'.

Harriet picked up the book of verse with a sigh; there was still something about Brucie that was absurdly touching. The print was almost obliterated by ink blots, doodles and annotations in a dozen childish hands. Harriet, flipping through it, realised that she was looking for some scribble by Brucie; silly enough, as she didn't know how Brucie shaped her letters. Was it in here, the little verse about a sparrow flying up the spout of something she imagined as a giant teapot? Not that she could see. Nor Edith Sitwell's Jane, tall as a crane. But Robert Burns's mouse was there, homeless, pathetic – she began to read it, pulled herself up short:

> I doubt na, whyles, but thou may thieve;
> What then? poor beastie, thou maun live!

'Thou maun live!' That's what Brucie would think about any wickedness! That's what Brucie thought about Robertie's crimes. And about Ammu and the child who died in Port Louis she said only that 'it was not so very, very bad'.

Harriet shoved the book roughly back into the pile, exposing, half concealed by a copy of something called *The Pink Paper*, the magazines. Of course, what did she expect? Harriet covered them up again and left the room.

Back in the attic, the bottle of rum on the escritoire brought an image of Brucie scouring Brixton market like a sparrow in search of a spout. She flung the bottle into the wastebasket, and marched up and down, Brucie's boots resounding against the boards under the thin rugs.

Harriet felt imprisoned by the room now, the little room that had once filled her with such hope. Before, it had seemed cruelly bereft of the marks of Ammu's habitation. Now, in the rum, the dead plant, the soiled counterpane, the cheap black cloak so reminiscent of de Haas's witch-like garment, the lingering smell of jasmine, there was too much of Ammu everywhere. Even the invisible box of horrible things under the mattress seemed to pulse with Ammu's presence. Harriet paced up and down, trying to forget that she had let herself be unmade by Brucie; she needed to force herself to think about Ammu; at the very least, think what she ought to do about Ammu.

But then, she already knew what she ought to do. This was not something she needed to discuss with Brucie. Brucie was not part of it. Brucie was soft, loose somehow, too close to the corruption. Whatever Harriet had given to Brucie in that now inconceivable fit of madness, she would take back again. With grim ferocity, Harriet reminded herself that Brucie was at least five years her junior and that she demeaned herself by yielding to a feeling that Brucie knew more about the world than she did. This was something Harriet had to think out for herself. She forced her mind to think it, think it out loud.

She had to go back to Highgate. Even though it was early evening and de Haas, his henchman and Robertie might well be there, she had to go. She had to march in and demand words with Ammu, alone. She had to force Ammu to call the police. She had to make Ammu surrender herself, Robertie and de Haas to justice. That was what she had to do. That was her duty. It was the one thing that was clear. It was the one thing that was whole in the wreckage of her life.

Harriet paced faster, the boots ringing louder. It was the decent thing. Harriet would give Ammu this last chance to redeem some scrap of her honour. But, if Ammu would not do it, Harriet would. Because it had to be stopped. Otherwise, if she, who knew, let it continue, more children would be fouled; more children might die; then Harriet too would be guilty of the death of that innocent child in Port Louis.

An image of Dr Ramgulam, leaning over the steering wheel to speak solemnly to her, came into her mind. Dr Ramgulam was waiting by the phone. 'No!' said Harriet firmly, turning her eyes away from Brucie's rum slouching drunkenly in the basket, 'for once, I will do what I have to do by myself!'

So, would Ammu give herself up? Would she hand over to the law de Haas, the wretched Robertie? Then why hadn't she done it, long ago? It couldn't take anyone five weeks to look up a telephone number.

If Ammu couldn't do it, could Harriet? Could she send to prison the woman she had loved, and followed, and made the light of her life? She paced, bashing her palm with a fist. Could she? With a shock she realised that she would not care if she sent Ammu to the flames of hell. Brucie ought not to have doubted her. Harriet was not a crying lady; she was a hard professional, an armadillo. She would do what was necessary. She would do it now.

Suddenly infused with energy, she stuffed her two remaining five-pound notes and few coins into the back pocket of Brucie's jeans and rushed down the stairs.

Sophie stood in the hall, barring her way.

'What'cha doing?'

'Going out. Going to see Ammu. Let me by.'

'You can't see Ammu.'

'You can't stop me.'

Sophie looked at her carefully. 'I can call de Haas.'

Harriet stopped in her tracks. 'Like you called him before, to tell him if he hurt Ammu you'd fight?'

Sophie nodded. Without a further word, she elbowed Harriet aside, and made her way back towards her den. Harriet, her head suddenly clouded with doubt, turned as if to follow.

'First get me something to drink,' Sophie called over her shoulder.

On the street, the wooziness of her legs made Harriet aware that she hadn't eaten since de Haas's breakfast, well over twenty-four hours earlier, and most of that had gone down the sink in Sophie's bathroom. The calorific value of Brucie's rum couldn't have been more than two or three spoonfuls of sugar. The people at the bottle shop seemed to think she was drunk. Still, they remembered her from late the previous night and, before she could ask, got out a bottle of the same scotch. It was, mercifully, only a third of the after-hours price, but still left her with barely enough for the tube fare to Highgate. So what. She could walk. On the return, if she ever did return from a trip that felt like going to a death, she would prefer to walk. She expended another handful of pence on a bag of crisps. But, when she opened them in the street, their smell reminded her of her own body hot under Brucie's mouth and made her feel sick. She shoved them deep into a hedge and tried to rub the smell off her hands against its thin winter foliage. The whisky, in its plastic bag, clonked against her legs, hard enough to bruise. She knew what she had to do; she could wait to hear what Sophie had to say.

'It was them letters that did for me,' Sophie said,

cupping her hands around her tumbler of scotch, 'I didn't get it before, your measure: could be you look like a stiff, but you was trouble. There was going to be waves. And then I had to get level with you, so I opened them up.'

Harriet nodded. Sophie had kept the letters, unread, for weeks? Harriet believed she had. Brucie and Sophie's preference for ignorance amazed her. But then, so should her own surely culpable five years of preference for ignorance about Ammu.

'I guess I always thought Ammu had something to do with Robertie's business. After all, the fart never stops talking about her, it's like he couldn't tie his shoes without her. But I didn't know till then that de Haas was after her. I guess I didn't want to know.'

Now that Harriet knew what she had to do, she wanted to know it all. It didn't hurt any more; now it was part of an important process with a beginning, a middle and an end, and the end was soon. She questioned Sophie closely. Sophie was, for once, more than willing to talk.

'Yes, de Haas and Robertie sent her to my place to get her away from someone. I dunno who. Never heard of any Ramgulam. Who'da thought a place sick as this was crawling with doctors? I dunno why she said she'd come here.'

Sophie lapsed into silence, then, as Harriet began to stir in her seat, added: 'I didn't fancy it when they turned up, though, and there was this little wog, shivering, wrapped up in Brucie's jacket. Brucie said ''Robertie told me to tell you it's le Maréchal, his orders,'' and that was that.'

' ''Le Maréchal'': Do people have to do everything that man says?'

'Sure. Like with God. Anyways, you know this is his house?'

'This is de Haas's house!'

Sophie, it turned out, was caretaker of one of a dozen de Haas properties in London. Like the others, this house was a brothel, but there had been some scandal, and it had to be taken, temporarily, off the market.

'Oh, God, not a scandal about children,' Harriet muttered.

'Dunno. Didn't ask.' Sophie's job, she explained, was to look after the place till the dust settled. Robertie had been staying there himself until just before Ammu's arrival. His removal to Highgate, the London nerve centre of the de Haas operation, was not a promotion. Someone of Robertie's low rank would be taken to Highgate only to serve at table or be kept under surveillance. Through Brucie, he had said as much, asking them to 'soften up' Ammu, something that would help get Robertie out of trouble and away from Highgate.

Harriet butted in: 'Then you lied. You said you didn't know how she came to be here or where she came from. Why?' (Sophie shrugged.) 'And that first night I was here, you told me you didn't know where she was.'

'Well I didn't bloody know, did I? She just walked out. I was just cut in pieces because I wanted to have her around me. How was I supposed to know she was in trouble with the big man? Think I'm some kind of clairvoyant?'

Harriet snorted. Ammu was hardly 'in trouble' with de Haas. But she kept her eye on the story. 'You could have guessed; after all you knew he had sent her here. But you didn't; and Brucie didn't either.'

'Brucie never had nothing to do with de Haas. He wasn't interested in her. I wanted it to stay like that, y'know; Brucie's just a kid.'

'Yes, yes,' Harriet muttered irritably, 'but you must have at least suspected that Ammu's disappearance had something to do with de Haas?'

'Around him, you suspect every damn thing. Yeah, okay, I had a funny feeling about it. Guess that's why I was stupid enough to ask Brucie to give you a leg up. I guess I thought somehow that Mozambique business might be a way out for her.' Sophie put down her glass, still untasted. 'Chrissake, it was daft enough to be, and so crazy it hardly hit me there was no place in that scene for me.'

Harriet dropped her gaze, then turned her head away from the reminder that she was still wearing Brucie's boots. There had indeed been no place in Harriet's scheme for Sophie.

Sophie sniffed. 'And you, stuffed shirt and all, I could see Ammu really mattered with you; you did want to get her out of a hole. So I asked Brucie to help you. But then, it all changed. You cheated on me. You thieved. No big deal, but I couldn't trust you no more.'

Harriet was calm. She had already apologised to Sophie over the letters; her apology had been rejected. So what? She *was* a thief. She *had* been trying to cheat on Sophie, and out of far more that really mattered than Sophie knew. Sophie was right not to trust her.

'Then, when I read them letters, I knew you was going to make nothing but trouble for Ammu. You was too wild. You was acting like you thought you could handle de Haas. Who in hell do you think you are? Do you know what a conceited little sprat you are?'

So much for Dr Ramgulam's belief in Harriet's fundamental innocence! This innocent was a thief, a cheat, and a conceited little sprat with crazy fantasies about saving the poor and wretched of this world. What would Sophie say if she knew that the sprat was also another of Brucie's 'bits of stuff'? Harriet could almost have laughed. But none of this was of the least importance. All that mattered was that, this time, the sprat would set Ammu the mackerel to catch the shark de Haas.

'But even so,' Sophie added in a softer voice, 'I'm kinda glad somebody tried to get Ammu out.' Sophie held out the bottle. 'Here, have a drink.'

Harriet shook her head slowly. It was sinking into her mind that what she was about to do would not only send Robertie, de Haas and Ammu to prison. Sophie was involved in de Haas's business as some kind of brothel keeper. Sophie would also have to face charges. For no very adequate reason, Harriet didn't want police poking and prying into Sophie's poor life. Ridiculous as it was, she didn't want to hurt Sophie because Brucie had taken such pains to spare her pain. Then it struck her that Brucie too might be implicated in these crimes. 'No thanks. I don't like whisky. But tell me: what exactly is Brucie's connection with Robertie?'

'Friend. She used to bike him home from the Fires in the mornings. Poor bugger was often too drunk to walk, but never too drunk to hang on to Brucie's jacket. Why d'ya want to know?'

'I thought they worked together?'

'Like friends. He likes her, says she's the one boy in his life who'll always be faithful.'

'Yes, yes.' Harriet had been made uncomfortably aware of Robertie's fondness for this 'boy' when they took him home to Highgate. 'But how exactly do they work, like friends?' she pressed.

'He gets dope and porn for her at stupid prices. It's stuff that falls off the back of the de Haas lorries.' Sophie grinned. 'De Haas may have the bugger by the crop, but Robertie can get in the odd kick. He's not finished yet, not yet.'

Harriet dropped her gaze, but it met Brucie's boots innocently cradling her feet. She looked up instead into the stare of the cat on the mantelpiece. Robertie would be finished soon. It was 7 p.m. In an hour or so, Robertie, de Haas and Ammu would be sitting down to dinner. She would walk in and say –

'Brucie didn't just bring Ammu here because Robertie asked,' Sophie said. 'She fancied her. Brucie's mad about skirts, especially long ones, and she says saris make her think of the Virgin Mary. She left off Ammu when she saw I seriously needed her.'

Harriet quickly changed the subject. If she wanted to know about Brucie's past, she would ask some other time. 'Is Brucie at the Fires now? Is that why she isn't here?'

'Naw, Brucie won't be at the Fires. She needs to keep clear of de Haas for quite a while. She's made him feel small; he doesn't like that a lot. She's probably at some pub trying to flog dope. She needs cash for rent; she hasn't worked since you came on the scene, she just dropped everything. She made a bit off you, y'know, that night at the Fires and again, but not much; tanking Robertie worked out quite expensive. Le Maréchal don't approve of shirkers and if I can't give his Oblomov eighty quid by morning, she's out.'

Brucie out of it. Harriet was ashamed that she felt relieved. 'Brucie shouldn't sell cannabis,' she said coolly, 'it isn't good for people. It isn't even a very effective painkiller. Aspirins are better, and, in England, they're cheaper.'

The words startled her as they came out of her mouth. Why was she saying this? She had long since stopped saying it to her student nurses because Ammu favoured the use of cannabis – for toothache, premenstrual stress, arthritis, depression, and as a substitute for the home-distilled spirits which sent so many cases of poisoning to the clinics. But mostly, Ammu had encouraged it because this was a medicine people could make for themselves, without any connection with the medical practitioners and pharmacists she hated. Harriet had seen the logic of this at the time. She had even, at Ammu's suggestion, tried it, though she didn't like the washy feel it gave her body.

But that wasn't why she had said it. Harriet recognised that her mind was distancing itself from Ammu. She thought carefully. She wanted to do what she had to do as a pure act of justice. She had to be fair, objective. She had to try not to hate. Ammu had done good work. Brucie had reminded her of this. Many people, many, many children, were alive today because Ammu had done good work. And now Ammu had placed a great deal of money in an account in Harriet's name to allow her to continue the work that Ammu could no longer do, because even she knew she was ruined. 'Ruined'. Why did that word give her a grim pleasure? 'Oh Ammu, if only it was something else, anything else; because anything else I could forgive,' she whispered to herself.

'Brucie seems to think a lot of you,' Sophie said, into the pause. 'She says you're brave at facing danger and such. She likes that. You know what a kid she is; course she'd like you better if you could ride a horse, bareback.'

Harriet looked up from her thoughts. That was a surprising and generous thing for Sophie to say! Her heart, icy cold from the thought of Ammu, was warmed.

'Oh, God, I nearly forgot to tell you.' Harriet's hand flew to her mouth. 'A message for you from Ammu. She's put her personal money into a bank account for you. I'll give you the address. And she asked me to say,' Harriet swallowed hard, 'that she liked being with you. She said,' Harriet swallowed again, 'she said you gave sweetness.'

'Why?' Sophie looked stricken. 'Why? She's not *leaving* me her money, for Chrissake?'

'De Haas has plenty. She won't be short.'

Sophie fiddled with the knobs of her kimono. She still hadn't touched her drink. She was a difficult woman to understand. 'Sophie, listen –' Harriet leaned forward in her chair. 'You know what Robertie's business is, don't you?'

Sophie nodded.

'You know Ammu is involved in it?'

Sophie waved her head uncertainly.

'You thought as much?'

'I dunno. It's nothing to me what she does. Shit, I just

want de Haas to get his winkle-picking bloody fingers off her.'

'Why?'

'He's bad news. I love her.'

Harriet chose her words with care. 'Perhaps de Haas should be sent to prison.'

'Prison – don't make me laugh! I told you. He'd run the world from there. He'd have a cell kitted out like the Dorchester's Royal Suite. Name me a prison, and he owns it.'

Harriet's stomach lurched. This, if she had to believe it, was unpleasant hearing. 'And Robertie should be sent to prison.'

'Robertie? That poor shit? Why?'

'He makes pornographic videos. He takes pornographic photographs. He takes them of, um, of …'

'He's got to.' Sophie was looking at Harriet with a crooked smile; it was the first time Harriet had seen this smile. 'He's got to make more and more of them. They say his stuff's imaginative, sells well. He's got to grind on till he drops. Because de Haas has got him, right there.' Sophie wrapped her hand around her throat. 'De Haas has so much money he's gone to metal himself. Nothing can turn him on except getting more. De Haas would lift a blind man's wallet. He bleeds Robertie dry. He bleeds me, everybody. When they sued for the rates last year, he paid, but I had to sign a piece of paper that he owned the cats in exchange.'

Harriet nodded encouragement as Sophie paused for breath; this was what she needed to hear.

Sophie's face was now hot and red. 'He even put up Brucie's rent a few weeks ago. I mean what's a few quid to a mega-millionaire? That few quid is his kicks. He doesn't drink. He doesn't do dope. He don't do sex. He just makes money, and buys old carpets, and plays war games in Angola and Liberia and Chad and anywhere people are in trouble. He likes Africa. It's what he likes to talk about. He wants to own it so he can set people to killing each other. He said once he wants to make it a grand opera.'

Sophie gulped another breath, then continued: 'He's especially deep in Mozambique, loves it. He's working with a bunch of bandits there, training them in how to maim without killing too quick. They made him a colonel, you know, but he says he's their field marshall.'

Harriet was now wildly excited, ready for action. 'Sophie,' she said, leaping to her feet. 'I'm going to stop all this. I've got to. I'm going to make Ammu get the police.'

Sophie, lumbering like a charging hippopotamus, seized Harriet's wrist. 'You can't do it. I won't let anyone hurt Ammu.'

Harriet twisted and turned, but Sophie's grip was iron; Sophie was by far the stronger – a beanpole body has many points of vulnerability. Harriet began to fight, thrusting her knee against Sophie's belly, kicking Sophie's shins. Then they were rolling on the floor; Sophie was on top and her fist was bouncing off Harriet's face and head as she rained blows that surely had enough power to crack a skull. 'You can lay off Ammu. Got that? You can leave her alone.'

Then Sophie, pinning Harriet by the hair to the carpet, paused to suck in a desperate breath. Harriet, judging the exact position of the solar plexus, launched the heaviest punch she could muster. With a croak like someone having a heart attack, Sophie rolled over and lay beside her, groaning. Harriet leapt to her feet and was gone.

In the street, she paused to check her pocket. Still intact, still containing one pound coin and eighty seven pence. Then she checked her face. Her nose was bleeding profusely. She wiped it on the sleeve of Brucie's black sweater. She felt her eye: yes, it was rising up fast; soon she wouldn't be able to see out of it. The other was not much better. Too bad. No chance to slip back into Sophie's house to douse it or get a cold flannel. Somehow, she would have to manage the tube without getting herself arrested as a vagrant. She had left Brucie's big leather jerkin behind, and had nothing to hide under. It was freezing. Too bad.

There were lots of stares on the tube and, though it was packed, people moved away from seats near her. Harriet squinted fiercely ahead, feeding her furnace of anger with contempt for this milling mass of people. At Tufnell Park (where the lifts were out of order), she had several worrying spells of faintness on the stairs. She fell, too, in the street; something was wrong with her balance: was it the blow Sophie had given her ear? The people turned away; nobody tried to help her or hinder her. At the Highgate house, the gates were shut and locked. She climbed them, her bloody hands sticking to the ice-cold iron. Hearing the alarm ring wildly all over the house, she hauled off a boot and used it to smash the door of the little control box and then the delicate electrical works inside. Silence fell.

The boot still in her hand, she barged, limping through Robertie's still unlocked door. Perhaps he was in the room – the light was on and there seemed to be a shape on the futon. The communicating door still hadn't had its chain replaced. The hall, lit, was empty, but something was going on upstairs: a woman, not Ammu, was singing; opera or some such.

The dining room was empty: no Robertie and Ammu being served at dinner by de Haas, no television screen, no video; not even the tureens and big silver candlesticks. But the remains of the little glass she had broken glistened in the fibres of the carpet, and the doors of the false bookcase that Ammu had opened were still wide. In the heat of the house, her nose began to bleed again. Big drops fell onto the pale, silvery carpet, marking her passage through the room. The place had a defiled feel, like something a burglar had visited. She banged the door to.

Upstairs? She looked at the wide staircase, the deep green carpet that snaked up and then divided into two, smooth as pythons in a pit. Something was going on up there; the opera, vaguely familiar, was still ranting on. But, no, even now, some part of her prayed that Ammu would not be up there with him, but down in the basement with the ivy in its plastic mug. The burglar alarm began to rage again, blocking out the opera, blocking out thought. Hurry, hurry; they were after her. Not much time. Find Ammu. Make her do what she had to do.

Though alarmed by her unsteady balance, Harriet crashed down to the cellars, charging through the stockroom, the wine cellar, the little chapel, to Ammu's room.

Here too the light burned, shining on the big, bare, stone-flagged, very quiet void. It shone too on the bed. There was a shape. She hesitated. Yes, it was a small, very small shape. It was Ammu, lying flat on her back, with the covers pulled right over her head. She was still. The ivy sprigs were laid on her breast. 'Oh my God, Ammu.' Harriet hurled herself at the bed, stripping off the cover. A strong smell of burnt almonds engulfed her. Ammu's face was pale, the skin of her cheek relaxed and faintly warm. Furiously, but already knowing there would be none, she felt for a pulse. With a cry that seemed to come not from her own throat but like a ghost of that other terrible cry from the dining room above her, Harriet lifted into her arms a body that had no more weight than a little girl.

'Put her back. Let her sleep. Don't hurt her.' Robertie's voice, so horribly like Ammu's, wriggled like an earwig in her brain. 'She was on the floor.' Robertie came close. His face was streaming with tears, but his breathing was even. 'I put her in the bed.'

Very slowly, Harriet loosened her clasp and returned Ammu's body to the bed. She smoothed her hair, still as wild as it had been in life. She caressed the skin around her eyes, limp now, as if exhausted by a terrible agony. All these acts seemed, in some strange way, familiar, rehearsed, as if some part of Harriet had, somehow, known that this was what she would find.

But why? How? When? What for? It came to Harriet that Ammu may have lain writhing with death on this floor while she threshed about on another floor, fighting over Ammu with Sophie. Perhaps. What was more certain was what the smell told her: that Ammu had been given, or had taken, cyanide. Without any doubt Ammu had died knowing that Harriet had abandoned her.

All Harriet's injuries now throbbed together, throttling her consciousness to a single, thin thread. One thing more to do before she could let herself think, feel – find the telephone, call the police; make them get de Haas. She laid the little body back in the bed and got to her feet, pushing Robertie aside.

'Harriet, wait for me.' As she dragged herself up from the cellar, Robertie was slithering up behind her, putting a slip of paper in her hand.

Harriet let it drop. Feebly, she shoved past him. He picked it up again. 'You must take it,' Robertie whispered at her back, 'it's the number for the police station.'

Her fist closed over it. 'My eyes have swelled. I can't read the numbers.'

'I'll dial for you. I'll do it. But first you must come with me, upstairs. You must see.'

'I've seen enough.'

But he was pulling her up the stairs, and there was no energy in her to resist. Even her dripping nose had run out of blood. He was leading her to the south side, to the bedrooms of de Haas and his Oblomovs. She lacked the strength even to shrink away. There was a door. He tapped respectfully, then opened it.

The music was deafening: a woman screaming rather

than singing, a man groaning, a thump as he fell to the floor, a crash of instruments joining in the woman's triumphant response. A video machine, perhaps the same one that Harriet had seen in the dining room, flared in the dimly lit room. Robertie switched it off, and the room came into focus. '*Tosca*,' he said, nodding his head respectfully. 'Le Maréchal's favourite opera. I put it on for him.'

There was a carpet, curtains, a bed, a figure in the bed. Robertie pushed Harriet forward. It was de Haas, a silk sheet grey and shiny as his strangely sweaty skin pulled up to the neck. Ammu's exhausted little features faded from her vision and she stood and stared.

Then somehow, from somewhere, despite shock and swollen eyelids, sight and consciousness cleared and the nurse in Harriet leapt into life. She put a hand to the brow, then quickly grasped the wrist, feeling for a pulse. 'He's alive!' she whispered harshly, 'but deeply unconscious.' She pushed back an eyelid. 'And his pupils are widely dilated.' She turned sharply to Robertie. 'What happened?'

Robertie shuffled his feet. 'You sure he's alive? A few minutes ago he was breathing like a mad rhino; you could hear it all over the house. But he's alive?'

Almost angrily, she pinched his ear lobe. No response to pain. 'Only just. But how did this ...?'

Robertie looked vague. 'Seems like his lunch disagreed with him.'

'Yes, yes: but what *happened*?'

'We ate downstairs, about four, maybe five.'

'And -?'

Robertie looked irritated. 'How should I know? He went up to have a nap.'

Robertie was useless! Harriet fought an onset of panic as her nose began to bleed again – she was not in command of herself. She needed Ammu. She didn't know what to do! She tried to think, to think like a nurse. Whatever had happened was serious – a heart attack, a stroke? 'Robertie, call an ambulance, for heaven's sake.'

On heavy feet, Robertie shuffled out of the room, closing the door quietly behind him.

As she was once more checking his heartbeat, Harriet started: this man was diabetic. 'Robertie' she yelled, 'tell them he's a diabetic!' Yes, she thought, surely it's a diabetic coma. Or was it an insulin coma, from an insulin overdose?

Harriet moved her face close up to his blanched lips, to smell his breath. She withdrew sharply: she smelt not, as she had expected, the sweetish scent of acid drops indicating too much sugar in the blood, but the harsh reek of brandy.

'Like a nurse, objectively, think!' Harriet hissed at herself. She still shuddered at the thought of those skeletal arms embracing Ammu in the dining room, quietening the dreadful grief; she found drunkenness ugly and frightening. She didn't want to touch him. She struggled to think of this man as a patient, just a very sick person in need of help.

How? Harriet knew the ambulance would be at least ten minutes away and that de Haas could well be less than ten minutes from death. Harriet straightened the sheet she had rucked up when checking de Haas's pulse. How neatly the man had been laid in this very neat bed. How strangely saintly he looked, his ascetic, bony face unworldly as the death mask of a Christian martyr. These thoughts floated through her head in parallel with another train of thought – the growing conviction that de Haas was in an insulin coma. Symptoms were less marked at so advanced a stage, but they were there: rapid (though in this case feeble) pulse, dilated pupils, cold, clammy skin. If this was an insulin coma she could perhaps save his life with a glucose injection.

But if she was wrong, and the condition was a diabetic coma, a glucose injection would, at this late stage, surely kill him.

Robertie shuffled back into the room. 'Shall I play him some more *Tosca*?'

At least Robertie had some idea what to do!

'No thank you,' she said mildly. Harriet was out of her depth. She was raking her memories of nursing textbooks, trying to reach a decision. Again she smelled de Haas's breath, trying to get past the brandy to whatever smell lay underneath. Not, she was almost sure, the smell of acid drops. Again she checked his pupils. Yes, dilated, barely responding to light. She nerved herself. 'I'm going to give him an injection,' she said tonelessly. 'It's an insulin coma.'

'Insulin?' Robertie seemed to revel in the word. 'Yes,' he said, 'you give him insulin ...'

Harriet ignored him. She now knew what to do. Find de Haas's glucagon and inject direct into a vein. She glanced at the bedside table, tapped at his pyjama pockets – strange – surely de Haas had been trained to keep it near at hand? Irritably, she turned to Robertie. 'Where's his glucagon kit?'

'It's insulin he needs.'

Harriet was again full of doubt. Robertie knew the patient well. 'You think he needs insulin? Did he forget to take it this morning? Do you know how much he needs? Please, Robertie, concentrate. A coma is caused either by too much or too little; it seems to me he's had too much. In fact, I'm sure, I'm almost sure ... But if you think ...?'

Robertie walked solemnly around the bed, and picked up a stainless steel tray from the bedside table. This he offered for Harriet's inspection: a pair of silvery spectacles, a glass of (apparently) water, and a used ten millilitre syringe, laid neatly in a dish beside a vial of insulin, just under half empty, its rubber seal showing the mark of penetration by only one needle.

'Oh,' she peered hard at Robertie's tear-stained face: 'This syringe is too big – it must be far too big. Did he fill it, inject all this? That whole lot?' (Robertie looked vague.) 'When? You don't know? All today? Had he eaten a big dinner first? You don't know? How much did he have to drink? Has he been in a coma before? Heaven's sake Robertie, cat got your tongue?'

Robertie was looking apologetic. Harriet felt her face flush with anger. 'Tell me how much he's taken – don't stand there like a dummy – surely you know *something*!'

Robertie rolled his head. 'Ammu knows.'

'Oh God!' Ammu was dead. Another death would probably happen within minutes.

'Quickly, help me now; where's his equipment? Where does he keep his glucagon kit, his glucose? Does he have a black bag somewhere?'

Robertie reached out a hand and, still without speaking, led her into the dressing room. He pointed to an elegant little refrigerator flanked by glass cases filled with ribbed, brown bottles. 'He doesn't need a black bag. He has a whole damned pharmacy to himself.'

Harriet reached inside the fridge: still no glucagon kit but her hands fastened instinctively on a bag of liquid glucose. 'I'm going to assume it's an insulin overdose, got that? I'm going to inject this, not into a muscle but direct into a vein. If the veins in his arm have collapsed – and I think they have – I'll go straight into his neck. Do you understand?'

Robertie shifted from foot to foot. Harriet realised that she was staring at him as she had seen so many doctors stare at some bemused relative, trying to explain that they were about to take some desperate measure which would almost certainly not succeed.

'It's the only chance.' Decision taken, she walked firmly back to the bedroom. She had forgotten to look for a syringe. She picked up the used one from the tray – for this, at least, it was big enough!

'Okay Robertie, you can go now. Phone the ambulance again … No, first call Dr Ramgulam. You want her number? Find the phone book; its R-A-M-G-U – Gunnersbury; tell her to come straight away; no, it'll take her ages to get here; tell her I think it's a massive overdose of insulin; tell her I'm injecting glucose; tell her I need help.'

Robertie didn't move. 'Give him more insulin,' he muttered.

Harriet, squinting through her swollen eyelids, punctured the bung and drew off some glucose. 'He's had too much; that's the problem, at least that's what I think it is. Please God I'm right. Go and phone now.' With her other hand, Harriet was already feeling for a vein. 'Run.'

She spoke calmly, but her heart was beating wildly with the old, familiar excitement of taking up arms against death. Strange that Ammu had never seemed aroused in this way by the presence of death; in the end, she always waited on it respectfully, as if seeking to do the will of a deity. But Harriet couldn't think about Ammu. Her fingers probed a flaccid arm, then the stretch of neck from collar–bone to ear, searching for a functioning vein.

Robertie wandered off, but not down to the hall. The door of the little refrigerator banged shut and then he was back, with another vial of insulin. 'I've brought you more of this.' His voice regained its force: 'This is what he needs, more and more … And here,' he proffered the tray, 'still quite a bit in this bottle if you put the needle in deep. If Ammu didn't finish off the job, you do it.'

Harriet's fingers were now tapping the throat, trying to raise the vein. 'Ammu?' Her fingers stopped short. 'Oh my God. Ammu did this? Then she, then she …?' Syringe and glucose pack fell, with a clonk, onto the tray.

Robertie nodded. 'Yes, she did.' He squared his

shoulders. 'And I haven't called that ambulance. If you want an ambulance, you can call it yourself.'

Robertie and Harriet looked hard at each other.

Out of the depths of the worst horror she had known in her life, a strange feeling rose up in Harriet, something like a triumph. Ammu had done it! She had done what had to be done – she had avenged the child who died in Port Louis.

Robertie nodded; point taken. Harriet noticed the stiffness of his nod, and then the heavy bruising on the side of his neck.

'I'm sorry about hitting you,' she said.

'No offence. You don't look so good yourself! But just show me how to do an insulin injection. I want to put that needle straight into his heart; I want to finish him off.'

'No, don't touch anything. Ammu's done all that's needed. This is Ammu's work. Keep your fingerprints off it. Ammu wouldn't want you to face a murder charge. Ammu's paid for you, Robertie. Ammu's taken it all.'

'But he's not dead. Make it another injection, a bigger one. Let's be sure. I want to do it. You just show me how.'

'No need. He's dying now.' Harriet's head was now clearer. 'We almost certainly couldn't have done anything for him anyway, almost certainly ...'

Supporting each other in the quiet resignation of relatives who had sat for days at a death-bed, they went downstairs together. Surely de Haas was well past anything medicine could do. Surely Ammu, a professional, would have measured the dose like an economist, like de Haas himself – just so much, no vulgar excess.

Followed by Robertie, Harriet made her way down to the basement. 'I want to lay her out properly,' she said, 'you can help me if you want to.' And the nurse who was allowing a man to die, untended, silently, only twenty feet above her, cleaned and prepared for burial, without visible emotion but very carefully, a woman who had already gone through a violent, extremely painful, but very quick death.

There was no point in trying to disguise the cyanide. The little container for the capsule, strung, not on a silver chain in the style of guerrilla fighters, but on a piece of string, she put back around Ammu's neck.

When it was done, Robertie called Dr Ramgulam, then returned to the basement. Silently, they sat side by side on the floor beside Ammu's body, waiting for the sound of Dr Ramgulam's car. Then Robertie gave the dangling electrics of the control box another yank to switch off the alarm, opened the gate to the good doctor and, at Jasbir Ramgulam's instruction, telephoned the police, and ambulance, himself.

Tuesday afternoon,
8 November

'Harriet – it's that girl Brucie on the line again. What do you want me to tell her this time?'

'The same, please Mother.' Harriet rolled over, wincing against the pain in her back: Sophie had given her a terrific thump in the kidneys. It was afternoon and the sun was shining. She could sense both these facts – despite the drawn curtains and the pads taped over the eyes – by the contented hum of cars drawing up beside the plane trees, letting out well-mannered little girls and boys to play on the green for an hour before settling down to their homework. Harriet's fingers outlined the escapades of Bunnikins on the wallpaper, then reached down towards the duffel bag on the floor, delivered to the house by Brucie.

Feet padded up the stairs and Mother was at the door of the little room that had been Harriet's since the Whittington Hospital had released her as a squalling baby. 'A lightly-boiled egg would do you good, Harriet.' Then Mother was inside, fluffing up the pillows. A faint scent of lavender rose, from the pillows or perhaps Mother's cool, brisk presence. 'Bear in mind what Dr Ramgulam said: you're malnourished, overwrought and dreadfully stressed, and that will slow up your healing.'

'I'm healing nicely, thank you, Mother.'

Harriet heard her mother sigh, then pad softly back to

the morning room, where she was engaged on a very complicated piece of embroidery – a cushion cover worked in silk in a Tree of Life design. 'It's for you, Harriet. I wanted to do something Hindu. I know how much you like that sort of thing.' Harriet didn't explain that this pattern was Muslim; her mind's eye was running over the dozens of similar silky designs all over the house in Highgate.

Those beautiful rugs would now be spattered with the chalk dust of forensic scientists, following, ghoulishly, Ammu's last voyage: to the insulin stocks in the fridge, to de Haas's bedroom, where she laid the used syringe neatly on its tray beside the half-empty vial, then down to the cellar. There was no need for all this police fuss. Ammu had let each action tell its story more clearly than any suicide note could have done.

It was all there, even on de Haas's body. The sheet pulled up so neatly to the neck echoed her instruction to him to sleep well, sleep long. There had been no struggle. De Haas, for once in his life innocent as a lamb, had allowed the doctor he trusted (and perhaps, in his way, loved) to do as she liked with him. Ammu had respected this; she had given him a painless and dignified end, and herself the death of a poisoned rat.

When had she planned this end? Some time before, judging by the letter Ammu had delivered into Harriet's mother's hand; the letter that had waited at the house in Palmers Green all the time Harriet had been searching, and longer.

Checking to make sure that Mother was now out of range, Harriet felt under her pillow for the single sheet of thin paper covered on both sides in Ammu's loopy hand. Like a photograph of someone long dead, smiling for the camera and thinking about lunch, Ammu's letter made it impossible to feel her death, even though it was a letter about death.

Harriet had no tears left. Her swollen eyes oozed, but

not with tears. Wearily, she loosened the sticking plaster
and lifted the dressings. Prising the sticky lids apart with
her fingers, she read:

Dear Harriet

You have to go to Guija without me. The matter is
urgent: you must take the first flight to Harare. Save
the Children has a crate of supplies to be put on the
same plane. Father Emmanuel Chipani is meeting every
plane from London pending your arrival. He will take
you, with a convoy of soldiers and food rations given by
Zimbabwe, to Guija. It is a ghost town now, but the
mission is still functioning, and the survivors from
Renamo's last 'burnt earth' foray have gathered there.
They have rethatched and repaired the schoolroom and
converted it into a hospital for you.

Father Chipani tells me that, although they have no
trained medical staff, no medical supplies and very little
food, morale is high. You will bring new hope, and
organisation. You are a good administrator. I believe in
you. Harriet, you must forget me – forget me but
remember what I taught you – that health comes from
the soul.

I need not remind you that the people are weak and
dependent because they are victims of a cruel war not of
their making. Try to help them revive their own culture
of health, don't foist on them a cheap copy of your own.

I cannot go because the time has come when I have to
settle the score which has been waiting for me all my
life. I have to let go of the hope you gave me, that we,
you and I, could ease some of the pain of the world.

I have done things that I cannot undo, and this
retribution was waiting for me. I cannot say the words
to you, but you must believe that it is evil that leads,
and has led, to death. Two deaths must now follow –
pray that they will break the chain. At the very least,
they will make life safer for you, and a lot of other
people, in Mozambique.

Do not try to know more about this – it would be a knowledge of no use. But believe that I know that you have

been very good to me. I hope your concern was for my ideas and not my person, which is not worth your love.

I pray that you may do great work, because in that is the only happiness.

Ammu

Harriet folded the letter again, and put it back under the pillow. Should she feel glad that Ammu was at least spared the sight of Robertie being shoved, a policeman's big hand pressing into the flesh of his bottom, into the back of a van? Why did they need to insult him like that? It was Robertie who had called them, Robertie who had put up his hands and said, 'You'll have to take me, but first you must listen; you must listen very carefully.'

Robertie told the story so simply and coherently that it was difficult not to think he had rehearsed it. There was no boasting this time about 'international connections'. There were tears in plenty, always about Ammu, but none of the sentimental gush that had so sickened Harriet at the Fires.

The inspector, a greying sort of man from the local police station, was polite; he offered Robertie a chair, listened for a while, then motioned a constable to get Scotland Yard. But Robertie wanted to go on talking, down there in the cellar, while two other officers poked about the bed where Ammu lay not listening, and another two were, pointlessly, carrying the brain-dead de Haas to hospital.

Robertie's first photographs had been touted round the hotels by the infant Ammu. Whatever sold well, they made more of. Children were best – a smaller but more profitable market than women – and a few chapattis were sufficient payment for a hungry child. The business grew;

then big money came from glossy books and films for the multi-media company owned by Monsieur Yves de Wet de Haas, a Mauritian-South African, then starting to build his empire. Robertie was one of his earliest freelances, and the only one of that first crew not yet mad, helplessly alcoholic, or dead.

Things started to go off the rails for Robertie at the time of Ammu's pre-med year at the university in Durban. Ammu's drunken father was frequently in trouble with the police, and he talked. Nobody prosecuted Robertie, but more and more officials of one sort or another called on him, 'protectors' who increased in number, and in greed. The cost of protection and counter-protection became a distinct irritant to de Haas – always one to count the pennies – and he began to see Robertie as a liability, though he was still too useful, and knew too much, to be discarded, at least discarded alive. So Robertie was constantly under threat of 'conscription', being sent to the front at the de Haas-financed wars in what was then the Congo, later Rhodesia and Uganda. Long after old Du Deffand's death in South Africa, Robertie continued to be regarded as, in some unspecified way, unreliable. De Haas liked cruel jokes, and often made Robertie the butt of them: 'Some years ago, le Maréchal ordered his best tailor to make me a special uniform. It was chic, with green and red flashes on the epaulets and the jodhpurs had an expandable waist-fastening. I liked wearing it; people said I looked quite butch and all that. But when I wore it at a big dinner he said it was for my posting as outrider and scout for Idi Amin – you remember that madman in Uganda? Amin was fat and liked other fat men. Then le Maréchal made me run round and round the table with my napkin stuck in the carving fork, like the natives had to do carrying messages in battle, and he shot at it with his little silver pistol.'

There were many humiliations of that sort. There was

also an enormous amount of work to be done, de Haas dictating exactly what pictures Robertie was to make and how. 'Le Maréchal never desired anyone, man, woman or child, but he always knew what the market wanted.' Robertie was lonely, unhappy, frightened and cowed. Without Ammu, he doubted that he could have survived. But Ammu, although she too worked hard at his business, was another source of insecurity. During her adolescence, she began to develop ideas which filled Robertie with fear – for her and for himself.

'My Marie-Louise, she told me one day she hated white people; she said she hated the three-quarters white part of herself. Then she said she hated her father. She never stopped yelling how much she hated men.' Robertie thought for a moment. 'But even while she was hating whites, she showed no love for blacks. She used to want to hit any one of them that said ''yes baas''. She got mad just seeing them standing in queues. By Our Lady, inspector, she hated everybody. She hated rich blacks and poor blacks. She hated the Indians so much she couldn't bear to look at them.'

Often, he told them, she talked of going to Banares to live among the lepers on the banks of Ganges; sometimes she threatened suicide. At other times, she wanted to study nuclear physics and blow up the world. Instead, she learned to speak and write Tamil, adopted Indian clothes, even an Indian accent. But she made, then, no Indian friends. Robertie was her only friend.

At this point, Harriet had burst out with, 'So she stopped working for you – when?'

Robertie seemed surprised to hear another voice in the room. He spoke abstractedly. 'When she went to the University, in Durban. That was just after we made the film you saw. Afterwards, she took money from me to start the clinics. She gave it back, though, at least some. She didn't earn much.'

Harriet, lying between covers scented with lavender, took a deep, slow breath, to help her memory drop its burden. She lay, longing for the merciful dullness which had blanked out her mind for so much of the past twenty-four hours, or twenty-four years.

But mind refused to switch off its tormenting machine. Robertie was now standing up, pressing his hand against the breast of the greying man, wailing, 'You're wasting time. You've got de Haas, but you haven't got his Oblomovs. They'll be starting another war before you've finished writing in that damn notebook. For my Marie-Louise, her sake' – pointing at the ivy leaves – 'You've got to get them. It's why my baby girl died. She died to call their number.'

Officers in the background, came, listened, went into corners to make calls on their portable telephones, returned. Out on the terrace where the oil spot still marked the last place of Brucie's bike, cars and vans, sirens and flashing lights came and went. The house, the gardens, even up and down Highgate West Hill, everywhere crawled with police. And down in the cellar, Robertie was still talking:

Ammu arrived in London for the conference, saw Robertie and discovered, for the first time, the extent of de Haas's business and his involvement with Africa. She gave Robertie an ultimatum. 'She just said to me, "Get out of it, or I talk to Paul".' (Paul, the quiet friend in Camden Town, had contacts at Westminster.)

And Robertie, sick of the unending drudgery of making more money for de Haas, wanted to do that and more, he wanted to go to Guija to cook and clean for Ammu. He offered to give up drink, give up boys, become the lowest slave in the clinics. Ammu said that was not necessary.

But de Haas did not welcome resignations from the firm. When he succinctly outlined to Robertie the consequences (Robertie in a jute sack at the bottom of the

Thames) Robertie changed his mind instantly. But Ammu didn't. And Ammu made it no secret that she meant business, was dangerous.

De Haas's letter led to their first meeting. De Haas was charmed by Ammu. He didn't take her threats too seriously – after all, the life of a beloved uncle was at stake, and, he reasoned, his fondness for her was a gift of such value she would surely be overwhelmed by the honour. He offered her a high position in the firm; a position of the greatest trust – she was to be his Eva Braun; and she would personally take charge of the health of le Maréchal.

'Le Maréchal, he said he was so moved by her interest in the health of the poor that he'd give Save the Children enough money to fund a hundred clinics. They had to be, though, in countries where he had business interests. He told everybody he was "captivated". He said he was never going to be parted from Marie-Louise in her lifetime. He only worried about her lifetime; I guess he never thought he could die himself.'

Until this meeting, le Maréchal had been a shadowy figure to Ammu. After it, he became an obsession. She questioned Robertie minutely about every detail of his work. When, as often, de Haas was afflicted with insomnia, she would sit all night with him, encouraging him to talk. Robertie looked thoughtful. 'I think he told her everything.' The Oblomovs were uneasy, but dared not question the power given to this new figure on the board.

Even though De Haas opened his heart to Ammu, he also, if only from habit, took precautions. To make sure of Ammu's loyalty, he had Robertie trailed day and night, often, as on the night Harriet met him at the Fires, doing this humble job himself, since he took a personal interest in the matter.

'How could I know when she decided to kill him?' Robertie said irritably in answer to the inspector's question. But Harriet knew now. Ammu had given her letter to Mother on the day of her disappearance from Sophie's, perhaps even called in at Palmer's Green on the journey across London that she must already have chosen to be her journey to death. Doing it that way, Ammu had protected Robertie, protected Sophie, even kept Harriet safe from any implication.

Ammu – so many people loved her. Apart from Sophie, they had all failed her. One, Harriet, had done worse than fail: she had hurt someone who was already so badly hurt that that additional pain could have felt almost like relief. But, then, perhaps that cruel end with an incomprehending, disgusted Harriet had been a signal, given Ammu the power to overcome the habit of twenty years of saving lives, to do what she needed to do, to take one, to take two.

The door bell rang. Harriet heard Dr Ramgulam's booming voice, then her firm step. She was too tired to face Dr Ramgulam. She would have turned her head to the wall if movement of the neck were less painful. Good, they were downstairs, making tea. Let them talk. That tinkling was Mother's best china. Harriet was out of it, out of everything.

Once more, she took out Ammu's letter and – not so much read it, for she knew it by heart anyway – but smelled it, though it gave off no trace of jasmine.

Mother's voice sounded from just outside the door. 'Harriet?' Harriet felt like a prisoner in chains. A little trolley of tea things was wheeled in. Then Dr Ramgulam was looking at her eyes, her back, her neck, saying soothing things about shock and rest.

Harriet's wrist was gripped in Dr Ramgulam's firm grasp, and both women were talking, together, about things that had no place in Harriet's mind.

'I phoned the British Council, Harriet my dear.' That was Mother speaking. 'A young man has been sent to replace you. I am told that he is unhappy in his work. The student nurses call him "Brother Frigidaire".' Harriet spluttered.

Dr Ramgulam seemed to be pleased at this reaction. She broke in: 'Harriet, I have news. Civil war has broken out in the de Haas empire.' Dr Ramgulam waved Harriet's wrist. 'The Oblomovs are fighting for top slot, killing each other all over London. The murders yesterday of a colonel in the South African police, senior officers in one or two other countries and a whole heap of drug barons are being linked with the affair.'

'Is that so?' Harriet closed her eyes under the dressings.

'Indeed it is. The dear creatures are doing much of the work of justice all by themselves. Ammu, it seems, planned all this, like setting up a long queue of dominos; extraordinarily thorough. I never realised how good an administrator she was.'

'You didn't?' Harriet said dully.

'Or how elegant her planning could be. Forensic told me this morning that she gave de Haas just enough brandy and aspirin to knock off his liver – so that it couldn't deal with the insulin – and an amount of insulin that would have been inadequate if she hadn't, at lunch, allowed him only a light meal of artichokes. Her own death was virtually simultaneous with his occurrence of irreparable brain damage. A truly literary feat. For all her crazy ideas, Ammu certainly understood good old scientific medicine. They want to write it up in *The Forensic Scientist.*'

Harriet tried to pull the covers over her face. 'Oh, please,' she groaned.

Dr Ramgulam paused for a moment. Harriet heard Mother shifting her feet, whispering. Harriet prayed that they would go away. But Dr Ramgulam continued. 'Unfortunately,' she said in a quieter tone, 'in the carnage, Sophie's house was burnt down.'

'Sophie?' Harriet suddenly came to life. 'Is she all right?'

Dr Ramgulam was pleased, too, with this reaction, judging by the tightening of her grip on Harriet's wrist. 'Sophie is shocked. Slight burns; she tried to save some cats. She'll be all right. She's getting good medical attention. She's staying at a women's hostel, a decent place; it'll do for a while.'

There was a long pause, then Dr Ramgulam continued. 'It would be nice if you could see her.'

Harriet let her head sink into the pillows. She wanted to say, 'Yes, I will see her', but those wretched, painful tears that burned her bruised tissues and soaked her dressings were starting up again.

A silence fell. Harriet waited; perhaps Mother and Dr Ramgulam would go away. But no. The hand was still on her wrist and Mother was talking.

'And, Harriet, I've been in touch with Martin. He's at the same address and still unmarried. He says he now wants to repair medical corps vehicles. If you would like to go back to Mauritius, my dear ...'

'If you want to go back to Mauritius,' Dr Ramgulam took up the story, 'I ought to be able to arrange things with the Ministry.'

Harriet tried to shake her head.

'But I also need to tell you, my dear,' Dr Ramgulam's hand tightened on Harriet's wrist, 'that I had to contact Father Chipani, to tell him about Ammu.'

'She told him herself.'

'You knew that?' Dr Ramgulam paused. 'How?'

Harriet rolled her head slowly from side to side.

Dr Ramgulam didn't pursue the point. 'Then perhaps you can imagine too what they would have said to me?'

Harriet was silent.

'If you are able to take on Ammu's work in Mozambique, my dear, it will be a very great thing.'

'No! Leave me alone!'

'I distress you. Forgive me.' The hand left Harriet's

wrist, shoes creaked as Dr Ramgulam rose to her feet. 'I
want to help you in any way I can. Sophie does too.'

'I'm sorry. I can't, I can't, I ...'

'But,' Mother took up the story, 'there is no need for
you to decide anything at all. At least not for some time.'

Dr Ramgulam finished the sentence, 'But it could be
valuable for you to know that you do have choices.'

'You're very kind.' Harriet turned her face to the wall.

The doorbell rang again. Mother went down to answer.
Dr Ramgulam's hand returned to Harriet's wrist, gave a
squeeze, and Harriet was grateful. This was one, perhaps
the only, human being that she still wanted to know. But
not now. Not herself to have love, friends, when Ammu
was – had been – so alone, so bereft, so ill-served by the
many people who loved her. Only Sophie, only poor
Sophie had been true.

'Harriet?' Mother's voice, calling from the hall, was
different, formal. This must be the police. Harriet had
already told them why she came to the house, how she
found Ammu and why her fingerprints were everywhere.
She had even told them that she had knowingly left de
Haas to die. At the station, she had answered every
question, and then gone meekly to hospital. She had done
everything that could be expected.

'Harriet; it's Inspector Swain. You remember
Inspector Swain? He'd appreciate a few words with you.'

Tuesday, 15 November

The funeral was delayed by the investigation. The police arranged it, a little Hindu nugget in a corner of the crematorium's bare and Protestant-looking chapel. The priest, dressed in white with markings on his face, regretted that he had never had the pleasure of meeting Ammu. In a small voice which echoed around the void behind the five mourners and three policemen, he spoke of the sorrow of dying far from motherland and loved ones. A pause. Then, awkwardly, the priest said this day was the birthday of one Charlotte Mew, a poet who had, like Ammu, died by her own hand, in pain and obscurity. But, just as Mew's voice had risen above the horror of her death, so would Ammu's cry for respect and care for the people the world despised. From this Harriet knew that Brucie had spoken to the priest. Then he bent his head to say prayers which, apart from God, only Dr Ramgulam, and perhaps Robertie, understood.

Another pause. Dr Ramgulam rose stiffly from her pew. She placed a lighted candle and two long-stemmed daffodils on the coffin, bowed, and returned to her seat.

Then Ammu went into the flames.

Harriet was wearing dark glasses to hide the bruises on her face. Not to hide tears. She did not cry. Robertie sobbed softly throughout the service, and left immediately afterwards, in an unmarked car with the policemen. There was no chance for Harriet to speak to him, but what was left for either of them to say when death had emptied both their lives?

She began to drift down the lane towards the gate. It was mid-morning, and Tuesday, and sharp rays of sun poured down between the bare trees. The frost had been heavy the previous night; the flowers left from half a dozen bigger funerals were pinched and sore-looking. It would be icy cold again when the sun went down. The begonia she had brought for Ammu would be dead by morning.

Sophie had looked terrible. The calf of her left leg was striped with sticking plaster and both her hands taped up. Her eyes, half hidden by the big black mantilla which covered her cropped hair and most of her face, still seemed swollen and sore from the smoke, or perhaps from weeping. She was frighteningly pale, leaning heavily on Brucie like an old blind woman. But then perhaps Sophie, who had lived so tight inside the dark house in Ladbroke Grove that was now a charred shell, could, like a mole, hardly see in daylight. At some later time, Harriet would find in herself the courage to speak to her.

She was almost at the gate. Behind her came the crash of boots running hard on the black tarmac. She waited for Brucie's hand on her shoulder.

It reached her. It was tentative.

'Harriet?' Harriet slowed. 'Harriet, I want to go to Mozambique.'

Harriet turned. Brucie's face, round and spotty, was pale as the moon.

'I want to do something with my life. I want to do something for Ammu.' Then, after a long pause, 'And for you.'

The whole world went quiet.

Then Harriet's eyes were flooding like the Brahmaputra, and the spindly arms of the trees were whirling as if in a great storm, and Brucie's leather-stiff arms were around her, and her fingers were deep in Brucie's coconut-oily hair, and she could hear Ammu's voice calling for life, life for everything that was denied life.

'You never know,' said Brucie hugging her tight as a bear, 'what talent we might find in a place where there's a war on.'